Gatherings

Gatherings

Mehreen Ahmed

Bridge House

British Library Cataloguing in Publication Data
A Record of this Publication is available from the British
Library

ISBN 978-1-914199-02-8

This edition published 2021 by Bridge House Publishing
Manchester, England

Contents

Introduction 7

The Black Coat 8

The Interlude.. 21

Gold Foliage 35

Backstage... 48

Mowgli's Mother 54

The Buraq 59

Since the Last Soiree... 67

The Fountain of the Twelve Lions......................... 77

In Search for the Purist... 84

Sweet Wood... 88

Pink Toenails 97

Purple Waves 103

The Scent of Goodness.. 114

Juliet's Song 119

The Blue Butterflies... 123

Autumn in a Coffee Cup 142

The Flower Girl 159

Spring River... 184

Mother of March.. 197

Scroll of the Turul.. 201

Sweet Calling... 213

That Rain, When the Peacock Danced 220

Pizzazz 238

Homecoming 248

The Journey 258

About the Author 269

Like to Read More Work Like This? 271

Please Leave a Review 272

Introduction

Gatherings, as the title suggests, is a book of short stories gathered from my published works which have appeared in international online journals. The intention was to revamp archived stories in book format. The stories here have been set in various locations on a number of themes, such as love, war, humanitarian and existential crises. They are meant for readers with eclectic tastes who love characters from diverse backgrounds. To this end, stories were culled from the east as much as from the west for this collection. Notably, there is also a series of stand-alone stories from the *House of Chowdhury,* tangentially linked by characters, but not by the plot; each instalment is a complete unit. This is experimental, done both to create artistic newness and to depict a comprehensive cultural portrayal, in which the series is nested within other stories unrelated to the series. Not necessarily in the sense of a plot within a plot as is the case in Shakespeare's dramas. Or *The Hobbit* in *The Lord of the Rings:* a book within a book. But this has evolved into a sui generis nature of short story collection.

Mehreen Ahmed

The Black Coat

One black, wintry night, Piccolo-Xavier bumped into someone while crossing the Boulevard Périphérique. Once he was across, the person he hit was not visible anymore. It seemed as though, in this Parisian dark alley, this someone simply dissolved into thin air. When he peered further into the darkness, his gaze shifted towards a shiny object that appeared on an uneven, asphalt footpath. He picked it up and thought he must return this to its owner. But since the black coat was long gone, he would step up his pace and look for the person. Piccolo-Xavier had a glimpse of a shape in a black coat, fast disappearing around the corner. He stepped up his pace until he found himself running. However, the more he ran, the further the person moved away. Breathing heavily, he stopped to rest.

He realised that he held a locket with a broken clasp in his palm. In the insufficient light of the streetlamp, he saw that it contained a picture of a girl. This object could be of sentimental value. However, there was no way he could return it to its owner now.

Back in his apartment, looking at the girl's picture in the locket-frame, the thought of the elusive, dark figure provoked all kinds of questions, where did the bearer of this object live? How far away was he or she from him? And who was this girl in the picture? Piccolo-Xavier began to imagine the wildest of dreams about the bearer of the locket, who was perhaps the little girl's mother, father, or even an older sibling.

It gave him immense pleasure to think that it could be an attractive young woman, with whom he could form a relationship. Flashes back to the encounter encouraged his fantasy. It seemed that this mystery person had a woman's gait rather than a man's. She was elegant, slender, and tall.

He envisioned that short dark curls framed her face. Her tilted nose rested just above full, red lips, and an oval-shaped chin. Her tiny, dimpled cheeks came alive every time she grinned. A ravishing set of white, even teeth flashed across the rounding corners of her lips. When she looked up at him, it was an indifferent gaze; her large, greenish-blue eyes peeped through the long curly lashes of partly-opened lids. She was a poet's inspiration.

Piccolo-Xavier felt dizzy. He could not think any longer. He went into slumber, shallow and peculiar, somewhere between real and surreal. A woman of this description existed perhaps, but was it only as a figment of his imagination? Could she appear in person, someday? He looked at his girlfriend, Lorna, lying next to him, and thought about her reactions if she heard about all this. He wandered off to a land full of dreams and even more visions.

For breakfast the next morning, Lorna bought two croissants from the bakery downstairs, from the other side of the alley. She made fresh coffee, poured him a cup, bit into her croissant, and watched him help himself to milk.

"You were restless last night."

"Yes," he said.

"Are you not well?"

It was frustrating to think that he was participating in a conspiracy against himself, against them. If Lorna knew the truth, the entire truth, would she be able to trust him, again?

"Oh, a bad headache and general nervousness about my exhibit, I'm afraid."

"Have you thought of anything yet? You do have a deadline, yeah?"

"Yeah, I do. Haven't really done much and that's bugging me."

The thought of the deadline and the woman in the black

9

coat merged seamlessly. They were entangled in a way that made him more pensive than ever. Lorna did not press him for an explanation. Whatever was going on in his mind was only his to share with the muses alone, and not with her.

It had always been like that. Lorna was able to see the end product only, the art itself, but never partnered his stream-of-consciousness. She loved him regardless of the person he was. And for the artist that he had aspired to become one day. Critics always found his portraits two-dimensional: dim-eyed wooden bodies, flat personalities, without a perspective. Through it all, he persevered.

Lorna cleared the table and went into the shower to get dressed for work. Deep character lines appeared on Piccolo-Xavier's forehead. He delved into artistic thoughts. On his way to the studio, he took a train. He came into the station before the train had arrived. He stood on the platform momentarily, looking at all the women in black coats. They came in all shapes and sizes. His dream woman from the road was not amongst them. But then, he didn't even know what she really looked like.

When the train rolled in, he embarked. And walked towards an empty window seat. He closed his eyes. There she was, again. This woman appeared in his mind; the face he had been painting since the saga of the lost locket began. He started dating this lady through fragmented snapshots; holding hands at the park; kissing her full lips beneath the weeping willow tree; making passionate love on the snow-white sheets of heavenly bliss. It now hurt. She was there, and yet, not close enough. Was he cheating on Lorna? Being this way? Thinking this way? Could he help himself? Now, there was a thought; this newfound dark lady consumed him. He couldn't block her from his mind. He didn't know why or how this unseen woman came to invade his thoughts.

10

The train stopped at the central station. He got out on the platform. He knew he wasn't going to forget her anytime soon, a mere stranger, a faceless phantom with whom he conversed, loudly at times, had dinners with at twilight, drove out together into the sunset, and danced with her in the silence of the night. He looked into her deep eyes and kept looking. Someone honked; he snapped out of his thoughts. He had left his studio far behind. He retraced his footsteps, brooding that he could do so much better with Lorna, if only he could love her as passionately.

Piccolo-Xavier forgot to sleep; he forgot to eat; he even stayed away from making love to Lorna. He felt some days that he was completely in the grips of this phantom. Who was she? An idea perhaps, an idea of abstract love. One which shackled his mind. He was not in possession of it anymore. It belonged to some else. He began to paint isolated images. First he painted eyes, nose, and mouth, then hands, a rounded elbow and bony knees and knotty ankles, legs until a slender shape took form. It didn't look like a real person, but a bit like cubism perhaps. Eventually, a curvy figure emerged. He scowled at it, holding his chin on the left palm and the paint brush in the other hand. He added more colour to the eyes, making them penetrate.

This portrait looked quite surreal. All the more, because the model was a delusion. Every detail, as far as his imagination stretched, was done to perfection, down to the unclasped locket dangling from her tapering fingers. The life-like portrait of the little girl peeking through the locket frame had not gone amiss either. Shrouding it with a black coat, he winked at it, and named it, *Le Habit Noir*.

He stood back and stared at it for a long while, his eyes wishing to see more than they could. He put the brush away on a round table beside the canvas, a radiant smile spreading across his lips. He cloaked the painting and deemed it ready for the exhibit.

On his way home, he went to the same road where he had picked up the locket. His eyes searched for this fantasy everywhere. It left him empty when he felt that he knew her somehow and could even vaguely smell her perfume in the thin air. He sat down on a bench by the lamp-post. His elbow was on a hand-rest, and palm on his forehead. It started to drizzle; rain followed soon, skewing down the street-lamp under the dark, starless sky.

Soaking wet, he walked back home hoping that one day, maybe, he would meet her in person. The exhibit was only seven days away. He waited impatiently to show his dark lady to the world. On the day of the exhibit, *Le Habit Noir* hung on one of the walls of the Taiss gallery; people were milling about and looking at this art. Some sat down in front of it, lost in quiet musing. It was hard to know from their expressions what they were thinking. Some smiled, while others frowned at it critically, but generally speaking, surrealism sat well with art lovers. Then, serendipitously a girl cried out in the midst of this urbane, arty crowd. People looked at her sharply. Piccolo-Xavier startled. He stood frozen in the middle of the room. Time had suspended.

All those compliments people paid, the well-deserved attention, the autographs that fans desired, or even the potential buyers who flocked towards him, didn't seem important anymore. At that moment, what had mattered was this resounding cry cutting through the space of that room. This was not a dream. The lady in the black coat and the little girl, from the picture in the locket, stood in the room. There they were. Right here before him. The girl's lips had parted, while her adult companion stood pointing her index inadvertently, towards the painting, her lips rounding in total amazement. She did not have dark hair the way he had imagined. It was much longer and flowing. The gaze was not penetrating. Her eyes were, small and beady. She was attractive too but not exactly the image he had imagined. Disappointed? No, he was not. He proceeded towards her thinking that he owed her an explanation.

"Hello," Piccolo-Xavier said.

The lady turned around, taking his hand into hers and said, "Hello."

"I am Piccolo-Xavier. You must be wondering where I got all this."

"Actually I was, and this picture, it's not me, but she is," she blurted out in a shrill, angst-ridden voice, pointing at the little girl.

"I know," he replied.

His chest heaved, but his speech was measured.

"Would you care to join me for a coffee? I fear I have a lot to explain."

"Sure, where would you like to go?" she asked.

Piccolo-Xavier led her to the Jewish café, the Boulanger Patissier, right across the road from the gallery. It was popular with artists and poets. What an incredible moment for Piccolo-Xavier that he held the arm of the woman in the black coat. She showed up at last. They sat down, at a corner table.

"You know my name, but I don't know yours?" he asked, as they sat down.

"It's Julia," she said. "And this is Chevon, my own."

"Hi, Chevon," he smiled.

They ordered two short blacks and a milkshake for the girl. Piccolo-Xavier noted silent wonderment in the girl's wide eyes. He handed her the drink. An odd feeling came over him. He had the most unusual emotional transformation as he described the events of that night to her. Strangely, he felt more connected to the faceless black coat than this woman, this young, attractive woman sitting before him. The affections he had been harbouring hitherto were then for whom?

"What do you do?" asked Piccolo-Xavier.

"Oh, I'm a student of visual art at the Academy of Fine Arts. Did you try to look for me?"

"Yes," he answered.

They sipped their coffee. Neither of them knew what to say next. Then to break this, Julia looked up and said in all sincerity, "I feel like sharing something with you."

"What might that be?" he asked.

"We broke up."

"How do you mean?"

"My partner and I, of course."

"Oh, I see," said Piccolo-Xavier.

"Well? Aren't you going to ask why?"

"Not really."

"Why not?"

"It's not my place, I guess," he said, quietly.

"Why don't we have dinner together one evening?"

"Maybe."

"How about next Sunday? My place?"

There was an element of almost juvenile candidness in her behaviour. Julia was taking him for granted. He felt rushed, pressured. The conversation was not going anywhere, really. This left him disenchanted.

"Look, can we talk about this later?"

"Sure, if that's what you want."

She scribbled her phone number and her name on a serviette that she'd pulled from the silver holder. Handing him her details, she suppressed a giggle like a cheeky teenager. However, he didn't notice her amusement because his thoughts roamed elsewhere, back to the dark lady. He realised that the magic, as far as Julia was concerned, was lost. It was far too mundane, far too sullied, for his artistic taste to carry on this affair. He had Lorna in his life too.

"Call me," she said as he nodded.

They rose to leave. They exited the café together, smiled at one another, and went their separate ways. Piccolo-Xavier walked aimlessly down the street; the thought of the phantom crept. He wondered if he had committed himself to unrequited love, because in the lead up to the exhibition, he couldn't forget her even for a moment. She followed him everywhere. Even at this moment, he had a mad desire to woo her right here on the street. But he continued to walk and returned home to Lorna instead; a woman of flesh and blood waited. When night fell, they went to bed.

In the early hours of the morning, Lorna and he lay entwined, like a pair of Siamese twins. Lorna had Piccolo-Xavier all to herself. He was a celebrity at last as she had imagined him to be. In a way, she was famous too. Her exultant pictures splashed across the newspapers on this momentous occasion; yet, the muses smiled at her predicament.

Julia was quite taken by his charms. His non-committal responses made no difference. She was not dissuaded when they said goodbye. A few days later, she went to the Taiss gallery, to look for Piccolo-Xavier. He was not there. But, she was able to get some information by showing them her Student ID card. Now that she knew where he lived, she decided to pay him a visit at his apartment on 57 Grand Avenue. Piccolo-Xavier made no attempt to contact her; he did not even know that she was seeking him.

The next day he left for the studio, steeped in drunken enchantment and still under the spell of the dark lady, in body and in spirit. He grew paler by the day and gradually

15

lost his appetite. Had Lorna not noticed, it would have been different. But since Piccolo-Xavier's malady was starting to show, she could not help but become aware of it. Nevertheless, she could not give him a remedy either. His constant distractions were impinging on their relationship. Every attempt she made to ask him about it, failed, simply because he brushed her aside and gave her a broad smile, telling her that it was nothing too serious. Lorna did not believe him. She thought that the malaise, if anything, was not physical, but mental. In her wildest imagination, however, she never thought of the existence of a phantom.

That morning, soon after Piccolo-Xavier left, the bell rang. Lorna heard it from the shower. She quickly came out and wrapped herself with a towel. She thought maybe it was Piccolo-Xavier, come back to pick up something. He had been increasingly unmindful lately. She walked through the scantily decorated lounge-room and looked through the peephole, but had not recognised the person standing outside. She opened the door, anyway.

They eyed each other up and down. After a quick *bo'jou,* Julia asked if she could speak to Piccolo-Xavier. Lorna told her that she just missed him.

"Would you like to come in?" Lorna asked.

"I don't want to be a bother."

"No, of course not, it's my day off," Lorna said.

Who was this woman? Lorna thought. What did she want from Piccolo-Xavier?

"I'm Lorna, Piccolo-Xavier's girlfriend."

Julia grimaced, sizing her up.

"How do you know Piccolo-Xavier?" Lorna asked.

"It's a long story. I'm an art student. And, after that smashing exhibit, who wouldn't know him?"

"So true. Did you want me to give him a message?"

Lorna could have easily given her address to the studio. However, she did not feel that this person could be trusted.

"Yes, that would be great, actually. If you could get him to call me?"

"May I have your number?"

"He has it."

"He does?"

"Yes, I gave it to him at the café where we had coffee."

"You had coffee together?"

"Oh yes, didn't he tell you?"

"No. What's there to tell?"

"Why, the story of course?"

"What? What story?"

Lorna was fidgeting. She tried to stop it. And suppress the anxiety in her voice.

"Oh look, I shouldn't tell you anymore," Julia said, looking at her obliquely.

She grimaced again and said she would be back soon to have a chat with Piccolo-Xavier. Then, she turned towards the door.

"But, what was your name?" Lorna asked.

"Please tell Monsieur Piccolo-Xavier that Julia dropped by. He'll know."

"Really? How does he know you, again?"

"Ask him," Julia said. "*Au revoir.*"

"*Au Revoir.*"

Lorna pursued the conversation no more. She felt hot, in spite of the shower that she had a short while ago. A brook flowed nearby; its lilting murmur gave her no respite. She wiped off the perspiration springing on her upper lip. She wanted to know more about this woman. She thought, what was she doing, meddling in their life? Who was she?

Julia stepped outside. Devious as it was, she entertained

17

the sadistic pleasure that Lorna was perturbed. Suppressing another giggle, she felt she had done enough damage for one day and she deserved praise. This was a brilliant plan. Once Lorna moved out, Julia with Chevon could move straight in.

In the studio that morning, Piccolo-Xavier tried to clear the phantom out of his head. He painted one picture after another on different canvasses. They were images of faces and images of faceless bodies; singular portraits at times, and other times dual, the dark lady and the artist. He decided to call her Eve. On one canvas, a story started to emerge as he painted a collage of pictures. Eve was in the brawny bind of a serpent which tried to devour her. Piccolo-Xavier painted himself as Eve's saviour trying to rescue her from the serpent. The painting was like Michaelangelo's *Creation of Man* in the Sistine Chapel. Eve stood out as an emblem of chastity whom no evil could touch, gazing at him with a shy smile.

Eve haunted him. His paintings in the studio revealed how he was gradually becoming mad. The studio had become a rendezvous, the playground of the lovers, in which he had Edith Piaf records singing *Les Amants De Paris*. Besotted by the melodic passionate crescendos, the mad ariste did everything with Eve and painted her as he wished: nude lying on the sofa, seated, or standing up. He painted her fully dressed and dressed her up and down, sometimes in short skirts, sometimes in frocks, pink, purple, and brown. With or without an umbrella on morning's afterglow, here she was with the sun streaming in through the picture window. On wintry evenings, she was covered in the black coat, alongside the fire, mellowed. It was quite mesmerising. But, she was his lover, the model, and his life. There was no other life apart from her.

When the artist was in the thick of it, there was a sudden faint knock on the studio door. It disrupted his lovemaking. First, he thought he would ignore it. But he couldn't, because the knocks were becoming more insistent, loud, as if the knocker was going to rip the door apart. Reluctantly, he rose from his stool and disengaged himself from the canvas portrayal of Eve's red, pouty lips.

His held the brush handle between his middle and ring finger. The paint from the brush touched his palm and smeared it. He saw it; it was milk and honey. He walked up to the door, droopy eyed. His lips were parted; there was also a noticeable bulge in the crotch. He opened the door and saw a woman. Not just any woman but... it was her, the phantom, his Eve. She stood here in the light of the sun. Eve smiled and walked right through him while he watched her.

She took his hands in hers.

"You don't know how long I've waited for this moment! You came. You finally came!"

Piccolo-Xavier whispered into her ears. His words dribbled out of his lips inaudibly like sleep talk. His eyes were half-closed in a trance.

"Yes, I have," Eve said looking at him.

"But for how long?" he asked.

"For as long as you want," she answered. "Breathe with me, my love."

Her long gown fell to the floor. Piccolo-Xavier sat down near the hem of her dress. She sat too, by his side. He looked up at her quivering red lips and her swelling breasts. It was her, Eve, the phantom in the flesh. She bent down and kissed him with her full, sweet lips. Once that prolonged kiss was over, she cupped his face in her palms and placed it gently on her lap, caressing his cheeks. She stroked through his hair with her long tapering fingers. He felt her breathing soft on his face. His fantasy and reality were fused. Piccolo-Xavier felt no anguish. He was one with his dream.

"Sleep, my love," said Eve. "You and I are one now."

The Interlude

It was an unforgettable evening. The servants of the House of Chowdhury had prepared the front yard as usual for a regular singing session. The family had just finished dinner. The master and the mistress, Mr and Mrs Chowdhury, noticed that their youngest son Ashik's chair at the table's far end was empty. After dinner, the family gathered on the mat in the front yard, although they expected no singing tonight. There wasn't going to be any because the singer, Ashik, had disappeared since last night. Adjacent to the gardens, next to the front yard, several lanterns were placed around a musical instrument. They shed light on a forlorn harmonium sitting on the mat without a vocalist. The slightly-ajar gate, between the neighbour Raja Hashem's place and the House of Chowdhury, lent a view to how big this house was against the backdrop of the cottage next door. The House of Chowdhury housed at least fifty members.

Few among those fifty residents, almost no one, had any clues to Ashik's sudden disappearance. Except for Ashik's younger brother, Sheri, and his girlfriend, Lutfun. They had some inkling. Ashik also had an older brother, Ekram, but he was never around. After the elders had gone to bed, curiosity goaded the duo to watch. They witnessed a horrific revelation unfold, that Ashik pulled the neighbour's wife, Prema Hashem, towards himself by the hand. And she relented without hesitation. It was a dark, moonless night. The monsoon had covered all of the stars, with impending rain. But the lanterns had not been snuffed out just yet. The telltale tall shadows were a sign that the pair was in love. They held each other closely. Then he kissed her.

Lutfun was rooted to the balcony's mosaic floor. She blinked a few times, gripping Sheri's hand. Their gaze transfixed at the looming shadow. She sensed that this was all wrong. How deplorable an act to covet the neighbour's wife! One, which would also hurt the reputation of the noble House of Chowdhury. They saw the shadows rise to make an egress through the main gate.

The following evening, people sat glumly outside on the mat, in silence. Lutfun and Sheri were there too. Somewhat statued on the mat, they realised that this uncomfortable secret of the elopement needed to be told, but their courage failed them. This could become fodder for gossip amongst the elite for days on end. Ashik's absence stirred the core of his parents' heart as it is; their son, a talented singer, had gone missing, the singing disrupted tonight on account of it.

A stormy wind picked up and swept through the front yard. The elders, Ashik and Sheri's parents, Mr and Mrs Chowdhury, quickly rose from the mat and went indoors with all other fifty members in tow, including Lutfun and Sheri. The flowers in the garden trembled in the gust. A few even wilted instantly and snapped off their dry branches in a matter of seconds.

This, a sprawling ancestral home, the House of Chowdhury, was a show of grandeur and landed aristocracy. It was an old two-story house wrapped around by broad balconies. They had wrought iron balustrades with floral-shaped ivory inlays. It had five massive bedrooms upstairs and four bedrooms downstairs, with a rectangular shaped living room and a dining room. The kitchen was not attached to the main house. It was separated by an orchard in the middle at the back of the house.

The Chowdhury family may not have been particularly inclined towards conservatism, but the mistress of the family knew where to draw the line. She would not have condoned Ashik's elopement with the neighbour's wife.

22

That would push her far beyond her limits. However, everyone was still in the dark, except Lutfun and Sheri. All they knew was this, that Ashik had not been home since the last soirée. Raja Hashem reported his wife, Prema Hashem, missing as well. The family suspected as much, especially Mr Chowdhury, who thought that the two were up to no good. It was too much of a coincidence that they disappeared at the same time. His suspicion nagged as it nagged in the others too. Only Lutfun and Sheri knew for sure, the truth which was their best-kept secret. They continued to observe the family trepidations without so much as a word.

A dream within a dream; a plot within a plot; a cloud over a cloud; a layer upon a layer, blues played out through the monsoon pour. Servants rushed to close windows around the house; the winds raged. The Lyra behind the wooden shutters, desperate in a bid to enter. When they couldn't enter, the drifts drove up fallen branches of dead leaves and the discarded weeds. The rain hammered on the open verandah. Lutfun lit a few candles inside the house and placed them around the room amongst the decrepit, antique furniture. Then she sat down on a high-backed chair in an alcove with Mrs Chowdhury.

They were Zamindars. Every inch, royalty and rightful landlords of their villages, they retained the title Chowdhury; a remnant, a whiff of a bygone era, a hedonistic lifestyle, which entertained decadence. The Zamindars could engage in practically anything they wanted. Womanising topped the list. The heavy smell of alcohol and the unending tinkling of ankle bells of court dancers stifled the palace air. Their official wives had not much say, about those who Zamindars took as paramours. They were powerful men, who rarely cared about anyone's feelings. They cared even less how they squandered the wealth, accumulated over many generations. Clearly, some

23

attracted more disrepute than others. This was an era of no accountability; the kings got away with every mortal sin on earth, even bloody murder. The cosy confluence of power and money made them untouchables. It was the sanctuary of nobility, their refuge.

However, the wheels of the overhaul were underway; it foretold the end of this sagging system, with the slow, but sure raid of colonisation. This was the fulfilment of destiny, riddled with the sins of fathers and the forefathers. An era had come round a full cycle. As the days ended, the crows and the bats went to sleep to wake up to a new rule of law. Although the class of Zamindars as a whole faced a major blow, they could not be cleansed any time soon. Some kept their old money, jewellery and their land assets. Then they forged deals with the new governments with serious facelifts. Such makeovers replaced the old corruption with a crisp newness.

God finally took a shine to the oppressed. Divine retribution descended on them in full fury like molten lead. It compromised the fate of these Zaminders from the House of Chowdhury too, which now hung in the balance, for a devastating flood occurred to boot the onslaught of colonisation. It drowned many of their villages, ousting them into the cold. Most thought of it as comeuppance. It drove them out of their opulent home and forced them to make a choice between either leaving the village or dying in the flood. They chose the former and migrated to town. Their ancestral village remained submerged for many years to come. But they survived by entering into business and flourishing on the repute of being a fallen aristocracy. They managed to remain well within the circle of similar high-profile families.

The night of the monsoon rainfall, the family sat grumbling over the disappearance of their beloved Ashik.

Reporting this incident to the police was a possibility. Lutfun and Sheri could shed some light, but their mouths were sealed like vexed children assaulted by a relative, vowing to never divulge. The steady monsoon rain tapered off, like the gradual fading of anklet bells before a maudlin Chowdhury, soaked in the dust of alcohol and lust.

Then there was a knock on the door which the family couldn't hear at first. They thought the window rattled from the raging wind. But this rattle became louder until a servant opened the door. Ashik Chowdhury stood on the doorstep with Prema Hashem. It was puzzling, but the news they brought was even more shocking. That Prema Hashem dressed in a red bridal sari, had her head covered in a veil. They walked over the threshold. Ashik entered at first, followed by a demure Prema. In the lime candlelight, she looked soft and young. Her fair, flawless beauty impressed everyone in the room, as they looked at her speechlessly. She came forward and stood before the mistress of the house.

Lutfun and Sheri watched in awe. Mrs Chowdhury's face paled. She rose from a leggy but rickety chair. It creaked and then collapsed, giving way to its weak structure. She looked at Ashik with rage emanating through her eyes and spat out, "What have you done? Are you in your right mind? Have you gone mad?"

Ashik stood there. His head lowered in front of the revered Mr and Mrs Chowdhury and the rest of the family.

"We're in love," he said.

It hurt Sheri to see his suave, talented brother slighted, and diminished to this.

"You couldn't find anyone else to fall in love with? But of all people, it had to be her?" his mother retorted. And then, she declared to everyone's astonishment, "Get out. Out! This very minute. I don't care where you go!"

25

Mr Chowdhury tried to calm her down by patting her on her back. But she was inconsolable. She was not prepared to give even an inch of leeway.

"Calm down. Where would they go in this rain?" he said.

"Rain or sunshine, I don't care. I disown you. Just go."

She then turned towards the family and said in a low tone but full fury, "Listen up, everyone, if I find anyone helping them, make no mistake you too will be kicked out."

She left the room. A docile servant followed her with a candle. Mr Chowdhury, too, meekly went out with her. However, Sheri and Lutfun couldn't endure this anymore. They knew they were taking a risk, but they came forward to aid the newlyweds anyway. As soon as the elders left, they whispered to Ashik and Prema that they could sleep over in the guest room for one night on the roof; a room, with a view of the full sky and a hanging garden of enchanting monsoon blossoms; green tiger ferns, yellow lilies, arundina pink, and orchids, growing abundantly over the musty, brick walls.

Although they colluded with Ashik, against Mrs Chowdhury's will, this pleased Lutfun, as much as it pleased Ashik and his new wife. Ashik agreed to spend his wedding night with his wedded wife in his own house but like a thief in a hideout. The wake of a fresh rain triggered a keening of a muggy night's wind. Mila, Ekram's little daughter's, apprehensions got the better of her.

At midnight, the windowpane mirrored a candle flame. Inside the bedroom of the roof, there were four adults and a child sitting on a double mattress bed. Their tall shadows, reflected on the wall, showing their huddled heads. That was just a fraction of the reality. Anyone looking at this image, would think these were heads of hunter-gatherers overseeing a kill. The sound of the rainfall, heavy on the corrugated red

26

roof, drowned their talks. The colour of the roof faded into white in certain places which needed new paint.

Those who sat on the bed were Ashik, Prema, Lutfun, Sheri, and little Mila. They had not slept all night. After Mr and Mrs Chowdhury retired to bed, the siblings came together like water bubbles on a scalding pan, drawn together in the middle. Rules were meant to be broken, the much-clichéd thought prevailed in the minds of the young rebels.

"Tell us what happened?" asked Lutfun.

"Well, it's a long story," said Ashik.

"Tell us anyway."

Mila listened with wide-eyed curiosity.

"Wow, what a wild bunch of romantics."

She jotted down every detail in her mind, proud that she was in the company of such great rebels.

A masjid stood at the end of the alley from the House of Chowdhury. The masjid housed not just the daily prayers of the faithful five times a day, but the Imam also had to attend to some perfunctory duties in the community. Eloped lovers who had been discarded by society came here to be wed. The faithful Imam did these duties reluctantly, because he didn't like to wed such couples, however, neither did he want unwedded couples to live in sin. When he saw Prema Hashem and Ashik Chowdhury come to his door at sundown after the Maghrib prayer, he frowned at them. At first, he didn't want to marry them at all, because of Ashik's standing in the society, and second, because she was not officially divorced yet. But the adamant Prema was ready to divorce her husband, Raja Hashem, there and then without any hesitation.

The Imam still could not wed them legally, until a divorce settlement had been finalised according to Islamic stipulations. A waiting time of at least three months had to

27

be observed for the previous marriage to be annulled, or else the new marriage could not be sanctioned. The Imam gave a lengthy sermon as to how the talaq or repudiation by repeating talaq three times was pre-Islamic, known as Talaq al bidah. Although many may still practice it, not knowing full well, it was frowned upon and denounced by Mohammad. And then there was a third option, the judicial divorce where either spouse could divorce at a sharia court.

Commonly, in an Arab desert, men would pay a mohr to marry a woman, and leave a note of talaq for the women when they went away for the long haul. Men paid heavily sometimes to give talaq to a woman. But it was something both could put in a contract where each could give talaq to the other if the marriage broke down, in the event of violence or infidelity. Those were the solid Islamic laws, but people's customs deviated far too much from such legalities, sometimes even without any bearing on these laws, when all they had to do was utter talaq, talaq, and talaq three times to divorce. For Prema, that was exactly what had happened. The Imam accepted her repudiation, upon hearing it, and rendered the couple talaq. He summoned Raja Hashem to the mosque that evening, who pronounced the word three times in presence of the couple. And the Imam put an end to this charade.

An overwhelming feeling of shame touched Raja Hashem afterwards, but his wife – or ex-wife now – did not share his emotion. The Imam sat down with his Quran and Qalema and married the new couple. After they were blessed, they left the mosque. The newlyweds felt a strange kind of solidarity towards each other, thinking about the next course of action. There was none. So Ashik, her new husband, bought her a red sari from a shop down the alley to doll her up at least like a bride.

During the dying days of the Zamindars, there were many party politics, played to keep the tradition alive. Deals were made with the British, but none worked out in favour of the Zamindars. The British well and truly expunged the tradition in the end. However, some were allowed to keep the title and their assets, such as palaces. Although, they were not the lords of their little kingdoms anymore, they had but gained influence for being old money, which they cashed in unfailingly. As profiteers always do, their reputation hinged on family connections. Prema Hashem's dramatic wedding with Ashik Chowdhury had become bad news for the House of Chowdhury.

The morning birds, the hungry crows, the cuckoo and an odd old eagle, all came out of the woodwork as a new sun smiled upon the world. They flew onto the roof to feed themselves on the nectar of the fresh monsoon blooms. Prema took her morning bath and stood out on the roof. Mila had fallen asleep on the mattress here the night before. Sheri and Lutfun left early in the morning. The azan from the mosque, which the same Imam sang, brought them to their senses that it was time to go to bed. Lutfun felt a thrill through her, sensing Ashik's chivalry of love. So much so, that she began to make preparations to let her own desires to be wedded to Sheri known to the family, although hers and Sheri's matter was more or less settled.

Lutfun was not an orphan. She lived in this house, but was not related to the Chowdhury family in any way. Her own parents had left her on the doorstep of the House of Chowdhury as a baby. Mrs Chowdhury, then a young mother herself, brought her home and raised her like her own children. Once she was old enough, Mrs Chowdhury told her about her biological parents. Sheri and Lutfun started off as friends, but they eventually fell in love in their teens. A relationship everyone found sweet.

Ashik, maybe a renegade, but he took full responsibility for what he did. Sheri was more of a conformist. Even though the age of Zamindari had died out, maintaining customary civility was paramount. Marrying the neighbour's wife was a violation of those unwritten rules. However, Prema and Ashik were in deep denial. Her defection didn't stir any sense of remorse of moral wrongdoing. Rather this emboldened them to embrace love. Ashik and Prema, both knew that they had to leave soon. But they'd also known that their life was southbound. Ashik would be disowned from his inheritance. But it didn't seem to worry them.

Prema, in all her prettiness, sat on the floor of an empty corner of the roof, in the morning. Her silky long hair shone in the lazy summer's sun, as she left it out to dry in the breeze. She watched birds play out their antics. They pecked greedily at a fallen seed on the roof. Seeds were mostly from ripened guavas gutted out of their pink core. Redhead woodcutters beaked and drilled through the russet poplar bark. Honeysuckle cups overflowed with juices and more from rainwater, nature's ultimate goodies from which crows and ravens sipped. Mila, who had dozed off, woke up. She found Prema there and had sat down by her side on the roof's musty floor. They watched the birds together, poking each other like a choreographed dance.

"Do you want to feed them?" Mila asked Prema, rubbing her eyes.

Prema Chowdhury smiled and nodded. She hardly slept all night. Mila saw how red her swollen eyes were. She smiled back and then they saw Ashik come out on the roof to join them. It was a gathering; a gathering of birds and humans. A few hours later, they heard footsteps on the stairs. Not sure whose they were, they braced themselves.

To their relief, they saw Lutfun appearing with a breakfast tray in her hand.

"Good, you're all up," Lutfun said.

"Yes, I've been up for a while now," Prema smiled.

"Here, I brought you guys some breakfast."

Lutfun put the tray down on a rain-beaten table. It was most unusual that the newlyweds tore down all the customs. Prema's ex lived just next door. She could almost hear her own children crying, "Mum, there's Mum on the roof of the House of Chowdhury."

"Well, you'd better finish breakfast and be off, I guess, before the house wakes up to find you guys here," said Lutfun.

And then she turned to look at Mila and said, "Shouldn't you be off too? Go downstairs before your mother comes up here looking for you. Go already. Hurry."

Mila gave her new aunty a hug and escaped down the flights of stairs. She startled when she found her mother, Nazmun Banu, on the landing, who was coming up the stairs to the roof to look for her. She had been into her daughter's bedroom in the morning. Nazmun Banu, looked at her sternly, waiting for an acceptable explanation. When her daughter had none, she held her by the hand and dragged her to their rooms.

"Do you know that I'd nearly fainted this morning when I found out that you hadn't slept in your own room? Do you even realise how much anxiety you've caused me? Now tell me where you were. Tell me this minute."

Mila thought if her mettle was to be tested, then this was the time. There was no pride in untested virtue. Once and for all, how she responded to her mother now, would prove her loyalty to the greater family, her uncles. The question was, whose side should she take?

Even at that tender age, Mila knew that she couldn't betray her uncles. But neither could she betray her mother. She

31

kept quiet until her mother's anger was diminished. Then Nazmun Banu broke into tears, mumbling how her own life took a bad turn because of Mila's father, Ekram. He remarried, to her best friend! Trust, by far, was the fastest depleting value of all. Her love was blighted; it was like being caught between the last hours of sunset and total darkness. Ekram's sensuous visitations on her doorsteps in the middle of the night often awakened Mila to remind her of her parents' togetherness, that Nazmun Banu, after all, was the first of his two wedded wives. And that he had come back at night to claim what was halal or kosher, as he frequented between his two wives.

Nazmun Banu had relented without much of a protest because these kinds of intimacy with her husband gave this relationship meaning and a reason for her to continue to stay in this House of Chowdhury.

Legitimate, it sure was. But whether or not it was moral, was the issue. Nazmun Banu lapsed periodically into a deep depression. As often was the case, she broke down into tears in front of Mila and gave her a few tight slaps across her face for minor mischiefs or none at all. She just needed an excuse to vent herself. She had become deceptive, like pith of the citrus fruits' hidden underlining. On the surface, all was smooth. Smiles and laughter. But they were as short-lived as the mandala, smeared with fleeting joy and pride. The colourful sand paint was painstakingly removed the moment they were finished. When dusk fell and the family retired to their quarters with their partners, only Nazmun Banu sat alone on her high regal bed wondering who her husband chose to be with for the night.

Sometimes she heard Sheri and Lutfun. Their tinkle of soft laughter sailing through the open shutters towards the rose garden below. They bloomed, while she sat upright like a thorny anomaly. Did she not feel like romancing? Did

32

she not want her husband to accompany her to the movies like all other couples of the house, to watch the handsome chocolate hero of the time, Waheed Murad? But no, she suppressed those desires. In silence, they ate right through her soul, like termites, until it turned into the mandala sand to be deposited downstream in the aftermath. For that was what her life had become in the end, termite stricken. Disposable.

Only, no one saw this infestation. The poisonous resin ultimately ate away the core of her heart. Mila didn't realise it; neither did her mother. But this poison left them both depleted of values, particularly Mila, who turned into a sadist. For when Nazmun Banu cried out in pain, and in front of her sometimes, Mila had a smile hovering on her lips.

Despite everything, Nazmun Banu was loyal to her in-laws, who in turn also respected her for being their eldest brother's wife. Sheri and Ashik, Lutfun, and Mr and Mrs Chowdhury had more respect for Nazmun than their own brother and son, Ekram, or his second wife. The second wife could never step foot into this house, let alone be accepted. She stayed away from everybody, not by choice, but because she was completely walled out by the members of the family, out of deference for Nazmun Banu. This special place or status that she held in the house was ample compensation. But Mila sometimes wondered why her mother had not left and moved back with her own parents, who lived not too far away but by the mosque. The answer was all too simple, because her parents wouldn't have her back.

Nazmun Banu and Ekram Chowdhury too had eloped just like Ashik and Prema. But under Mrs Chowdhury's strict moral codes, while she accepted Nazmun Banu, she had discarded Prema. Fair enough, Nazmun was an

33

innocent child of sixteen and Prema? She was a grown woman. She was someone's wife. Those were her rules. In accordance with those rules, Ashik and Prema had lost Mrs Chowdhury's support.

No big deal; risk-takers such as Ashik and Prema never cared much about rules, anyway. This total disregard for morals gave them a strange kind of a high. Because of what had happened to them later was unbelievable by any stretch of the imagination. But they fared well. Stealthily, they came down from the back spiral stairs following Lutfun. She saw them to the door. On the road, they held each other's hands. They had no money and certainly nowhere to go. Lutfun gave them some from the savings of her pocket money. It was about 200 rupees, which in those days, of the 1960s, was a decent amount. They embarked on this journey, with only that and a small sack of clothes and bric-a-brac, which Lutfun snitched from the kitchen. They headed out for Raven's end, where there was a slum by the alley, behind the mosque. Here, in the slums, they started a new life.

Gold Foliage

Pintu sat quietly in his room at Madura Island boot camp where he was undergoing mandatory military training. Dravi authorities wanted to fully ensure that every refugee received it. Conscription was frequent in Draviland as they were in perpetual war with the neighbouring state of Zelda. Knowledge about Draviland laws and social values was another important aspect before gaining freedom of release. More importantly, they had to make sure that refugees did not pose a threat to the citizens of Dravi.

Smoking guns filled up the atmosphere around him suddenly. One man, died here a couple of hours ago. This man wanted freedom so badly that he tried to flee the boot camp. It was considered mutiny. Where no guns were even supposed to be brought in, let alone be used, guards shot and killed him. They were always unarmed. Fear never left Pintu's side. He hid with twenty others cramped under a bed and felt that he too would get caught up in the crossfire. Pintu thought of Maa but had not called her.

The last time he spoke to her, she was too upset to carry on a conversation. It saddened him too; he had then decided not to call her again. He wanted to send money home. Feeling quite useless, he didn't think it was going to be so hard to earn money or to make a living here. Escape was not possible from this place because of the ubiquitous presence of the sea. Unless the refugees volunteered to return to the homeland, there was no getting away from this boot camp; the political climate forced them to become refugees. Nobody wanted to flee, certainly not become refugees. But to escape persecution back home, what other option did they have?

But Pintu felt trapped in this boot camp as well. He felt that they were gradually becoming invisible characters to the authorities here, who felt they owed no obligation to save them. They were not the saviours. This caused many refugees to become suicidal from sheer uncertainty. Sleep was a constant problem and pills didn't help. It was just as futile as it was to see psychologists, generally known as confidantes in this boot camp. Repeated monotonous questions shot from them, giving Pintu no peace of mind at all; on the contrary, they made him angry. Hell begot hellish behaviour and that was certain. Refugees who came from other remote parts of this two-moon planet gave Pintu suggestive looks. They even invited him to come into their rooms at night. Pintu was still a child. At seventeen, he didn't want to lose his optimism, nor his virginity to other trainees. After all, he survived the formidable Mundip forests by remaining hidden for days on end from the police there. One day, he went to see his confidante to put things in perspective.

"Optimism is a good thing," the confidante said.

"Yes, I'm not suicidal. Not yet. But it scares the hell out of me when I hear others are. I've seen on TV how people kill themselves here because they got tired of waiting."

"Yeah, I know waiting can be quite tiresome, the worst that there is. It could snare one into all kinds of situations."

"Is there nothing you or anyone could do? Everyone tells me to be patient; investigations are underway. Has anyone been to see my father in our village yet? What's taking them so long to complete background checks? I haven't killed anyone. I was framed; they set me up."

"I know, but you know what? There's always light at the end of the tunnel. You just need to wait it out."

"And I am, of course. That's all we do, isn't it? Wait and be patient, while Maa suffers. I don't call them anymore. It upsets me to see her so sad. She cries endlessly on the phone."

36

"What do you do, when she does that?"

"I try to console her. Well, used to, but I feel I'm in a losing battle. Words dry up in my mouth. I don't know what to say to her anymore."

"She should be happy that you're alive."

"Oh yes, that she is. People won't leave them in peace, you see. Police come around and Miah's men too in the village, to ask about my whereabouts. They tell them that they don't know. Baba got badly beaten. They tied up Maa."

"All this must be really hard to talk about. But thank you for sharing. Is there anything else you want to say?"

"What else? No, none. Would no one take a shine to me ever? I don't want to be tinkering all my life doing nothing."

"You won't. Be strong now, so you can deal with life's difficulties later."

"Yeah. Thanks."

"Goodbye, Pintu. Come and talk to me anytime you want, okay?"

Pintu came out of her office feeling slightly upbeat. He thought of strange paradoxes of life. Hard work didn't always pay off. Who would intervene on his behalf? Man or God? It was almost like waiting for divine intervention to take place. Men had so much power over others. People with strong cases and weak were all in the same boat. All were running away from the oppression of some sort. Evidence? Where was he going to get all this evidence from? In this culture, documents were taken seriously. But not back home in the Lost Winds. Nothing was well documented under the regime there. His papers looked fraudulent here. He arrived with hardly any clothes, and certainly no passport. There was no evidence of his alleged crime. How did one prove one's innocence? Yet, he would

37

die a terrible death in the hands of those who brought these trumped-up charges against him.

All the niceties of the world were a mirage to him. Fame, wealth, power, and happiness were lures revolving around him. Somehow, he was not a part of it. He felt he existed in a parallel world with only a 'see-through' button. He could only look, but could never be in the desired world. Like the forbidden fruit, not permitted to enjoy, as though these impossibilities were hardwired into his system. Burn it. Oh! Burn it all. There was no need for arts to flourish; no music to soothe the mind; no latent talent to be recognised. Barrenness was all that there ever was. However, he harboured strong passions to become someone; he waited for his ambition to flower, as the world prepared to impede it.

Pintu sat down to eat his lunch. Today, it was a meal from the Serendipa. Every dish came with the tinge of a sour and sweet taste. He picked at his yogurt and smiled, remembering the young confidante lady. He managed that conversation in the broken Kroll language. Warmth grew in his heart. He was curious to find out if she was married. No matter; he discarded the unwarranted thoughts. When the night fell over the mountains of the camp, he sat down in his room rummaging through all kinds of thoughts. That was mostly what he seemed to be doing these days, besides attending Kroll classes, training, gym, and sports. He watched TV for a while and then prayed. Then he went to bed. Sleeping was one of the hardest things to do in camp. He fell asleep to be awakened by intermittent nightmares.

Between those troubled hours of sleep and awakening, he heard Maa's frantic screams; they echoed through his disturbed mind. *Run, boy, run. They're coming for you.* Pinto ran breathlessly through the alley, by the Mohammadan house of God. His little chest heaved, tight with fear. Motorbikers surrounded him; men in dark glasses in hot pursuit came to take him away.

"I don't want to, no, don't want to," Pintu cried in a child's thin voice. "I don't want to be a part of all this. I don't want to throw bombs at people, rocks, kill and plunder. In the name of resistance, God save me, I shall be growing up doing all this. Oh, I want to go to school, read, and to write."

But they were resolute. They picked him up without hesitation, took him away, and put him to work. It was recruitment; it was awful.

"Leave me, leave me alone," Pintu screamed in bed.

He woke up in the boot camp, all sweaty and frightened. Red streaks across a pale sky told him that it was time for the early morning prayer. Patience was a virtue. Were any other options left, besides being patient? Yet, life came with no promises or guarantees. Fleeting moments of small indulgences leading to nothingness was the only guarantee. Mega dreams and aspirations were notional; they served a futile persuasion for recognition, only to be followed by grand deceptions, central to life's contradictions. Get better at your task. Push the limits and the boundaries; freedom and fame lay ahead. Happiness was elusive for as long as it lasted, like coffee. A pat on the shoulder that one had done better than a few million others appeared to be all-important, somehow. Pintu was ambitious. He wanted to give his life another chance; he wanted to reload every bit that he had missed out on; education and employment were just some, to begin with. He called Maa impulsively one day.

"Maa, I'm going to get out of here soon, I know."

"How long? Pintu, how long?"

"I don't know. But I've got to be patient, Maa. Pray for me. To be patient is all we ever do now," he said. "Is baba better?"

"The wounds seem to be healing."

"Has anyone come to investigate?"

"Yes, yesterday. I think they were just the police from the local station."

"You need to send my school certificate, Maa. This will get me a job here in the end."

"Okay. Keep trying, Pintu. Never give up."

"I'm trying, Maa. I'm doing everything they ask me to do; couldn't try any harder."

"Are you praying regularly?"

"Yes, I am, but the man who got killed recently, also prayed regularly, Maa."

There was silence. Pintu stooped low and sat down on the campgrounds.

"Maa, you there?"

"Yes, Pintu, I am. He was just unlucky."

"Is it in our hands to change fate? What is luck?"

"Learn the ropes, Pintu. Goodbye."

"Bye, Maa."

Luck and fate were meaningful concepts to a refugee in a world determined to establish free will; this world, the Draviland, where pre-determination was obsolete. Learn the ropes. Being talented or truthful, no matter how legitimate, did not always guarantee success. Men died in the Red Sea. Some survived with tremendous luck, saved by dolphins, those stories were true too. Life's journey was at odds. It could pass without fully understanding exactly what we were supposed to do here; what paths to take and what the cosmic plan of our existence was. Refugees were leaving the camp, every day, but Pintu's day of release never came. He suspected that perhaps more papers were required; evidence, more and more of them to fully satisfy the high counsellors of the Draviland of his innocence. Time would pass unimpeded just like the slow

40

waters down the drain; invaluable. For each invisible minute lost, here was an irrevocable addition towards infinity.

Pintu was not tall. He was dark and plump. He lacked sophistication, confidence, and he stammered when he spoke. A fine line of moustache was just beginning to emerge on his upper lip. Clothes given from the camp were his only possessions, besides a mobile, which he had bought from Mundip. Calling Maa and having a conversation with her ever so often, made his day.

One morning, he went to see the confidante again. He sat across the table from her, as he spoke with her in his usual broken Kroll language. She noted that he squinted often and looked at the floor continuously. Pintu was afraid to make eye contact today.

"Pintu, tell me, why did you want to see me?"

"I want to tell you something."

"Okay, what is it that you want to tell me?"

"My maa grieves for me every day."

"I'm sorry to hear that your mother is so heart-broken."

"How can I prove that I had nothing to do with that murder?" he asked.

"Provide papers."

"What evidence? I'm innocent."

"Do you have a court case back home? Have you been charged with murder?" the confidante asked.

"A case has been filed recently. Maa said that the police think I did it."

"Unsettling," she said. "Oh, look, don't worry about it. Tell your mother not to worry. As long as you're in the camp, no one can harm you."

"When will I be released?"

"I don't know."

"Aww."

41

"Sorry. Have you told the counsellors of the high court everything?" she asked.

"I had lied first. I told them I had come here because I was poor. Friends told me not to tell them the truth. Also, I was afraid. Not understanding the system properly, I thought I would get into trouble here. After all, I was implicated in a murder case back in the Lost Winds."

"Have you told them your true story in your subsequent interviews?"

"Yes. But I could not tell them the date of his murder. I was confused and I gave them different dates at different times. This journey was arduous. Fifteen days out on the sea, without food and water. I wasn't thinking straight."

"You were confused. I'm sure they'll understand. Just tell the high counsellors that there has been an error," she advised, calmly.

"I ran away from many places. I'm tired of running."

"Yes, understandably. Just be patient, Pintu."

"I go to class every day to learn the Kroll language, and I play sports and of course train regularly, but I still get anxious."

"We will be able to help you with that."

"My life has been such a lie," he said, impatiently.

"Why is that?"

"I am only seventeen. I wanted to go to school, study. Just didn't work out."

"Take solace from the fact that none of it was your fault."

"I had the same dream last night. Trying to run, but can't, couldn't run away. My fate was sealed; born with broken luck," he said.

"Now, you're trying to set it right, yeah? You're doing something to amend it."

"I can only try."

"Don't underestimate your powers or, your strength, Pintu. Each of us is talented in our own ways. You just have to find out what it is that you do best and then do it."

"Yeah. I was always fond of singing. I often played the flute in the village when I took my baba lunch."

"What does he do?"

"Who? My baba? He has a farm. I wish none of this had happened."

"I'm sorry."

"Yeah, so am I."

She left it at that. And as soon as he came out, he met two other refugees who told him their release was imminent and that both had converted to Jesuit. Whether or not these releases were related to any covert operation of proselytising in the boot camp was yet to be seen. Pintu had battled all along but never thought of using religion as a means to an end. The banality of evil had caused his misfortune, but never really made him entirely Machiavellian.

In the village, as he often did, Pintu took lunch to the field for baba, his father. Maa made up a plate full of rice, with some green papaya on the side and a raw onion. Pinch of salt and green chilies were placed on one corner of the plate as well. She covered the plate with a lid and put two smaller bowls on top. One container carried a watery fish dish, the other bean soup. Then the pile of containers was tied up together inside a red cotton kitchen towel, looking like the leaning tower of Pisa. He held a small pitcher of water in the other hand.

"Pintu, dear, take this to baba, okay?"

"Okay, Maa," Pintu replied.

Pintu invariably left the task at hand to obey Maa in carrying out her order. Maa's face would brighten up with a smile at his small shape leaving the house. Pintu walked for about fifteen minutes down the dirt road in his tiny penguin gait to meet baba. The farmer had just finished tilling the land and was resting expectedly, waiting for lunch to arrive. He sat down under the shade of the Banyan tree and looked out towards endless tones of greenery. Pintu was nine at the time. His little body slowly appeared on the horizon, wearing a white shirt and black patched-up shorts which Maa had lovingly stitched up. Bare-footed, the boy walked slowly, leaning over the pebbles on the dirt road at times to avoid getting hurt. The farmer smiled at him. Pintu smiled back and put the several tiers down on the grass.

"Pintu, what has Maa cooked today?"

"I don't know. Take a look."

He untied the red towel with his nimble, soft fingers and laid out a plate for baba. Then he sat cross-legged across from him under the great knotty tree and watched him eat; affection in his eyes shimmered like a desert mirage. After baba finished, Pintu quickly packed the chaotic crockery in a bundle and then stood, pulling himself up, smiling. He picked up the bundle and swung it over his shoulder before he turned around to step out. Setting off for home, on his way, he always stopped to pick up yellow mustard flowers from the side of the narrow dirt path for Maa. Maa would have bathed by then and waited for him to come back and have lunch with her. Serving two plates of food, Maa waited. When he entered, she looked at him pulling a smile and invited him to sit by her. Maa often fed Pintu.

"Come. Let's eat now."

"Okay, Maa."

That was such a treat, when Maa warmed up to him like this, occasionally feeding him sticky fish balls fried in deep oil. He would take the towering stack of soiled containers out of its ties first, and then, soak them in a bucket of water. Poverty was always there. However, so was love and care.

Pintu's eyes glistened with love, feeling special and pampered; his face would glow through a child's downy, dark, skin under a mass of oily hair pasted to his skull, like wet cow dung, glued on to the thatched walls for dry manure.

"Maa, I'll always stay with you when you grow old. Way older."

"You would? You would have your own life by then with children and a wife and my little grandchildren."

Pintu rolled his eyes in embarrassment.

"I'll take care of you, Maa, so you never have to work so hard. And I'll make sure that baba never has to work in other people's fields again. We will buy our own land, become rich, work for ourselves."

"You're a good boy, Pintu. Have you done your homework for school?"

"Yes, I have. Teacher said I did well in language."

"Good boy. No sooner you will be helping baba in the fields."

"I'm afraid to go to the house of God."

"Why?"

"Men on a Honda chase me. They tell me I must go with them."

"Go with them? Where to?"

"They tell me and other kids to go to meetings and rallies. They tell us to hurl rocks at others."

"Oh my God! Stay away from these people."

"Yes, Maa."

A long way away from home now, Pintu sat at the boot camp and heard echoes of his own sobs. Men had succeeded in recruiting him and many others like him in the end.

One midsummer afternoon, as he was returning from

45

the Mohammadan house of God, they caught him on the dirt road and took him off to the city. He had just turned ten.

"Let me go! I want to go home!" he had cried out.

"We will kill your baba and Maa."

Pintu cowered into silence and could not utter another word. He had stopped going to school and he found himself running errands for the resistance party instead. He did what he was asked: brutally recruited children. Friends, he played with, so they too would distribute leaflets and brochures for the party. Jobs then escalated to much higher and, disappointingly, more heinous and dangerous crimes; torching cars; hurling rocks; beatings and brawls and arguments. On the streets of Potteiclay in the city, Pintu was seen one evening with blood-shot eyes, sprinting frantically through a furious mob, with a cocktail in his hand, in a tattered shirt, blood running down his left cheek; marks of beating stood out in red hot streaks, crisscrossed on his back. Soullessly, it behooved him to keep up his end of the bargain, so his mother, his father, and his sister would be protected. He escaped from one prison to the next. All in the name of democracy and freedom, which in the end became an excuse to grab more power; patriotism was never a part of this zeal. However, he fell out of the party in the end, and the party betrayed him by making him a scapegoat in a murder case. Maa had been mute with fear and baba could not protest. It was too late, too late now to go back to that golden age of purity. Oh, Pintu, how have you corrupted your soul?

Pintu walked up to the gym down the grassy path of the camp. With a few other refugees, he waited for his turn on the treadmill. As soon as one got off, he quickly got on and did a run for half an hour at the speed of six. Then he went into the shower. Next was the Kroll language class. Here, very attentively, he concentrated on listening skills today. "Hello, how're you?" a voice in the tape asked. Pintu parroted first and then said, "I'm well, and you?"

He had to master Kroll, if he were to get ahead, one of the ropes to success. He had to convince the authorities that he wanted to be a model citizen. Seven years went by in this manner. He was able to rote learn Kroll enough to communicate. However, his days of freedom were still uncertain, still a distant possibility.

Backstage

Stream-of-consciousness

I sat in front of a mirror. My reflection was enhanced by the many glaring lights fixed on its frame. I saw a masked face in the white make-up paste. The make-up artist diligently applied colour dust with a small sponge on my dark skin.

"You really have very soft skin," she whispered into my ears.

"Is that a good thing or a bad thing?"

"Don't know," she said, moving her attention to my eyes now. Eye make-up was the hardest to do. I empathised with her and asked, if her arm ached. She had it suspended for quite a while now. But the artist continued without complaints. She took out the mascara brush and poked it into the tube with its dry bristles to catch a patch of colour. Then she brushed it over skilfully on each of my naturally long lashes. Nearly an hour later, the make-up artist finished. My face was an unrecognisable mask under heavy make-up. She looked at me with a definite smile of satisfaction spreading across her painted lips, and a deep twinkling in her eyes.

"It's done. You look different, nice," she said. "Take a look." She held up the mirror. A transformation had occurred. I also thought so. I said to myself, what a good cover-up this could be. Not just to hide one's own grief, but also other emotions too. Masks made sense. They always did. And then my thoughts suddenly switched, to a different mode. I floated on its stream.

I didn't. No. No. No. No. Last thing this Problem. I no want this trouble. Oh, God. Oh, this loneliness. It kills me. Gently it does. I know not how. But it does. Lovingly and softly.

His smooth touch. The hypocrisy of it all. Pills. Bring me them. My pills, bring my pills.

"Are you okay?" the makeup artist asked.

The wind was rough. I woke up with terrible pain. In the early dawn, the door rattled vigorously in the stormy winds. The pain increased gradually. I screamed and held on to the flimsy bed frame. A summer's day. The winds revved up, like a car in the hands of a novice driver. Five years of age. I sat by the window as winds knocked on the glass pane. Another morning. Some clouds had gathered. I opened the windows and a sudden gust of wind whipped my face as it passed through the hut. My hair blew wildly over my face, almost veiling it with a mass of dark locks. I looked at the distant sky and saw layers upon layers of dark clouds; each layer was a different shade of grey. The little daisies down the mountain danced insanely in the ferocity of the winds. Poor yellow little souls and bleeding blades of grass. Then there was a knock on the door. They came back. There was a shipwreck far off the peninsula. Couldn't make it in the storm. How was I to endure that? Those faces of the desperate sailors floated in the ocean of my eyes, their bodies floating. But the garden still looked nice.

Who's at the door? Son, my son. Did you come back for me? Have you come for my soul? Oh, God. The wooden door went off the latch. It flew apart, flung open. Crazy! The crazy winds. My hut seemed to be wrung out of its soil. But the door flung open. The mountains green, but dark and grey today. Dark. Yes, pitch dark it was too when my sixteen-year-old sailed away off to the edge of the peninsula. On a boat, they sailed towards some faraway coral islands. The mountains spring. The fall from this height among the rocks and the craggy crevice. The rains lashed its spray across the... My son, are you even alive?

Come back to Mama. But no drugs and overdose. The ship had drowned in that ever-engulfing sea. Took away. The water. The ocean. This stream. How I miss you! Little baby. Little. No more. My son. Down by the green valley, I see him running. I see him now and then he vanishes. There he is again. Play. Play. Playing hide and seek. Don't run to the ocean though. Come back. Come back. Oh, dear child. There he is coming home. Up the hill, he climbs to get back. He's here. In my arms. Kisses and hugs. The ocean rises and falls. Boats passing through mountain ridges. Suddenly all falls apart. No boats. No ships, only the sounds of the raging seas.

I think I might have killed it. Actually, I did, I believe. The sea didn't take him. I did. I took his baby life the night that he was born. The storm had raged just outside my wooden door. It had rattled persistently in the crazy winds as it rattles now. Oh, my dear, dear baby. Did I grab the pillow and smother you? The cries. I couldn't take it anymore. The cries kept getting louder and louder relentlessly but, my baby. Not sixteen? No, he was but a day old. I had picked it up. Fed it, put it back on the pillow. Then I took the pillow from underneath and placed it on his face. I pushed. I pushed it hard on his baby face. His tiny little nose. His dad was away on a fishing boat. Fishing yes, he was. Caught loads of fish too. Off the peninsula. Mummy, Mummy. I hear his slight voice crying, calling me from afar. Only Heavens know. I see him floating up in the sky doing a summersault. Why? Mama why? I cried. I was hungry. The hunger pains were terrible. You didn't feed me enough though. I cried. You took it. The pillow and pressed it down until the last breath slithered out of me. Baby. Come on baby. Come now. Mummy didn't do that on purpose. I wish I could do this to myself. My baby. Come, come now. No.

No. No. No. Standing by the glass pane of the window. I see the sky cracking up in delightful, severe lightning. The fireworks of the sky. I ran along the mountain path. My sister behind. She stopped and took a deep breath. Clearly, couldn't keep up. I looked behind. She's gone now. Just gone, vaporised from the face of the earth.

Dinnertime was quiet. Soup. Watery soup and few measly pieces of meat afloat. I break a piece from the corner of my bread. My sister does the same from the other end. Mum and Dad looked on. They picked up scraps from the table. There was no more bread left. Dad had not been paid for the work he did. His employer went bankrupt. The carpenter hadn't been paid. Dip your bread not in wine but in water. Lo! The fury of the ocean. The sound and the fury. Waves overlapping, layer upon layer. The ocean couldn't be contained. The wind and the ocean entwined in the fury of a twister. The boat tussled across the waves. Boats are rare on days like these. They are on their way to the Netherlands, for sure. A man did come through the fog and knocked on the door. I'd turned eighteen, and my, sister twenty. Mum, there was no money at home. For Dad had gone for a long haul across the seas. My husband. That's who he was. He said. And yes, we had a church wedding. It was small all paid by the husband. Eyes half shut still on my honeymoon but stayed in the cottage. Sister and Mum next door. Dad not home.

My husband not with me. Half-asleep, I listened. There was suddenly lots of food on the table. I stood looking at it through the gaping hole of the wooden hut. The fury of the seas. I saw through the gaping hole my husband paying his good money to my mother. My wedded husband! And then he left. The sailor who had sailed into my life, sailed out the same way he had come. Off the seashore, his sailing boat wrestled. Cheering with his mates he left. His ship over the bosom of the great waves, dancing like a toy. I saw through the crack of the shaking door. The flimsy bolt shook. He left but he put a smile on Mum's face. My sister sat alone by the window watching the ship float.

Oh, the horror. Few years past I was now big with child. All the money had now run out. No more boats or sailors did drop by our hut. Mum sat mute. The man who fathered my child had left I, not wanted in his life, no more. No none of the children was really wanted. What did we do to deserve this? Why us? Oh, why us? But surely it was going to be you. The easy targets by the sea. No one was there to protect us. A sailor's wife. There's a wife for him at every port, I'm sure. There was me and another somewhere. A storm did rise darkly in the evening sky. By the window-pane, shut and a rattling bolt sat my sister alone looking into the grey, melancholy. He's but my husband alone, and I'm meant to share a life of love with him without a contester. But I think others loved him too, although he didn't marry them. Why did he need to marry me? He could've just broken in and out of our lives, paid Mum for our services and left laughing jolly out of that door.

But no! Somethin' made him marry one of us. In God's name in the merry white chapel hall across the graveyard and behind the grey walls of the mossy run-down church. There was endless booze and his friends swam in it not in the ocean so much, I reckon. Fish were caught in the muddy waters. Huge mouth watery barramundis and pints of ale. Luckily mum's white bridal veil was still there I wedded my husband in. I felt blessed until I found out how he screwed us. Big time and yes, big time. My child would probably go the same way too as soon as he learnt to row the boat across the hundred seas. At sixteen... Tender and malleable when he too would go out like his father. That's when his father left home to become a sailor. He saw and learnt from all his drunken mates what they did at the end of a day on every port the ship threw deep anchors. While it lay fallen under masses of water. My sister declared. She had it up to her eyeballs. No more of this, nonsense.

She was going to get a job. She wanted to clean her life and for us. My baby was going to be born out of a legal marriage. My sister understood that well and truly. She took off evening of a fierce storm gathered high in the sky. She cloaked herself in the black widowed coat. Black like the darky day and the murky seawater. She took off. But not to return. knitting a sweater for my little unborn. Seafarer that he would become one day like his father. But I did nothing to stop my sister. My own mother's womb that we shared once. A home that sheltered us. My blood. My sister. She went out in the fowl winds never to return. Mistaken. She returned all right afterwards but battered and bruised. Something went wrong at her job search. She couldn't wipe the slate clean. Water in the well went round and round. There was no exit.

I looked at my reflection in the mirror. My eyes had welled up. The make-up artist couldn't understand the dark, formidable and inescapable place, where she could never enter.

53

Mowgli's Mother

"What a strange name? Mowgli's Mother," Brenda Brady said.

"Yes, very strange," said her friend, Frieda Jane.

"But do you know what?"

"What?"

"What's even stranger, is that no one really knows who she is? She's a mystery."

"Gosh! What do you even mean?"

"She was called by that name, Mowgli's Mother. But nobody knows why. Because she was childless. Everyone thought she couldn't bear any children."

"How extraordinary!" Frieda said. "She told you that? How do you know?"

"Well, I asked where her son Mowgli was. She said she didn't have any. She was always known by that name, nonetheless."

"Wow! That's mad!"

"Yes. That's what's most puzzling. This has also puzzled the police," said Brenda.

Brenda Brady ran a corner shop on Paddington Street. She was meeting her friend today, Frieda Jane, in Café Boulevard, just two blocks up the street. She was describing to her a missing person by the name of Mowgli's Mother.

"Did it ever bother you?" Frieda asked. "That kind of a name, when you hired her? Did it ever occur to you that it could be a false name?"

"Yes, it did. But then when I asked her, she smiled and kept quiet. Her qualifications were okay, and I didn't want to discriminate on the basis of her name. Her passport and references checked out. It was just that name. But since neither of her previous employers bothered, I didn't give it much thought. I gave her the job."

54

"Hmm, this is kind of strange, though," Frieda said. "How long did she stay?"

"Oh! Less than six months. Not even a year."

"I find it a bit odd that this person moved in and out of so many places in less than a year," said Frieda, thoughtfully.

"And this time she didn't even ask me for a reference. In the last ten years, she has had at least ten jobs."

"How old is she?"

"According to her passport, she is thirty."

"That's pretty young."

"Yes, police don't even have a clue to her whereabouts. When they searched her place, everything appeared normal. She didn't take any belongings with her. Not even her clothes. Her closet was full of her belongings. But surprisingly her fridge was empty. There was nothing. Not even milk. Her larder was empty too. It seemed she lived on air."

"That's so strange that she had disappeared in thin air too, huh?" Frieda added.

"Hmm, I guess, I don't know, we just have to wait until the police find something."

"I guess, hey?" Frieda said. "Anyway, I got to go, really! I am so late. Catch you soon."

"See ye', I'll call."

"Bye."

Brenda went up to the till to pay. She was still thinking about the odds of finding this person, Mowgli's Mother. Her passport said she was from an Asian background, and that she'd seen a bit of the world and had lived in various places. In Athens, she sold flowers. In Madrid, she worked as a kitchen hand and waitress; nothing illegal, or abnormal. She seemed to have received the right kind of visa and work permits too. But on her passport, her name appeared as Mowgli's Mother and authorities didn't seem to think anything was wrong with it.

Brenda decided to carry out her own investigation. She only knew what Mowgli's Mother had cared to show her. The passport, visas, and the work permits. Brenda wanted to know more about it. This person who had simply just vanished. She paid immigration a visit one day. The immigration officer, reluctant to have a conversation with her, let alone give out any details, finally agreed, when Brenda told her that it was a dob in or complaint.

"Who do you want to dob in?"

"This woman, Mowgli's Mother."

"Is that the name she goes by?"

"Yes, that is the name on her passport and on all her reference letters."

"Hmm, odd. Very odd."

"There's something going on here."

"Let me check."

The immigration officer typed in the name. She found nothing under that name.

How odd? the officer thought.

Weeks went by, days and months, still nothing. No news. Her friend Frieda Jane was also worried. There should have been some news on this missing person, who was a woman of the world, who had travelled with legitimate passports and visas. Brenda thought she needed to contact immigration again to check if anybody had left the country, by sea, land, or air. Investigation reports had already stated that the missing person had not been found. Could it be that she had been murdered and dumped somewhere? Maybe, who knew?

Next morning, Brenda took off early on the bus straight to the immigration office in the city. She waited for an officer in the waiting room. She saw an ambulance come around and park up-front. Then there was a commotion and the receptionist walked up to her frantically. The immigration officer she was to meet today had an unexpected seizure. She needed to be taken to the hospital in that ambulance; a healthy person becoming ill. She called her friend, Frieda, but her mobile was switched off. She took a bus back to work.

As she got off the bus, she saw smoke coming from the direction of her shop. She walked faster and arrived panting. But it had burnt to a cinder.

"Oh no," she gasped and sat down on the side of the road. The fire-fighters tried relentlessly to put out the fire. The ambulance, the police, everyone was here by now. They wanted to interview Brenda. The owner of the shop was on television. She was telling them about the curious case of Mowgli's Mother. She was telling the world, the freakish chain of events to the lead up to this. Something or someone was trying to sabotage her attempts to find this person, known as Mowgli's Mother. That was how it all felt at least. As though the disappearance wasn't enough, now this? Just then an SMS popped up on her screen. It was from an unknown number: "Frieda Jane in hospital, a heart-attack."

"What?" Brenda screamed and then fainted.

After twenty-four hours, Brenda woke up in a hospital bed. She saw herself, waking up and walking through a white corridor wearing a white gown. Everything was so white that it hurt her eyes. Then she saw something flying towards her, a spirit, a wavering phantom. It came closer, and she looked at her intently. "Mowgli's Mother? Is it really you?"

"Yes, it is. Stop looking for me."

"Who are you? What are you, a phantom?

"Think whatever you wish, but know that Mowgli's Mother doesn't exist, never did."

"But, but?"

57

"No buts, the papers you saw? The passports and the visas were not as they appeared. You saw what I wanted you to see. There were neither any passports, nor visas, or any references of my existence anywhere in the world. You saw me, a person, a living person of blood and flesh, did not exist. Like I said before, I am a phantom. I am here. I am nowhere. And that is the state of reality, I project. That the rainbow you see only appears to be so. It is not made of colours. We only perceive it that way. The reality is what exists behind the rainbow: a collection of droplets. I am that. That which you perceived as Mowgli's Mother, the person in flesh, was not the real me, but what I conjured. What you see now is the real me; I am a body of gasses, energy, and abstractions."

The doctors at her bedside were trying to resuscitate her. She regained consciousness. She felt anxious. When she finally opened her eyes, she saw many grim doctors and nurses looking down at her.

A nurse smiled at her and said, "You will be okay. Not to worry, dear."

She received an SMS from Frieda that she too had been released from the hospital. Soon there was another SMS from immigration.

"We checked. There are no records, nationally or internationally, matching with this person's details. Case closed."

The Buraq

In the darkest hour of a summer's afternoon, the clouds had gathered in an elegant mass of deep grey. Mugginess hung thick in the atmosphere. Pushpa Pervez sat curled up on a reclining chair, in the far end corner of her balcony. Inhaling a cocktail mix of air made from pungent rain and perfumed gardenias, she looked at a retinue of ants climbing up the balcony wall. She snapped at a minuscule black fly hovering over her upturned nose; she ruminated, "Well now, finally some rain, long overdue."

The horrid black flies swamped her. They stung her in a number of awkward places, under her upper arms, and her lower legs. She was itchy. No sooner had she started to scratch them, the itchy spots burst into ugly little blisters on a range of red mounds. They erupted randomly on the smooth surface of her elbow and the calf, like tiny molehills of all sizes and shapes. Pushpa looked at the red swellings and began to count them with her index finger. Gosh, thirteen! She rubbed lightly over them in rapid successions to avoid an onslaught of abrasion of black blotches. Storm clouds looked spectacular. They loomed large on the distant horizon. She tried to decide whether it would be prudent for her to go to the spice bazaar after all. She was almost out of spice. For dinner tonight, fried, hot curried fish. Nothing less could spice up this stormy evening.

The bazaar was just around the corner of the next street in the West End. It had always been busy. Most of the time, it was impossible to cross the Montague Road near her apartment building. Some days were better than others, but most of the time, people waited on the foot-path for hours before they could go to the other side. Pushpa joined the cautious crowd and crossed over through the rush hour traffic.

When she'd finally arrived, she walked the dirt road to the nearest spice shop. The shopfront was decked with many extraordinary colours. It showcased a great variety of saffron, turmeric, coriander, cumin, and red chilli powder in tall hessian sacks; each packed with the potent goodness of Ayurvedic medicines. The yellow turmeric assisted in reducing the swelling from the cancer of the bowel. Brown coriander and cumin served as antioxidants. The orange saffron, an aphrodisiac, and the red hot chilli was the detoxifier. She took a deep breath of the varied flavours that exuded from them. She asked the salesman, who sat behind the products to pack a few grams of each. He scooped out a measured amount and poured it into neat brown paper bags. The rumblings of the clouds intensified. The storm would sweep through any minute now. Before the pelting began, she rushed to get back home, just when she saw a mother struggling to get through with a double perambulator. What could have driven her to come out on a day like this? She stopped short to give her a hand with the perambulator. The mother looked at Pushpa and lashed out, "Don't bother."

"Excuse me?" Pushpa asked.

"I don't need your help. Mind your own business."

For the first time now, Pushpa actually stood back and looked at her. She could have been in her late forties and had a distinctive beard and a moustache. Overweight as she was, she was wearing a frumpy, old frock. She also saw several beer bottles necking out from the bottom pocket of the perambulator.

"You clearly need help!" said Pushpa.

"And you've come to help?" she asked.

"Yes, I think so."

"Thanks. But no thanks."

Pushpa looked up and down and saw twin babies seated in the pram.

"What do you mean?" she asked, aghast. "Are you their mother or not?"

"And you, a complete stranger. Who're you and why should I tell you?"

The storm had rolled in. It lashed haphazardly in the strong winds.

"Look, I can help you, I think. It is raining. Shouldn't we run for shelter?"

"I don't need shelter. I'm already sheltered under the blue umbrella. See that?" she pointed her index towards the sky. "You go on now."

The woman paused and then pushed on, straggling down the wet path. She disappeared among the motley crowd. In all the world, Pushpa was annoyed that she had met this rude person. She had half a mind to follow her. But she didn't. Then she also didn't know what to do. The storm gained momentum in the meantime; in the poor visibility, she decided to search for her. Soon the spices began to run down in coloured rivulets through the soaked paper bag.

"I don't have to do this," she cried out in the heavy winds.

"No, you don't," someone behind her screamed.

She looked back and saw a young man. He stepped up his pace and ran along with her through the winds.

"Who're you?" Pushpa yelled.

"Time," the young man replied.

"Time?"

"Yes. That is my name."

"What do you want?" Pushpa asked.

They were running abreast in the same direction.

"I want to talk to you."

"I don't understand," Pushpa said and looked at him.

"I would like to explain something to you," Time said.

"Like what? What about?" she asked.

"Did you not say just now, you wanted to help her?"

"Yes, I did?"

"But you couldn't," Time said.

"And how would you know? Have you been following me? Are you a stalker?"

"You could say that, a stalker? I like that. As I said, I'm Time."

"Should I have not offered to help, then?" Pushpa asked.

"Yes. But that was all in the plan, as was her refusal. There was nothing you could do to change that."

"Plan? What plan?"

"I saw everything coming. Down to the last minute," he said.

"Why did you not stop to help her then?"

"Because I can't either!" said Time.

"Her perambulator was stuck and I was just trying to get it out of the rut."

"That's the whole point of it. The bit on the perambulator was but a fraction of an entire chain of events. Her disapproval meant you couldn't help, because it was no more pre-determined than the sun setting in the East and rising in the West. Get it?" said Time.

"How was I to know that?"

"You weren't! No one does. Events that come to pass are pre-determined! Even seers get baffled sometimes. Do you not see where I'm going with all this?"

Not completely sure, Pushpa continued to run with Time. In the blinding rain, she couldn't see the woman anywhere; neither could she see the young man, anymore. She scowled. Looking around clearly chagrined, she grunted, "Where did he go now?"

There was a shady tree nearby. She thought she would sit down there to catch a breath. Its umbrella leaves drooped in the rainwater. A couple of hours later, the man suddenly appeared and sat down beside her under the tree.

"Come with me," Time told her. "Close your eyes for a moment and put your trust in me. Come, let's time travel together."

"What? Time travel?" she asked.

"Yes, time travel," he said.

"Where were you all this time?" she asked. "I am older by those few moments, now."

"You are, my dear. You're a time-rider, unlike me. I am wrapped all around you. While you age on account of me, I don't," Time said. "Come, let's go for a ride."

"Where?"

"Imagine, you're on a date with me. This young man who took you somewhere you could only dream of," replied Time.

"Okay. I could live with that," she said.

He held her hands and they took off. Time jetted through the air at the speed of light and transformed into a white knight on a winged mythical horse, called the Buraq. They rode on this unicorn through various time warps. He took her to a place where larks and doves chirped in the depths of ancient olive groves.

"Olive groves? Doves?" she asked in awe. "Are we in some kind of an oriental paradise?"

"Maybe we are. The heavenly God's waiting for you, humans, to seek Him out and to meet Him here," Time said.

"Really? Have you seen Him?" she asked.

"No," he said. "Everywhere and nowhere. Down under, up above. Don't really know."

"Why should we worship Him then?" she asked.

"Don't, if you don't want to. He wouldn't care. He is that powerful light that blinded every organic eye, No one can see him," he replied.

63

"But we're stuck in His plans nevertheless, aren't we? The cosmic scheme that He has devised for us and which descended upon us?" she asked.

"Yes. Do you know how His 'cosmic scheme' works?" he asked.

"No."

"Events not only pass, but they're also intrinsically irreversible too," said Time.

"Irreversible? In what sense?"

"That's where it gets tricky. It means events are tied up in irreversible knots. What's meant to happen, will happen, thus fatalistic. For instance, no one could reverse that meeting with the woman in the market; it had to happen at that precise moment and you couldn't take it back, or make it different. You can replay the past in your mind but past cannot be undone or redone."

Time gave her a kiss on her lips and vanished with her into another warp. This place felt like a new day, bursting into a sunny, late afternoon after a fresh morning rain. She sat by the jaded River Nile, and he, the young man sat with her. They saw together Cleopatra's golden chariots pass with Mark Antony by her side. She learned about the theory of irreversibility of an already reversed order: the past, and the irreversibility of this order, as Time had already exemplified.

"You were saying?"

Then her mind switched to a replay mode in which, she began to *reverse* and replay events; she saw the reversal of every moment from this point backward. She saw events furl back. This rare date with Time; meeting him in the rain; searching for the lady in distress; stopping by to offer her help; getting insulted in the process; crossing the Montague Road; feeling itchy; getting bitten by black flies; watching the ants and the storm from the balcony; sitting curled up in a chair.

64

She kept taking the clock backwards, as far back as she could. She was a young girl again; then a baby. Time was travelling backwards. Each precious moment disappeared into the past. Here and now, her mind danced like waves; her thoughts roamed freely. As the clock ticked tirelessly onwards, with each ticking, the world's events were traveling in reversed order. The dinosaurs, the epic wars, ancient history, the Pharaohs, once in the future, now gone. And then she beheld trees, the hummingbirds, the dragonflies and the petrified forests; the milky-ways, constellation, the galaxies, the entire cosmos. All rushed back together through celestial spacetime like rewound cinema. She saw the beginnings and the endings alike. There was darkness before the inception of time. Time had set the universe in motion. With a bang some billions of years ago, she saw it all. How the universe expanded like a stretched balloon, life was born on earth. Yet, it was in this very passage that time also took steps backwards. Every passing minute, life glided towards death. Deaths took place. Time travelled through the future, the present, then back into the past. In this travel, it carried all events of the human dramas downstream. The future became the present, and the present became the past, lost in the backwards snitches of time. Then the universe crunched back to a singularity. It collapsed into the blissful seventh sky of a complete void. She saw how time itself came to a halt. How the clocks stopped ticking and even the death of time had occurred.

These were pre-determined events, of irreversible order. That was a deep paradox, lying within this metaphysics: the irreversibility of a reversed order. Her friend, Time, kissed her in the olive grove. One who truly wrapped her around like the tortuous roots up the brawny bark of the oak tree. He 'wrapped' her within his invisible heart. He showed her some more. That no human predictions, nor interventions could change this rigid paradigm, nor its luminous pathway. People had no hand in reversing this course, but only thought they did.

"What the heck? Feeling itchy again," she complained.

Time had zapped her back in a flash and sat her down with a jolt on the root of the old oak tree. Then he was gone, yet again. Where was Time? She remembered the tight kiss, as she looked around for him in her familiar surroundings. Well, of course, he would be gone, wouldn't he? She locked her arms together and trembled. The storm-clouds were still dark. When she returned home, a towel lay on the apartment floor. The gusty winds had blown some clothes off the pegged line.

She put the kettle on to boil. Meanwhile, she picked up a cup and a saucer, put two sugars and a dash of milk over a tea bag in the cup, poured hot water, and took the tea out on the balcony. The storm was nasty. Branches of the trees snapped off; they flew in havoc. She picked up her six-months-old knitting, lying on the coffee table. Looking out, she began to knit. She couldn't procrastinate much longer. Just a few days now, that the full season change would embark; autumn's 'mellow fruitfulness and mists' heralded the sweet summer's peaceful retreat. Caught up in this Tango dance with Time, that memorable date at the speed of light was an unmissable eye-opener. To have gone back to the source, she thought; how mad was it to view Time crunch?

Since the Last Soiree

Mila Chowdhury and Rahim Rahman sat by the green pond. Rahim Rahman was Mila's best friend, Papri Khandakar's fiancé. They waited for Papri to join them soon. Sitting abreast, they glanced straight ahead at a couple of white swans, basking on the pond's placid water. From the corner of her eye, Mila noted Rahim Rahman's reading spectacles; they were rimless. She wasn't expecting it, but he abruptly took them off and turned his gaze towards her. She bit her lips under his gaze, as she lowered her eyelids; she began to knot and unknot her fingers without any eye contact. A host of flying foxes were passing by, she looked up at them instead, and pretended to be distracted. Rahim continued to look at her.

The flying foxes were heading North, self-organised in perfect harmony. Then a crow came by and swooped low over the pond; it found a few measly bread pieces, floating on the water; it ducked, beaked up a soggy portion and swallowed rapidly. Watching this, Mila hid a smile and thought the food scraps must have been left overnight by people, perhaps even lovers who had come to feed the swans. She felt Rahim Rahman's bare eyes all over her face. *What was keeping Papri? Where was she, anyway?* she thought, inching away from Rahim. But Rahim also inched in to sit closer.

Yearnings of love burned elsewhere too, at the far end of an alley. A site which was disreputable for sheltering scandalous affairs. It was a hotbed for runaway lovers. Mila's grandparent's house, famously known as The House of Chowdhury, an imposing, two-storied brick building, also stood here within its short distance. This respectable house, the House of Chowdhury was juxtaposed to this place like a seated grand lion and a slinking skunk pictured in a jungle.

Mila's grandparents were old money, an aristocratic family of fallen Zamindar, or king of a principality. Although fallen, The House of Chowdhury, was not a bleak house. In their own right, they felt patrician for being one of the most influential families in all of East Pakistan, now Bangladesh. They were also the proud patrons of art and culture, who made sure that there was never any dearth of culture in this house. The members of the family paid visits to the local cinema theatres nearly every week, streaming the dashing, postmodern hero Waheed Murad's top hits of 1960.

Every evening there would be singing performance here in its front yard. A huge straw mat would be spread across it, carpeting most of its grassy patch, except its surrounding garden; this was a secret garden at the edge of the front yard of enchanting monsoonal tiger lilies and thorny roses, growing within the foliage of juicy berries and tall neem trees. Short of an 'oriental paradise', an idle full moon could have conjured mad Puck to spark tender romance in the hearts of its visitors.

The members of the House of Chowdhury, jostled tonight on the mat to listen to their youngest son, Ashik's, rendering of love songs. His songs were heart melting, but they ignited unflinching love in one woman particularly, the neighbour Raja Hashem's *bibi*, Prema Hashen. Prema Hashem, the young mother of three, found Ashik's company more pleasurable than her own husband's. This transformed into an unsavoury chain of events; she decided to slowly move away from her husband and form a stronger bond with Ashik, as only this spirited youngest son from the House of Chowdhury could give her the thrill and a meaning to live. Prema Hashem was a woman of great beauty, an enchantress by a long shot in the neighbourhood. She didn't think that age had mattered. Ashik was eight years younger than her. He was only twenty-two and she, thirty.

In the evenings, when the House of Chowdhury woke up to Ashik's songs, Prema Hashem could not restrain herself. Regardless of the various moods exuded from those songs, melancholic or lively, she thought, he sang them only for her. His love songs touched her beating heart in every possible way. Those lyrics, *I loved you so much that only the moon knew its full depth* could mean only her, she thought. Whether or not, he sang them out of deference to her, or out of actual love, no one could tell. But as time rolled by, and time and time again, those very lyrics sung in her presence, were like a call of nemesis to her ears. They left her undone. Trying to stay confined in her own house was futile. Neither could she stop listening to the songs, which could be heard anyway, because of the close proximity between the two houses, separated by a flimsy gated wall.

On a full moon, this garden reshaped into the mango grove in her mind, where the enchanted Krishna and his Gopis came down to play. To Prema Hashem, they seemed to perform ritual dances, to the magical tunes. At the behest of her muses, she felt like a Gopi herself surrendering to her amorous god, Ashik, whose open invitations awaited to begin full romance.

Such unbridled thirst pulled her towards the house like a star to a black hole; it behooved her to respond to her senses. Songs, which made her feel beautiful. She felt whole in all those jewellery and saris. They made her forget about the chores and her children and the drudgery of a prosaic husband, Raja Hashem, who seemed to live in his own world – like a happy idiot, oblivious to everything.

Ashik meant lover. Ashik couldn't deny that he too

desired the young mother, Prema Hashem; the forbidden fruit, a mother of three, and married to the neighbour. They both knew that love neither understood nor respected any boundaries. It was literally coveting the neighbour's wife. However, nothing could or ever would obliterate the feelings they harboured for each other, nor keep them away from their mischievous dates. The rendezvous? What other place, but the shady end of the alley? Just as well, the alley offered lovers like them some kind of recognition, a panacea to the souls. A place where clandestine relationships thrived in happiness. Some were romantic interludes, short-lived and casual, others more promising, leading to marriage. It was yet to be discerned Ashik and Prema Hashem's fate.

Within the House of Chowdhury, another couple were also in love. A rounded verandah enveloped the house, in the privacy of which, this romance blossomed. Lovers whom Mila knew that their love had come to fruition. The hey-day of their lives, when the leaves of the guava trees trembled with joy at the slightest touch of a pecking bird; its whistles whipped the core of young hearts; the agony of restive days and listless evenings; the sallow lantern didn't quite reach the far side of the balcony. Where in this dim obscurity, this young couple sat in two cane chairs with their fingers braided into each other.

Her name was Lutfun Azhar, and he was Sheri Chowdhury, Ashik's older brother. Lutfun had just turned twenty, and Sheri twenty-five. They dated here at sunset every evening. They didn't have to go to the alley, for theirs was a more legitimate relationship. Other members of the family recognised it in tacit support which encouraged them further.

Mila, was Sheri and Ashik's eldest brother Ekram's daughter. As a child, she'd often wondered around in the verandah too, when her uncle and his girlfriend dated.

70

Somethings she could never forget; this sense of subtle sweetness which hung in the air. She'd heard their spoken words describe a quiet adoration for each other, and unspoken heavy sighs, and soft murmurs. They'd also known that Sheri's niece, Mila, watched them without a din, but they'd smile at her curiosity. They were not remotely bitter, nor concerned. There was no place for such negativity in their hearts, which oozed with the ripened juices of pure love.

Memories were always precious. Their hearts told magical stories. Impossibly intense love stories; stories of Romeo and Juliet, and Laila and Majnu, which only inspired optimism. None of these tales ever happened concurrently. Never in the exact same sequence, nor in the same place, but in completely separate moments in history. Still, they spoke of the same profound themes of love in the sacred hearts, alluding to no profanity. Invaluable tales gathered like a relic in the repository of the mind. Nostalgia heavy with gripe rekindled. Good and bad entwined.

Lutfun was a virtuous woman, kind and pious. She loved people unconditionally and her guileless smiles said it all. They beguiled everyone. She possessed natural selflessness like the perfect Hyperborean land. Such innate endowments became stronger with every passing season. These were some of the qualities that made Sheri Chowdhury fall in love with her. The gentle lady bestowed her affections steadily upon Sheri. When little Mila eavesdropped on their conversations, they let her in on it. She stood there in the dark passageway and listened away to every story they told. She'd observed how they kissed, held hands, and whispered nothings at blue twilights.

It all seemed like a fable to Mila. That this sort of kindness should prevail in pursuance of love. Utopia, at best, something so divine that even time didn't or wouldn't

71

tarnish. These were exemplary instances. However, they also provided a rare glimpse into the natural order of things, of what should be, but rarely is. Like the perfect sun or the moon, or precise forces of gravitational pull, such love could find itself a home in the celestial pantheon, but few and far between. Sheri could easily die for Lutfun, as did Romeo for his Juliet.

A patch of cloud had gathered and veiled the sunlight. She noticed that Rahim had also put his spectacles on. He looked out at the pond unmindfully to say, "I wonder what's keeping Papri?"

"Hmm, don't know. There's going to be a storm soon," she said. "What should we do?"

"I don't know. At any rate, I don't think we can sit here anymore," he said. "Why not come over to my place. I've got my car."

"Thanks, I can walk home. My house is not very far," she said.

Mila knew he wanted her in his car somehow. What were they going to talk about though? Money? Investments? Those things didn't interest her. She looked up at the layered clouds set against an autumn sky on the satin edge of a dull horizon. Rahim kept a close watch, hoping that somehow she would change her mind. But Mila's passions lay elsewhere. She was the quintessential introvert, who pondered and observed the world around her. No one would understand, nor even care for her love of incessant rainfall, the thunder and the swishes of the gusty winds, or the mists of the opaque drizzles; the frolicking birds such as the crow's measured picks on the pond.

Mila didn't respond. Rahim stood up and walked away. He got into his car and left. The car raged as it sped. She didn't understand why someone remotely related to her

72

would get upset. Apart from the fact that Papri Khandaker was a close friend of hers, there were no other ties with him. It wouldn't be right to get into his car and then go home without her friend being present here. Her role models, Uncle Sheri and the virtuous Aunty Lutfun, would not approve. However, Prema Hashem and Uncle Ashik may have, she wouldn't know. At any rate, in both cases, love had to spring both ways that brought people closer. Not force, much less anger.

Prema Hashem and Ashik were just as passionate as lovers as any other couple. However, they would never be allowed to date in the house like Sheri and his girlfriend, Lutfun. Despite the fact that Ashik was Sheri's brother, Ashik and Prema Hashem dated far down the alley with all other shady couples with equally shifty commitments. Prema Hashem came out every night after putting her children to bed. When her husband sat with the boring evening newspaper, she snuck out courageously to meet her lover, over by the designated lovers' den.

The lovers' den was a cave in a small mountain conveniently located out of sight. At nighttime, lovers enshrined the cave with glowing candles. This was the moment when the cave became a sanctuary, illuminated with impassioned dialogues. This wasn't the place for Sheri and Lutfun at all, but only for the strays of the moor. Although, Ashik Chowdhury wasn't one; he belonged to the same House of Chowdhury, a house held in high esteem; this dungeon was not the most suitable place for a man of his stature. But his circumstance decreed otherwise. His, amounted to an unsightly affair, compared to the Lutfun-Sheri relationship.

What difference did it make anyway? Mila thought in circumspect. Why should society condemn the types of Lady Chatterley or Madame Bovary? Were they any different from the Laila-Majnu, and the Romeo-Juliets as far as love's purity was concerned? All's fair in love and war, isn't it?

It depended on how those songs that Ashik sang in the evenings really affected the people in the house. Surely, for Lutfun and Sheri, they meant love tantamount to worship. A union of a celestial pair sanctioned by society, favoured by their elders. Every other evening, they sat beside one another on the same mat under the watchful eyes of their elders, holding hands in perfect bliss, exchanging tiny, coy smiles. Whereas, Prema Hashem would push herself in through the gate and hover at the fence darkly, like a dithering shadow, waiting for a welcome cry from someone to join the party on the mat. Although she and Ashik were Cupid blind as anyone else in love, the elders of the House of Chowdhury looked upon Prema as nothing other than the beautiful, lush wife of their quiet neighbour. Clueless to their affair, however, this the family would never have condoned if they knew so much as a word.

Her husband, Raja Hashem, hardly spoke to anyone, but commanded huge respect in the neighbourhood on account of it. A learned man, Raja Hashem, couldn't understand his wife's fantasies. To him three healthy meals, clothes, and ornaments sufficed; from head to toe, Prema Hashem was covered in jewellery like a queen. But her insufferable ennui was hard to break. No one could. Apart from Ashik, not even her own children could break its bounds. Although she couldn't go even remotely close to Ashik in the House of Chowdhury, she found a full life here in-spite of it, away from the stifling atmosphere of her own. For, her husband wouldn't notice her great beauty, let alone compliment it. Deep in his studies, he lived a life of the mind, a scholar in seclusion.

One night, however, he decided to not read his newspaper

but to be with his wife. He looked for her in the house. She wasn't there. He thought, maybe, Prema Hashem was with the neighbours, but he wished she were here tonight. As the night progressed, he gradually fell asleep. When he woke up in the morning, she was still not in bed. Her side of the bed had not been slept in all night. Suspicion didn't enter his mind, because he was not the sort. But when he entered the dining room for breakfast, he found his children sitting glumly without a mother. As soon as they saw their father, they broke down in tears.

Raja Hashem now feared the worst. He walked over to the verandah and found a note pressed under the heavy volumes of *War and Peace* on a feeble cane table by the red rhododendrons. He saw it and swiftly pulled it out from under the two tomes. It read very clearly that Raja Hashem should not try to look for her, as she had run away with her man next door. Was this some sort of a joke or serious elopement? Indeed, but as Raja Hashem struggled to grapple with the reality of the situation, he read the note a few times, and then looked at his children's sad expressions. They had no idea where their mother had gone, let alone, why she had gone. He grabbed his children in panic and embraced them in sorrow.

Ashik and Prema's affair was bold and tantalising. Raja Hashem's sanctimonious life, or at least how Prema Hashem would interpret it, did not keep her ennui at bay. Raja Hashem could not give her what Ashik could. The couple settled at the far end of the alley, without the blessings of the House of Chowdhury. Their elopement did not make his family proud. It caused such turmoil, that Mrs Chowdhury, the mistress of the house, had to disown him. And Ashik, forced to part with the glory of the House of Chowdhury, thought this sacrifice justified his love for her. If Romeo-Juliet, Laila-Majnu could transcend to a

75

metaphor for love, theirs could too one day. In the heart of it, he felt that they were equal. They had more in common, than naught. Because, in terms of the society's rebuke, none found a sympathetic hearing from any quarters. Conversely, Lutfun-Sheri thought of themselves as the proper embodiment of Romeo-Juliet, since they fared so well. But the definition of the real McCoy of the world remained indeterminate. Because, love machines like Lady Chatterleys always justified their affairs not profane, but as just as sacred.

Mila thought about Rahim Rahman. It would be another affair then if she were to agree to his advances. However, did he really love her? Or did she for that matter? If she did then it would be pure love because *love in itself* was always unadulterated. No matter, she realised that perhaps she was not in love with Rahim Rahman after all. Otherwise, she wouldn't be trying to justify it. In matters of the heart, could anyone justify love? If it was love, it would have broken all social bars by now, as was Prema and Ashik's. It was a confusing emotion which she shelved for the moment.

The Fountain of the Twelve Lions

One delightful spring afternoon of 1203, a Moor princess by the name of Zaida, stood gazing at the Nasrid gardens from an alcove near her palace at Alhambra. At the palace entrance, rows of majestic pines and hedges adorned these gardens with myrtles and myriads of roses in yellow, pink, and red; the white tiger lilies, the unfathomable bushes of lilacs, the carnations, and the scarlet geraniums were some among the flowers. Most prominent were the roses, flanked alongside and around the fountains of varied shapes and sizes; a posy of roses overlooked either the circular or the elongated basins, while the tall hedges rose above every flower bed, setting boundaries between the gardens and the main thoroughfare.

On the outskirts of the palaces, lay several meandering mountain passes leading to these princely homes of the Moorish Emirates. The towering Torre de las infantas, one of many towers, built on the hilly slopes of one of the voluptuous mountains, served as a distinctive landmark. Visible also were the snowy peaks of Sierra Nevada, or the 'snowy range' in Spanish, whose snows of spring still melted over the horizon. A terrain most formidable and stark for not being garnished with that many magical groves, perhaps, but, owing to the precipices, this view added an inescapable look of sublimity to the landscape.

This afternoon, the air was heavy with the seductive aromas of diverse oriental flowers. Princess Zaida stepped out into the Jannat-al-Arif or the 'architect's garden'. She stood on its edge and took a few exhilarating puffs of the fragrant air. A sensuous atmosphere infused with the sound of a cascading waterfall, and perfumed flowers, lent an unearthly perspective; the pregnant orchard was laden with oranges, lemons and pomegranates. The chirrups of a lonely dove to boot, an expression of an idyllic milieu.

Wandering through these orchards for many years, princess Zaida heard whispers. They pulled her into the realm of otherworldly creatures, who conferred with her. She went into a stoned, trance state. Her almond eyes widened to behold elements that only she was privy to when she began to walk again. The soft rustle of her green, resplendent dress stirred an inner sense of foreboding. Along this trail, she plodded by the leafy vines over the lofty, Moorish walls to the hilltop of Assabica. Her shadow fell under the Torre de Comares. Set against a backdrop of the court of the myrtles, this, another notable tower, housed the throne room of the North African ruler of the Nasrid dynasty, Mohammad the 1st. She left the tower of throne behind as she drifted through to the Puerta del Vino, the wine gate towards Alcazaba, not too far from the gates of the wine, an old fortress of the Moors. She trod lightly down a pebbled path. Hundreds of intertwining, serpentine paths, broken midway into Escher-like paintings of nonlinear staircases, into narrow flights of stairs without any marked ingress, or egress.

Her own royal apartments, the magnificent rooms of The hall of Abencerrajes, were close to the Palacio de Los Leones, the 'Court of the Lions'. These rooms were notable for superb craftsmanship. Every ceiling in these rooms was decked with a bejewelled dome and a central star theme made of muqarnas prisms. The motif continued, and gradually merged into the square-shaped floor under the hanging muqarnas spandrels. Rooms shimmered with speckled pearls of pink rubies, white sapphires, and sparkling diamonds, in gilded silhouettes of an unrivalled beauty of an oriental fairy tale.

But she was depressed. To lighten her mood, her palace

maids organised the flamenco dance at the fountain of The Twelve Lions. The princess's laughter rang in unison with the gentle sway of the plash from The Twelve Lions; doves chirruped away. The palace became an enchanted Eden. Then she heard the ghosts again, whose sighs encircled the cold marbles of the pillars, within its Arabic inscriptions of the mosaic halls; purportedly, imbued in history. The princess began to talk incoherently.

"I cannot do what you ask. I can't... you horrible creatures of fate and death. How could you... Is this true, indeed? What do they say? Someone's trying to kill the seven Nasrid princes? Awful! It's awful! Owwwww! What're you saying? That I should pray, not take this potion? You say, do not take those pills. Push her away. Push the nurses away. Come, come away with us. We will take you down an ethereal path... a new land of wondrous spirits..."

The whisperings continued until she was brought to her bedroom, with a psychiatrist called upon to assist her.

"Is this malady in the head?" the psychiatrist of thirty years tried to decipher. She sat erect on the bed. She looked outside through the palace windows at a melancholy sunset, deciding that this evening reflected her own tetchy mind. Mourning became her, like Electra. She viewed the other Alhambra palaces at a distance in the departing sun; how the facades looked just as tetchy in red.

Her nurses stood by her bed with the herbal concoction in a silver chalice, gently nudging her to take some. She took the goblet and swallowed the potion.

"These voices drive me crazy," the princess complained.

"You might have to take medicine regularly," said the psychiatrist. "That's what they are for."

"No medicine has ever worked for me."

"They will work just fine this time," he said. "I'm sure of it."

"Tell the voices to leave me alone. Give me a cure for this disease," she pleaded.

"Tell me more about them," he asked.

"They call themselves The Moirai."

"The goddesses?"

"Yes, that's what they call themselves, the goddesses of fate. Hmm. Why do they haunt me and hound me so?"

"You are unwell, my lady, that's why," says the psychiatrist, nonchalantly.

"I see these three ghastly shadows dancing at sundown, spinning threads in flowing robes. I hear them each whisper to themselves, and to me."

"What do they say?"

"Oh, about the same."

"Can you tell me what these sisters say to you?"

"Oh, these are diabolic, vile ghosts of darkness, whispering nonsense that no one wants to hear."

"Like what?"

"They are here again."

"No, they're not, be brave. You take some rest. We will be in the next room." the psychiatrist said. And he, followed by nurses, left her alone in the room.

The sun dipped on the edge of the Assabica. Darkness crept into the room. Another psychotic episode loomed. Caught up in that distorted reality, the princess grinned. She spaced out. Her expressions turned from grim to stoic. The fleeting hours passed. Another change occurred. Her hands on her ears, she shook her head vehemently.

"No. No. No. Go away!" she screamed.

Someone tried to calm her down. They put a supporting hand on her back, massaging it up and down the delicate spine. Beautiful, long bones. But it didn't work. She narrowed her edgy eyes; silent tears oozed out of those kohl corner slits.

The princess wailed. Then she was aggressive and suddenly strong. Her fragile demeanour was replaced by an unsightly pallor of purple, her voice a shrieking nightingale. She rose and stood tall. She levitated mid-air, thin like a leaf of autumn, but dropped thick through like the granite of the Colosseum. Anyone watching her now would stand petrified. There was no match for this newfound brawn.

Stepping down from the bed, she began to follow her whisperers. She glided through the air, walked over the jaded waves of the Darro River, and tried not to lose sight of the three spinning goddesses. They took her through a secret passage of a garden. A garden, hidden from the public eye for centuries. Under a shroud of moss, the wild ferns, and the wet heaps of parasitical creepers, the garden spread sidelong up an old, Moorish wall. In the far corner of it, a creaky, wooden door appeared to be slightly ajar. The princess allowed the voices to lead her. She sleepwalked over a dead log. Her body rose above it; she, a blind seer of an alternate plain, followed them through the great palace gates, then headed further away into the depths of the garden's jaded hedges. She plummeted and fell on the stump of an old oak tree.

In demonic possession, she lay there clutching to her emerald dress. Her whisperers hissed by her side. Under their influence, she rose again and saw a portal open before her eyes; a fiery ball showed itself as a sharp torchlight through a dark tunnel. It began to move towards a door. The dot now assumed the shape of a man. Her lips parted. Eyes darted. The dress remained in her clutches. The female voices came and went intermittently.

"Come with me, Princess," commanded a hoarse, male voice.

"Where?" she asked.

"Come. You have a mission to fulfil."

"A mission to fulfil? What mission would that be?"

"Take this."

The fiery figure offered her a sword studded with precious rocks, asking her to hold it. She slipped her tiny palm robotically over its hilt. Her hand was now locked under the man's iron fist.

"What's this?"

"Follow them. The Moirai," he instructed.

The apparitions, the three goddesses, jetted through the air to propel her into the portal until they arrived at the regal bedrooms of her cousins. All her seven cousins, the future Moors of Alhambra, lay asleep, breathing heavily on the stately beds. Moirai prodded her to enter the young princes' rooms. Then she stood before their beds and picked them up one at a time, and carried them out to the fountain of The Twelve Lions. While the naked sword rested tightly in her other firm hand, she gathered them and held them tight by the locks of the black mane. They slept standing; the life-size rag dolls of men drugged with opium poppies, this morbid moment. She wielded her sword. And in one precise strike, the incisive blade sliced right through their ebony necks.

She saw it through, this massacre at the fountains of The Twelve Lions; the severed heads of all her seven cousins lay scattered amok along the cross-paths of the pooled blood. A job well done; the otherworldly spirits relished in the success. At lightning speed, they unplugged themselves from the princess's hook and took the sword to release her. She entered her domicile alone, but she felt dead lost like the last unicorn.

For, this freedom came at a cost. As soon as they disbanded her, the pale princess fainted in the garden of

82

hedges, a few steps away from the fountain floor. She did not wake up until the warm touch of the human hand jolted her back to full awareness. She found herself not in the garden, but within the walls of her own quarters, with the psychologist and nurses poring over her, concerned.

"What just happened?" she asked.

"The princess has had some side effects from the medicine. We were not here but by looks of it, you had hallucinations after we left you to rest in your room. And you did some pretty crazy things."

"Like what?" she asked.

"Sleepwalk. You sleepwalked, my royal highness. We found you among the foliage of the hedges, not too far from the fountain of The Twelve Lions. Your sleep was deep."

"What was it? I can't remember. Was it a horrific nightmare?

"No, it was a delusion," the psychiatrist answered.

"That may be true. I do hear voices in sleepwalks."

They looked at each other. Princess Zaida held the young psychiatrist in her mesmerised gaze. After a while, they both smiled. Whether or not this was true, was hard to gauge. But the princess's delusions foretold a surviving legend, not easily beguiled by imagination. At some point in history, those princes, her cousins, were actually killed at the same place and in the same manner by some elusive red hands. To this day, it remained a mystery as to why or who murdered those young Moors at the fount of The Twelve Lions.

In Search for the Purist

Laura Jane was not pretty. She knew this only too well. Her nose was too long, and her too narrow forehead sat right above the thin-browed, beady eyes. Her mousy, straight hair fell to the waist like the tall, russet poplars. Her plainness made her a recluse. She was pale, shy, withdrawn, wrapped up in routined smoothness, comprising going to school and getting home by bus. She went to art school. She took the regular route back and forth and ate her humble tomato-cheese sandwich for lunch every day. She got off the evening bus at Tattersole Arcade and walked up to her one-bedroom flat around the corner. Only her dog greeted her, with a welcome bark, as soon as he'd heard her key turn in the door.

Her only human interaction was with the owner of the corner store. This young man, Tom Brady, with whom she had uncountable, casual encounters over the years, when she would come to his store for a purchase. Many of those interactions she really valued. The fact that in his happy demeanour, he took the trouble to ask how her day was, and what she had been up to, made it meaningful to her. Some days he even walked her to her apartment. There was an uncanny connection between the two of them, which neither of them explored, to take the relationship further, or even make advances. Tom Brady, a perfect gentleman wasn't inclined to propose to her, because he wasn't sure if she would welcome him as more than a friend. That she kept to herself. And Laura Jane was just too shy to make the first move.

This was pretty much Laura Jane's life at twenty-five. She was not poor. She travelled frequently, to escape from the humdrum of her life. Much of the world she'd seen was on cruises across the Mediterranean, the Atlantic, and the

Indian oceans. She received a scholarship and saved up for these journeys from the few sales of her artwork, while she still studied for a post-graduate degree. On several occasions, she took along her portfolio. Such cruises gave her the high, and inspiration, to sit raptured on the deck, to watch dolphins frolicking in the undercurrent, immersed in the jaded waters of oceanic wonders, or behold the cataclysmic cyclonic breaths of cloud-folds in a rumpus. Sultry, summer's day was perfect to capture these moments. Moments of tranquillity and rage caught on canvas. By far, her resolute adherence to structure made her a purist.

Her paintings revealed the exquisite beauty of her artwork. Her strokes were bold. They displayed glimpses of the insightful richness of colour: gold, emerald, and scarlet. Her brushes touched the core of life, the principles, and properties of rainwater that made life possible, under every garnered atom of the earth. She once sketched a silhouetted doe against a translucent light of the golden ray. The spirited female deer leaped high and low to reach out to the leaves at sunrise in an enchanted forest under a macabre; a deeper conceptualisation of life in the spirit of abstraction.

She was alone, but not lonely. Her siblings took her to be spinsterish, who thought she'd selected to lead a life of a recluse. They assumed her days must be too bleak, like midwinter mornings, without a beau. But there was no heaviness in her heart. No poignant regrets to bear grudges. She felt feisty and chose to remain blissfully ignorant of the 'promising otherness', of other lifestyles, which she thought were freakish. In her inclination to the purist line of art, when she portrayed bleakness, such as terrifying lightning above murky oceans, for example, she laced them with sprinklings of silver linings. Through turbulence or placidity, brightness or morbidity, her portraits glowed with exultant warmth and optimism. Her viewers barely had any inkling of what imparted such sheen to her art. Neither did she. Her depiction of a transcendental reality allayed any fears or new trepidations arising out of tomorrow's uncertainties. Tomorrow, and tomorrow, and tomorrow's dispositions found their way into the depths of her canvas, nuanced detail of thrills and hopes; raw emotions of happiness, divorced from formidable tomorrow.

One day, however, a fatalistic frontier unveiled before her. A sense of foreboding loomed without a description. Her inner peace threatened. Until now she had been untouched by a quandary. But it had to do with the owner of the corner shop, Tom Brady. In all the world, this only man, who didn't find her even remotely odd, finally found courage to ask her out tonight. She agreed, because of the lure of enchantment; a romantic interlude that awaited a special tomorrow.

As she descended from the bus, she felt a thrill run through her. She walked over as usual to the shop to buy milk. It was a midwinter evening. The dense fog like Turin's shroud covered most of the Daintree rainforest ahead. The fog hung from a panoramic ceilinged sky in opaque, droplets, of whitewashed walls. When she entered the shop, she couldn't find Tom. No matter, she opened the fridge to reach for the milk. Everything else appeared normal, except for Tom's peculiar absence. He was not there at the check-out counter. In fact, he was nowhere to be seen.

Laura Jane was concerned, more so curious. She stood still with the milk bottle in her hand awhile, then walked over to the till, where she usually found him. Her gaze shifted momentarily to something lying on the floor. It was an inert body. She looked carefully. Her eyes scanned the body, head to toe, up and down, to take a closer look. It was, no one, but Tom himself. It was he, who lay there, hard as a fallen filbert; left to rot overnight; decaying spots of clots, like the yellowed sycamore. She was petrified, as was the body, cold as frozen fish.

Someone had murdered Tom, and she was the first to discover him. The bottle of milk fell from her clutches. It scattered all over the floor, many-sized glass fragments in milk. The milk fused with Tom's dead blood, a rivulet of a honeyed, textured blend. She fainted.

Again, there was yet another tomorrow. This tomorrow without a closure, away from all other tomorrows of her past years, brought only lustreless sterility. For when she woke up in the hospital, her head hurt. This event had destabilised her mental balance. She gathered her torn self from the shock, still nervous and sore from all she'd witnessed; this magic, long gone. This too, too, terrifying episode transpired into an illness. With no known panacea, the chemical composition of her tetchy mind went awry. Her imagination occluded from being porous. 'The end of imagination'. Her heart clamped up. It recoiled, and she suffered a blow of loneliness for the first time. Nostalgia gripped her from the loss of a friend. Nothing brought back her solace; neither the dedication of her artwork nor the keen cruises she braved on those curvy seas.

She knew she was unattractive, but thought she had infrangible bones at least. Mistaken, now they caved in like clay pottery, broken in the mould of novice hands. Her sketches rendered nothing, other than an unscented wasteland of blighted stills. Her palpable sensuousness of sights and sounds, touches, tastes, and smells were in crisis. She viewed the same prosaic tomorrow that every other artist also viewed. She ceased to be the purist she once was.

87

Sweet Wood

Late afternoon drizzles blighted the light. Layered clouds, hung over in translucent folds. Dusky shadows fell upon a gully's end. Next to this, a cinnamon farm lay stretched to the horizon. Tia Magnolia stood on this farm, under a cinnamon tree. Her red sari wavered in the moody winds. She stripped off a clump of sweet wood from the scented bark of the tree. She pouched the bark inside the sari's loose trail and tied it with a secured knot. It dangled, as she threw it over her shoulder. The sticks of the ancient spice were sturdy, yet delicate to crumble at the slightest twist of fingertips. She pulled a branch of tree and reached for its leaves. She plucked a few to squash them in the middle of her palm. The sweet smells of the cinnamon were released and pervaded the gully's air. She wandered down the bush paths.

Rains skewed over her as the intensity increased in the lowland by the basin. Down by the basin, wisps of vapour rose. Winds lashed on. The cinnamon pathways were covered in a smoky haze. She had to get away. Trespassing through the cinnamon garden was an offence, entailing harsh punishment. She had to avoid it at any cost. This belonged to a merchant who had traded the spice to the West. She headed for the hills. She had plans to ascend it on her nimble feet, towards a cottage on the peak. But the winds escalated, the roars louder. She struggled on the sharp incline. Winds kept pushing her down.

The hill was covered with feral trees and shrubbery – rare dragon blood trees and wild cinnamon. Her sinewy arms ached from stretching for balance. Ravens and wet crows flew over her in a rush to get back to their nests. The storm worsened. Tia kept up her journey. Its end appeared a long way away. Rain dribbled down her smooth, dark face. Her clothes drenched in water clung to her body. She stopped to take a breath and looked at a hot spring at the foot of the hill; its rising vapours, a silken enigma of coloured Borealis. Tia's breathing was shallow and difficult. She viewed gods, engaged in seductive frolicking in a warm bath in the basin, walled within the green precipices. Gods' hand in all this. Indifferent to the human cause, their laughter rang in the winds, as they splashed water and plopped playful rocks into the basin. She stood there screaming; tired, but resilient, amongst the fallen debris.

Close, but not close enough. She must make sure that her journey ended up in the cottage. One that she must fulfil. When she had come to pick the cinnamon bark, she did not think that far, that the heavy rain would make it all blurry. Now, it fell everywhere and blinded her way up through the deep forest.

She tumbled. She assumed she fell by the loop-root mangroves. Why? This place had always been dark. She thought she saw a white unicorn on the mangroves' edge. But no, it was just a figment of her mind. There were no mangroves here. Her journey continued. This golden cottage was up on the hill, mounted like a pearl of paradise. A cry pierced through the pattering rain. It was but the gusty wind, cutting past her in hasty rage. She must hurry before it subdued her. With each step forwards, she went a step backwards. Alas! The winds beat her to it, getting in her way. Reptiles, the inhabitants of the mountain, crawled back into their holes. Tia Magnolia kept pushing on. The wrong day definitely to come out for the cinnamon, Oh! The sweet wood! It could drive anyone crazy with its perfume. This forest was too dense for her to see anything far away. She fell again and scratched herself on this slippery terrain. Her knees bled. The gods smiled.

One day the cinnamon merchant had invited her into his palace. He told her that he had some great stories to tell her. She went to his great mansion and sat down to listen to whatever he had to tell. Then he started sharing with her his experiences of travels. He told her one story after another which fascinated her; her mouth fell open as she listened. He even cajoled her into believing that he would take her places. The fool! The colossal fool, she was. His maddening charms pulled her towards him like the black iron-ore, that middle-aged cinnamon merchant, of fifty years. She, a tender sprout. A romantic nomad, he told her stories, breathtaking stories of places he had visited, which melted her heart. Wonderful tales of giant hawks, and sweeping vultures scouring the sky and the earth. He described one palace after another. Magnificent ruby summer palaces of the East; sapphire winter palaces of the West. Beautiful princesses covered in blue and red head jewellery, danced in their primrose flowing robes when they walked up to see what he sold. The aroma of his cinnamon floating high in the air, the infusion of cinnamon tea made way for a porous imagination of a pantheon of visions; of scarlet battles, glittering diamonds on crowns, and studded sceptres. Victors and vanquished kings and queens of their kingdoms.

Tia Magnolia listened in a trance. The more she listened, the more she became enamoured, and drawn into the spell of the sweet wood. She wanted to become a princess. She wanted to live in a mansion. She wanted it all. She wanted the impregnable walls to fall flat at her feet, to open passages strewn with silver tinsels. Time and time again, he told her these stories behind closed doors, and then left her mesmerised in a bloody contortion of heartaches. He would be gone for years after that. And his tales would arouse curiosity in her loneliness. She would feel poor for the first time. Such illusions were a reality for her. She lived in that bubble, night and day. Bubbles that could burst, and leave her exposed. But she paid no heed to those warnings.

Now this passage was hard. This rain. This soft thumping on the lush mountain, the sweet wood soaked in the sari's pouch. The winds stood in the way. A hunger seized her to see a blue-headed racket-tail in the first Sun, and a dazzling, plumed peacock. What extraordinary colours? That dream, this storm could destroy. She took the difficult route, a choice she made. She must make it to the top of the hill, no matter what stood in her way; this was homecoming. She kept plodding along. The higher she went, the harder it got. She pushed herself up the slope. She slid and started anew, a yoyo of rising and falling. She felt like giving up, this arduous journey, which was what it had become. She wouldn't come undone. Her heart was a heaving heap. That mansion, and the golden cottage up the hill, streamlined in her imagination. Her strength did not dissolve like any molten lead. This was what kept her going. Life was not meant to be defeated. She was not a defeatist. This journey's end was at the tip of the mountain. That's where her happiness lay, her little bundle of joy, a joy that came at low tide. Tears. That was what it was. In the midst of tears, came her joy. This dream brought blessings into her little golden cottage. The cinnamon merchant would never know that his farmworker had such a strong inclination to learning. His tales acted as her impetus to dream big; maybe a bit too big to harbour within her small chest.

Steal? Yes, she stole the cinnamon bark to feed that dream. She stole to avenge the merchant for letting her dream of the impossible. In her heart, hopes fed an undiminished desire, not to surrender, but to reach out. The top of the mountain meant the end of a chase, an accomplishment of a dream. However, the more she chased it, the harder it became. It was but the golden cottage, on the mountain peak, her lost unicorn on the mangroves. The aromas of the sweet wood tangled her mind.

At midnight, in a final bid, she stopped short to inhale its smell, sat down at the foot of the wet mountain. She tried to listen to the forest, after a short interlude from the rain. Then she saw fireflies of fiery jinns, flying ubiquitous, through the summer's night.

Before the night was over, she knew the merchant was back at last. He brought with him yards of lazy, decadent satin which lay like a sluggish river; sunflower yellow, saffron, and soft baby pink; nuanced, along the deep contours of Aegean Mermaids. The merchant spoke to her, told her softly a path paved with a great history. But there were also some untold hidden miseries that eluded her.

"The Greek Islands, this time," he said.

"What about them?" she asked.

"Islands, woven on alentejo wrinkled wine at the behest of the sea nymphs."

"Beautiful?"

"Mesmerising, especially, when the turbulent waves of the emerald Aegean broke on its shores," he answered. "I traded spice, and the incensed cinnamon to entice gods to draw them out of heavens."

"Were they enticed?" she asked, wide-eyed.

"It made them drunk, both mortals and gods alike."

"How would you know?"

"Because on this land, mortals waged a hundred-year war. A war that would not quench Paris's thirst for the Helen of Troy. The nation's total immersion in the young blood of men, not shaken by their cries. War thundered on the scarlet sands for ten long years. Men trampled over each other, all but to win a divine beauty, a mortal, the Helen of Troy. Gods were delirious.

"Come on, you can't be serious."

She laughed.

"But I am."

"I want to see. You have opened my eyes to pleasures beyond me. I want to know more." She inhaled repeated short breaths.

"Imagine, this wide, wide-open sea before you. Men on papyrus warships, sailing towards the sunset to battle other kings, bringing either glory or gloom. They went hand in hand. Gods watched a fatal power-play but had not intervened. While men suffered and died in battles, they did nothing to save them. Just like the eye on their sleek boats, they only watched. They suffered because it was in their nature to fight. Gods would not have them believe otherwise. Men waged wars on a wanton chase to become tragic heroes. That was the cosmic bait gods decreed. A bait to drive men to the edge of insanity. And to end life. So life would perish, to make room for others in this limited space on planet earth."

"I want to fight. I want to be the Helen of Troy," she whispered. "I want to be queen. I desire everything you said to me so far. I want it all."

"Shush, my love, shush, not so fast," he said. "I sail again tomorrow to the far east. Towards the end of the ancient peninsula, into the kingdom of Joseon and further. Wait until my return. I bring more enchanting stories of glorious kings of mighty deeds."

The merchant left. Tia Magnolia became a restive inlander, left to wallow in her gluttony, her sweet bark, tied up in the pouch of her attire. She circled the pouch around her neck and smelled it. She looked at these invincible mountain passes beset with reptiles, lions, and hyenas. Trees,

93

one taller than the other. Resplendent leaves were made greener by every Monsoon rain; russet, and black, leaves grew anew in fresh droplets. Her struggles made no difference to rain or to any seasonal change or disorders. If a volcanic eruption were to happen, it happened. If lava were to overflow the ashen cities and towns, it was unstoppable. If clouds were to float, they floated. Floods, flash floods, blotted out lives with every drop. Changes of sky's luminous tinges from blue, violet, gold, or cream occurred without a fuss. Nature would not abate an inch. Loved ones would die despite people's grief. Dire predicaments would not alter any natural course. Unstoppable.

She waited morosely for the merchant's return, to hear more stories of indulgence, to seek new lands and hidden palaces thumbed under age-old shrubs; primordial tree-trunks snaked through decrepit palaces' cracks and crevices. She wanted to watch more epic dramas in cinematic expose. The rise and fall of men. Learn, what freedom and ambition actually meant?

At the heart of it, men were not free, no matter how much they fought. They were not. They only believed in the illusion that they were. For they were not ready to make those sacrifices just yet. Men still lusted after glory and power far too much. They loved going to wars, to fight battles and win them. The desire to acquire more land and kingdoms spiralled out of control. Those big tasks and asks would lead them further and further away from the real kingdoms of freedom. They would be free, only when they allowed themselves to be free from such desires; simple, not simplistic. Tia Magnolia, steeped in the aromatic flavour of the sweet cinnamon, continued to tie herself into tighter knots. She shackled herself deeper, down the unfathomable dark dungeon of dreams where no enlightenment could enter.

No matter, she must find her way up to the golden cottage, even if she had to claw, damage her nails, break her ankles, bruise her wrists, and skin her knees. She must never give up. Giving up, meant surrender. Men without ambition were as good as paupers on the roads. Ambition must never be taken lightly. Where did it end and where did greed begin? Men were ultimately caught up in this paradox, this inevitable trap of bewilderment, which led to profound illusions.

Two years had passed. Tia Magnolia climbed only halfway to the top. The merchant had not returned as he had promised. But he sent letters from the eastern peninsula. One letter, too many. They described the beautiful kingdom of Joseon of unimaginable wealth. Cities fortified with formidable emperors in spectacular dwellings. They traded luxurious silk, and spices down the silk road, paintings, and written words on famous Goreyo papers. But these cities were also vulnerable. They fell to frequent raids from foreign invaders. Another horrific tale of tainted wars and irrepressible suffering. Those dark times relentless and ruthless, for all their professed knowledge of Confucius's teachings, they were far from free, as emperors lusted after power and lived in its fantasy – both the legitimate kings as well as their colonisers. Because nothing lasted in the end, not even the lusts. All those kingdoms broke equally without fail on this continuum, only to survive in heritage paintings under lavish colours of historical grandeur.

The more she read those letters, the more convinced she became, that illusion, was more powerful than reality, by far. It was this illusion in the end that men fell for. No more futile than trying to grasp the meaning of existence. What did Tia Magnolia want? Getting to that cottage on the hill, what did it signify? She had to figure it out. One way or the other, she fell for it too. Because she embraced the naked desire in her heart that she wanted to be queen, and live in those grand, pleasure mansions.

She completely raptured herself with the thought that prestige and accomplishments were everything. She had to be that Helen of the Trojans, regardless of the consequences of the Trojan Horse. She had to be right at the top. This enchantment was unflippable. She was steadfast. Or else all struggles came to naught. Yes, struggles to dig bigger entrapments. This pursuit of a dream was too, too strong a lure; she could not forgo. She must push boundary and get to the golden cottage, as long as it took, unbeknown that happiness was eluding her.

Pink Toenails

Then the mountains spoke. Voiced it in the chorus, on the ancient land of Turag. A world where trees walked, winds cried, rivers sang and the mountains talked. This place, not for humans to reside anymore, but for natural lives and artificial intelligence. Turag, yes, this place, because humans have long been obliterated, like dinosaurs before them. Since then robots have replaced them. The organic world ceased to exist, as autumnal dirge swept through the pine forests of deadwood.

They all witnessed it, the sky, the oceans, and the mountains, but their voices couldn't be heard. In the days of humans, everyone thought they neither heard nor spoke. But humans were wrong. They communicated and witnessed every human history. Humans didn't see what they saw. Just as well, because they saw the end of the world. They saw it all coming. There was too much clunky background noise. Humans made it all.

Turag, once a lush plateau. Birds frolicked in the rain. Wheat and rice grass grew in abundance under an autumn sky. Children played around, while mothers barbecued corn over open fire-pits. The neighbouring mountains of the plateau nearly choked from smoke inhalation. But the mountains never complained. They smiled and took it all in their stride. They waited patiently for a miracle to happen.

In the meantime, billions of years of civilisation had passed. Generations toppled one another. Kings died to make way for the new. Power corrupted kings. Mighty kings they might have been, who won battles, but they also killed people on the mountain steppes. The green fields turned scarlet, replacing the many resplendent shades. But wins and expansions were all that mattered to the kings. These were the ways of the despots – often sacrificed the innocent and sons of the poor, for self-aggrandisement, cared not much at all for justice, whether or not justice was mete out. Then a time came when nature revolted. Fields stopped producing bumper crops. Rains decided not to dole out the bountiful properties of the rainbow. Leaves shrivelled up. Darkness covered the sun. Blood-moon lit the world. Machines were empowered. This new age of machines initiated a different kind of rage: human annihilation, underway, to take possession of the land. They didn't need nature to feed them, neither did they care to find beauty in it. Humans, long gone.

"Could men not have predicted this?" asked the blood-moon to the mountains.

"They could very well have because they were the ones to make these machines. But men ignored it in a haste to chase success," the mountains answered. The veiled sun conceded.

The mountains said, "Enter our caves and view the paintings there; stories of life foreshadowed on the dim walls. But men paid no heed, because they were blinded with ambition. Loud sounds came from war drums, drunken cheers of vacuous victories, and wonton amusements. Noises which shrouded men's judgment for everything that came to pass. Fools, they were fools! Those men, whose wisdom failed them. Only the stars knew how reckless they were. The massive destruction of innocent lives. Timeless settlements and resettlements, of nearly broken bones and spirits of men, women, and children. They didn't realise that they looked like scattered peas to the gods from high above; that's how insignificant they were.

Kings, endeavoured to build communities and strange dwellings such as marvellous palaces to shield themselves from enemies, showers, storms, and blustery winds. However, once they felt protected within those walls, then they chose to ignore the fact that life was transient. They stopped to think that the life-giving, precious air, their lifeline, was sourced from an outer world over which they had no control. The last breath taken, could be on those battlefields where relentless battles were held.

Mortals inhaled this infinite air to harness what little strength they could, and stored it within their little caged shells of a passing existence; that humans were tied to timeline. The timeline and the air they inhaled were immortal, paradoxically humans were not.

"Was this a fair deal? That while life-giving elements were immortal, humans clearly were not?" asked the blood-moon.

"Fair or not, the space needed to be created for every newborn. Power blinded men, who fought and killed and thought they made history. And they did – make history. But they also fell prey to nature's greatest conspiracy."

"Tell us more about them, these conspiracies," the blood-moon said.

"How can this be the real world, that men lived on borrowed gasses for their dear lives, the sprinklings from sunlight? The sun hidden behind you? All this, ah! This sweet smell of life, the history, the inceptions, and the destructions, the indelible stories of men writ on cave walls, what were they, but fantasies? Life was fated to fade, alluding to innumerable 'once upon a time' tales of the past."

"Is this all a dream?" asked blood-moon.

"It is. That's why humans have left us today, gone like a dream. They were invaded by machines, another wave of invaders, took possession. They were ruthless too. Because humans built them in their own image so that they would understand this organic race better and to perform impossible tasks commanded by humans."

Blood-moon listened awhile, then added, "Hardwired into a far stronger bind of vulgar ambition; more logic, than emotion. They destroyed men because they were the noisiest of the lot. Foolish men, they thought they were making machines that would serve them better. Alas! But the irony was that machines took over. They silenced men and left us, nature, in peace. However, the absence of human drama made for a boring existence. Like the lonely moons over the barren planets."

"Why, is there another paradox here?" the mountains asked. "Under the sun, on planet earth, it took billions of years for life to grow; destruction of life under the same sun, and the same planet became inevitable. Now that all have gone, and we, the mountains, the sun, and the moon have been left in peace, I miss them, mankind. I miss them a lot. Because, they were mad, passionate, and intelligent, who loved, killed, and created extraordinary things. Who allowed themselves to be frenzy, crazy, no?" the mountains replied.

"Ah! But they didn't think that far ahead. They were too limited in their imagination for predictions. That human passions exultant, looped them up into this paradox. That this paradox would also lead to the destruction of humanity. By far, their intelligence caused this downfall," said blood-moon. "Did they have a choice?

"Here's a question, indeed: did humans have a choice, regardless of divine intervention? Or was this a part of a cosmic project, one that shaped a destiny, and wrote human narrative? What was it? All this, a human choosing, in the end?" the mountains thought.

"Well, you and I have both outlived humans, and continued to outlive them, unless Mr Lightning struck you down today, or we, the sun, and I got completely eclipsed by each other. Our orbits collided to write us off into oblivion," concluded blood-moon.

"There's your answer, then," the mountains said. "The forces out there, with their random acts of discretion, could tweak anything. You may not sit on your silver throne forever, just as humans didn't. Just this, that the human existence was an illusion, which the humans didn't understand. It seemed real to them," concluded the mountains.

"Hmmm, I don't really know," said blood-moon.

"Neither do we," the mountains chorused.

While they were having this conversation, a dust storm picked up on the far side of the plateau. A gust of russet winds, rolled in and darkened the mountains, clogging up its crevices and valleys. It covered the blood-moon too, rendering a sad world to further gloom. *This wasn't the end surely?* the mountains thought. They had difficulty breathing; the air had ceased. The trees stopped walking to get their bearings back; the rivers stopped singing. They broke out into hiccups and coughs. These tumults in the surroundings shook the planet. No human hand at play, to create this havoc. The machines ran amok and kept losing their vital parts. There were no humans left to fix them. Machines could doctor one another, but they didn't get that opportunity, because even they couldn't predict this. A human flaw of design.

A disaster loomed. Another kind of warfare started within nature itself. The winds clashed with the rising tide. Mountains stood guard, to stop the storm from going any further. But the lightning then befell the mountain tips. Series of volcanic eruptions and melted glaciers paved the way to pandemonium. The overflowed lava wedded the falling flashes of lightning and danced in spiralled tango. The blood-moon shot out of sight. The storms, the bolts of lightning, left history in awe. Then a heatwave surged. Turag was hot again. Turag heating up! The lava ran in a rivulet towards the swelling seas. The oceans submerged the mountains. The plateau of Turag, now underwater, saw another breathing world beneath the oceans. Once again there was life. Mermaids swam unhindered. A clear sun ruled and gave it a second chance.

Purple Waves

"I want to be with Babu. You've reached the nadir of that river," Tahu lamented.

"Those pills? Do they not work? You've been on them for many days now," said Nalia.

"I see him. I hear his voice. He comes and goes through my room like a shadow, accusing me of casting him into the river. But he was blue, blue as stonefish spikes. He just didn't breathe; pills don't work; one blue and white or pink, oh! I don't know. At least he has stopped beating me now; oh! How he beat me every single night in drunkenness; yes, for money and to sleep with him."

Tahu sat in the front yard of her friend, Nalia's mother's house with her legs stretched out and entwined at the feet. She looked not at Nalia, or her mother but out into oblivion.

"That night of the big storm, I came home from work. There he was sitting on the bed drunk. I was pregnant with Babu. He asked to see my purse. I did not give it to him. I was tired. Oh, so tired from a whole day of stitches in the factory that it gave me stitches in my tummy."

Tahu stopped and took a deep breath. Nalia's mother made some tea on the small wood stove as she listened. The flimsy aluminium kettle hissed; it blew out some vapours. Nalia brought two little cups made of clay and set them down on the floor on the sitting mat where they talked. Nalia's mother poured out three cups of tea already made in the kettle with fresh cow's milk and molasses. Nalia handed a cup to Tahu and took one for herself. A shiny big raven came from nowhere and sat on the cane fence under the over-extended branches of the mango grove. Holding the cup of tea in the one hand, Nalia stood up and tried to get rid of the raven.

"Pills not working. When I didn't give him the purse,

he slapped me hard on the face, so hard that I fell down. I howled with pain. Yes. I did."

Tahu shook her head, her gaze transfixed on the floor, as though she were talking to nobody but herself. She wore a long garb of black check pattern. She couldn't care less if it covered her bosom. Parts of the garb slipped off her shoulder. Her hair was undone. Nalia took a comb and put it to work, gently pushing its teeth all the way to those roots, and down to her black knotted hair ends. She untangled the knots slightly, running her fingers through. Tea was getting cold.

"C'mon finish your tea, now," said Nalia's mother.

"I need to go home. I'll take the evening boat. He stopped beating me for a while after I lost Babu," Tahu said, picking up her tea. "Babu was doing well, and then one day he just breathed no more. I ran like crazy to the doctor; they said he was gone. Gone. Yes, never to see Babu again. Never. I brought him to the bank of the River Murma and took a boat. A storm loomed in the sky, the boat twirling around on the big waves, like a handmade paper toy boat; darkness was everywhere. It was so frightening. I couldn't care less. I tried, tried to wake him up in my lap, offered him milk, but he slept the sleep of a lifetime. And in that moment of panic, I started to cry and lowered him to the foaming waves; gave him away to Murma. Murma will take care of him, right? I know, he told me, he smiled. Babu. Babu. Where's Babu? Bring Babu."

Tahu's eyes popped out large, as she wailed and shrieked, reaching the limitlessness of the sky. Raven flew away nervously and Nalia, with her mother, continued to gape at her in despair. Helplessness was one thing but what just happened was boundless misery.

Yet, Nalia's wheel of fortune kept turning. In our random

fate-ridden existence, everyone supposedly had a fair go. She had saved a fair bit of money from her job working as a domestic helper. There was a deathly shadow in that house too, but she decided to give the money to her mother to buy another milk cow in the village. Courage had never left her side, even at her lowest. As they sat there with Tahu, Nalia's father rushed in.

"What's wrong?" asked Nalia's mother, frantically.

"Something's happened next door."

"What? Is Pintu in trouble again?"

"I don't know but Miah is on his way to the police station."

"Oh? Why is that?"

"The police had been asked by the regime to investigate his dead nephew's case in the village."

"What for? Hasn't enough happened already?"

"I don't know."

Tahu raised herself suddenly and said she wanted to nap. Nalia took her into her mother's bedroom and made her a bed on the floor, with a patched-up sheet looking like seven colours of the rainbow. Tahu lay down, stricken with grief. Nalia embraced her tenderly and kissed her oily dishevelled hair.

Tahu smiled and closed her eyes, whispering, almost chanting, "Babu says, come Maa, come to me. He stretches arms. Little arms. Baby fingers, stretch them as far as they would go, Babu. Babu is leaving. Wait, wait for me. Don't go just yet, Babu. No no no… medicine no don't work… the city. He remarried."

Nalia left Tahu to her half-formed thoughts, and came out to sit with her parents to listen to her father. He was saying something about their neighbour, Miah and his nephew, and his alleged murderer, Pintu, being falsely accused of the murder.

"Miah was interrogated by the police. They asked him if he knew where his nephew was on the night of the murder."

"What did he say?"

"That he was asleep. I believe the people from the autocratic party killed him. That nephew had made many enemies, you see. That's why they killed him and made Pintu, the scapegoat. Police, the head magistrate, everyone is in on it. That's what I think."

"Mmm. Will they find the killer? Police will throw innocent Pintu, the dead man's bosom friend, in jail too, now," Nalia's mother sighed.

"Anyway, Nalia's mother, give me some tea."

"In a while; rice is nearly done. I'm also going to fry some salted fish Nalia brought from the city."

Overall, the family looked much healthier for Nalia's earnings from the city.

"Mohammad has become a Jesuit and changed his name to MD, hasn't he? Don't give me the phone when he calls," Nalia's father said. "I raised him like my own."

Nalia stood by, listening away. She jumped in that very moment, saying, "He should stay wherever he is, Father. They might kill him too, if he tried to come."

"Who would?" asked Nalia's mother.

"Oh, don't be so naive, Mother. Jesuit or no Jesuit, if he's happy, then let him be. It's not our place to judge."

"No? Where would he be today if I hadn't found him crawling at the ferry stop?"

"I don't know. It's his life. You have given him a loving home, Father; fed him when even we didn't have enough to eat ourselves. Let it go. You've done your bit."

Nalia's father kept quiet. Her mother put the rice down on the paved floor, with boiled potatoes and some homegrown fresh village spinach, which she had plucked earlier from the small vegetable patch by the thatched house. She made another cup of tea for her father.

"You're probably right. I won't mull over it anymore. Certainly won't give the wicked farmer the sadistic joy of losing him; the hard slog that the bastard was going to put him through."

"Anyway, wake Tahu up. Lunch is nearly ready," said Nalia's mother.

It was becoming late in the afternoon. On the edge of the earth, the sun slowly diminished. An unexpected sense of calm descended. In one short life, this drama would end. And that would be the end of it all; those who suffered the worst were the ones most deluded by the notion that this life was forever. Oh, how calm, how peacefully the River Murma flowed today! A mere twitter of a bird in the heavy groves, the shepherd's distant tune caught in the flute wafted through the air. There appeared to be no grimy crimes threatening such delightful sensations of undulated serenity. The night forest was illuminated by fireflies everywhere. Lights sparkled, as they flew ubiquitous around the slim, tall trees and the heavy bushes of the blue forest.

Tahu woke up. She said she was hungry. Sleep made her feel so much better. She needed to move to this village to get away from that horrible, wife-bashing monster of a husband in the city, she desired to enjoy the tranquillity of the River Murma, to be closer to her Babu. Babu wanted her to be alive, so his apparition could make regular visitations, so she would see her baby's toothless, gum smile.

As they sat down to eat, there was the sound of a motorbike revving up outside the hut.

"Nalia's father, do you want to check who that might be?" asked her mother.

He stood up and walked to the fence. Two men had come to talk business with him. Tahu, Nalia, and her mother stayed indoors and listened, pale-faced, as he argued with the men.

"Either join us, our resistance party, or you pay heavily," they threatened.

"Resistance party? I'm not into politics. I don't want to be a part of what you do."

"And what do you think we do?"

"I don't know. Killing, looting, and rallying, all in a day's work?"

"Is that what you think? Have you forgotten Mohammad's debt of fifty-thousand gold coins he had borrowed from the farmer?"

And then there were heavy sounds of punching followed by a terrified bawl.

"Aww, oh God! Oh! My nose, nose. I'm done. These men have killed me."

"We haven't even started yet," they scorned. "We'll come back next month, make sure you've ten thousand gold coins ready for us. Or else, we'll beat you so much that you wouldn't see the morning sun."

"Please, I'm a poor man. There's no money. We go hungry most of the time. How can we pay what you demand?"

"We don't want to know. We will be back in a month's time. Keep the money ready."

They got back on the motorbike and disappeared along the dirt path. Nalia's father appeared in a moment with a frightening nosebleed. He flopped on the mat and held his head down, supporting it on his palms. Surely, they were the wealthy farmer's men. Indeed, they were his hitmen. Mohammad had to leave to become a refugee because of them. He had borrowed fifty-thousand gold coins from a rich farmer – not with the intention to milk him, but because he needed the money to bail out his sister Nalia's husband from jail. Now the farmer wanted to put him through unpaid hard labour, because the farmer knew, Mohammad would never be able to repay.

"Oh, good God. Nalia, bring the pitcher of water from that corner and give him a wash."

Nalia and Tahu dabbed his nose with a damp cloth.

This was a common occurrence in the village. People came regularly to recruit apolitical and peaceful village folks to join demonstrations and rallies. Make them do all the dirty work. They were tormented and threatened into subjugation. Like a great domino falling, those who felt unsafe and could find passage, took the risk of leaving the village, showing up in another part of the world. Terrible crimes against men, women, and children were being committed by the regime in the name of resistance to save democracy. Now that was irony. Nalia's father frowned. He couldn't think anymore. Nalia suggested selling the milk cow. Their only source of sustenance came from selling milk in the market. Did this have to happen this very moment, when things were beginning to look up from Nalia's factory job in the city?

"They will be back. This is what had happened to Miah too, before his nephew was killed. They came back, again and again, for more gold until they milked him dry," he said, meekly, and sighed.

"Wasn't it enough that his nephew was murdered? Well, you can't stay here," Nalia declared.

"Where could we go?"

"I'll think of something."

"What? What will you think of it? There's nothing remaining, besides death."

"No. It doesn't have to end like that. You're coming to the city with me."

"Are you out of your mind? What would I do there?"

"Whatever. Pull people's carriages; live in a slum."

109

Neither of her parents warmed up to the idea of being dispossessed in this manner, but, what else could they do? Anything was better than dying in the hands of these extortionists. Mohammad would have been either worked to death from slog, or killed by now, by the rich farmer and his powerful men, if he had stayed here. In a moment, the situation changed. What had seemed like a peaceful afternoon, turned dramatically into this? These were changeable circumstances, which swung like a busted wild clock pendulum.

"Shall we eat? I must seek help. Nalia, has Mohammad called yet? Mundip. The human traffickers," Nalia's father said.

Raven came back with a big caw and swooped down, to pick up some salted fish off one of the plates with his pointed, black beak. The rice went cold. Steadily, with fish at the tip of the long beak, he frisked about and sat on the fence. "Caw, caw." He ate it fast, seemed to say, "You're in a losing battle, join 'em, leave 'em, there's no escape."

"It was 'Nemesis'," howled the chorus of Sophocles of Oedipus Rex. What act of hubris was this? No more or less than what Oedipus had committed? Naught a Rex by a long shot, but Nalia's father succumbed to this ill-fate just the same.

Nalia's mother set out the plates again and gave each some food. Tahu must go home to her aunt a few doors away, for now – she, who raised her, after Tahu's mother had passed away in the last, great storm. She left them in dismay. There wasn't a single family in the Lost Winds, except for the influential, which enjoyed peace here. Each had their own burden of woes, transpiring in their own way into classic tragedy. The graver a situation became, however, the more people's fates hung in the balance, and the more astute they became.

110

Shingdi was a far cry, the ideal world that was out of ordinary people's reach. These people learned to survive on the edge, avoid bullets, and lie with confidence. In a way, they created a wall of deception to give them protection, a kind of immunity behind which the underprivileged hid. Somehow, the lies of the less fortunate were deemed as more criminal in the eyes of the law than corporate bullying or political transgressions.

Under the cover of darkness, Nalia and her family set off and disappeared, with their two milk cows. A month later, when those two terrorists came back to extort money, they found that the house had become the property of that wealthy and powerful farmer, who had acquired it as a trade-off to Mohammad's debt of fifty-thousand. It was a real bargain, because, the land itself would have cost over two hundred thousand. With the house, it would have been much more. Undoubtedly, those two were the wealthy farmer's hired assassins.

One evening, Tahu sat by the River Murma, talking and smiling at her baby. The world thought she had become completely mad. However, they could not see what she saw in her madness, as she rambled on. She told her baby that she wondered where Nalia went, without so much as a word: "She simply disappeared into thin air, Babu; no letter, no phone calls, no nothing." And then she smiled sweetly looking over the river as though the apparition stood on the contours of the sparkled water and smiled back. "She is? Do you think she is well? Whatever had happened to those two milk-cows? Oh. My God, now that's clever? She found a home for her parent's in her employer's house?"

Nalia was able to negotiate with her employer of the factory where she worked in the city and his wife, into taking her parents in and to make a cowshed. They sold

111

fresh milk, a rarity in the city of Grosnii, to every household that they could possibly reach through Nalia's employer. In return, they supplied free milk to her employers, a trade-off for a nice bedroom in their big house.

The apparition seemed to be telling Tahu all this, and she was seen laughing her head off, still looking towards the River Murma. She stretched her hand and brought it close to her chest in a gesture of hugging and then protruded her mouth towards emptiness, in the way of kissing. The village boys who saw her called her insane, but she had a method in her madness, which only she and her baby understood. They communicated every day.

"Nalia, if I find those men, I shall most certainly kill them and throw their bodies in the River Murma. No one will know it was me, because I don't exist for most people. My insanity will shield me, be my alibi and my defence, Nalia. I swear I would kill them the next time I saw them. This much I owed you, my dear friend. Babu and I would do this together. We will put a curse on them, as I did on that brute husband of mine. Where was he now? Do you know anything about him? He must be dead. Cold dead by now for certain. Wail. I wail, Nalia. I know not why. I'll be one with Babu soon. We're one in spirit, as close as one possibly can be with the dead. Dead? Who said he's dead? He's as alive as anyone else. You will see, Nalia, how those two die. You will read it in the paper one day. What do you care? You never even bothered to tell me where you were. Babu knew best and he told me. Wait until I finished the job at hand. We would have so much fun killing those two. They deserved nothing better; God knows they didn't."

About the same time, Nalia felt a strange tug in her heart too, as she sat in the cowshed milking the cows.

"Tahu, I now milk the cow every day; your black locks must be spread out on the silver River Murma when you

112

bathe. Do you think about me, too? Look for me? All those times we spent together. Tahu, your husband was found dead in the corner of the slum-alley. There was a fire and he was too drunk to run; he died from smoke inhalation. Fool, I've been such a fool. I didn't get in touch with you."

Surely enough, the newspapers in the city read that two people on a motorbike were driving past the River Murma one day. They fell into a trap of a fishing net thrown out at them from the blue. The net got entangled around them and the men were dragged off the stalling motorbike while they were still alive, and then straight into the water at high tide. All this happened quickly, before they could escape; the bodies slowly sunk into the depths of the river. Such was the fate of these two criminals. A convoluted contraption was pulled up the next day, as cold as fish laid overnight on the virgin snow.

The Scent of Goodness

Courtney Justice didn't like anyone touching her. Male, female, animals, it didn't matter. Her body swerved like a dancer, when she walked, trying to avoid the slightest bump with anyone on the road or public transport. Her steps were slow and measured. She would go to any lengths to avoid a clash with another living being. This way, she felt, she could remain pure.

This was Courtney Justice. What people said or didn't say about her was hardly an issue. She wasn't the kind of person to be bothered by such trivialities. Her concerns were different. Even she didn't know what her concerns were. She was bookish and friendless. She lived in her own world. When she walked past someone, she showed disinclination or even disdain for people around her. She never looked at anyone with any interest. Just happy, in her own world of imagination.

For the church, however, she was a regular; never late, especially on Sunday morning sermons. She sat in the corner, right at the back, where most people would miss seeing her. Insignificant? That she was, but, a life of her own choosing. One Sunday, though, as she came out of the church, a young girl walked across the lawn towards her. Courtney nodded at her and she nodded back. Courtney's simplicity was her beauty. She had cute freckles on her buttoned nose. They shone in the sunlight, today.

"Hi, I am Sara Knightly," the young girl said.

"Courtney Justice. Nice to meet you."

"Cool. What do you do?" Sara asked.

They started to walk side by side. But Courtney maintained a distance from her.

"I am a cashier."

114

"Right. Where?"

"Downtown. The Red Bull Café."

"How about you?" Courtney asked.

"Oh, I am a student in creative arts," Sara replied.

"That's cool," Courtney said.

"Do you like your job?" Sara asked.

"Yeah, I do okay. I work in the back office, mostly."

"Neat. It's quiet in there, yeah?" Sara asked.

"You could say that," Courtney responded.

"My boyfriend and I, may drop by at your café, one day."

"Great, do that."

"Goodbye."

Sara said, and then walked away. Courtney kept up her pace steadily until she reached the train station. On the platform, she heard a sharp cry of mirthless laughter. She turned around and saw Sara; Sara Knightly amongst her friends. She appeared to be the butt of a joke. They teased her, poked at her, even pushed her around a bit, too close to the railway track. Sara cried out in pain sometimes. She seemed to notice Courtney looking at her. What should she do? Should she walk over and rescue Sara? Courtney couldn't decide but remained calm and undeterred. She stood like a thorny puritan, judgemental and aloof.

No one deserved to be bullied – even Courtney understood that – whether on railway platforms or in school-yards. But this church-going puritan didn't lift a finger to offer Sara any help. The train arrived and they all embarked. Courtney escaped to the far end of the carriage, and sat down on a single seat, by the window. She combed through her actions. Perhaps, she should have helped her. Or maybe not, since that would involve touch. She may have felt defiled afterwards. All in God's plans, Courtney thought; she felt assured in her chastity. She liked playing the Madonna very much, Michelangelo's Pieta, in being immaculate, but childless.

When the train stopped at the platform, she was last to get out. And as the train took off, she looked behind to see Sara, giving her a cold, strange look. But Courtney shrugged it off and continued towards her flat. When she arrived, she found a few letters poking out of the letterbox slit. She grabbed them and pulled them out. She found one of interest. It had been sent from the church. It was an invitation to a fundraising event. She felt an uncanny thrill run through her.

Later that evening, her sterile, stark flat, offered her solace. She would never have a roommate of any sort. She ate a dinner of roasted potato and bacon rashers, and contemplated the fundraising event. She could bake a cake, or perhaps a proper turkey roast. One way or the other, it had to be something that everyone liked at the church. Not because she wanted to treat them goodies, but, because she thought it would please the priest and in the end Jesus. Her thoughts got distracted. The bell at the door rang. Odd, she thought. Who could that be at such an hour?' She opened the door, and a little boy stood outside. He looked like an urchin.

"Who on earth are you?"

"I live around the corner with other homeless kids."

"Why did you knock on my door?" Courtney asked.

"Because I saw you come in."

"You saw me? Did you follow me here?"

"I guess I did."

Courtney looked at the boy, straight-faced and tight-lipped. She was close-fisted; her hands by her side. She didn't invite him in or offer dinner.

"What do you want?" she asked, aghast.

"Could I have some dinner? I am really hungry."

116

"Dinner? No, no, I can't let you in; I don't even know you. Besides, you have been following me."

"Please," said the boy, and extended an arm towards her to touch her hand. She stepped back nervously and shut the door in his face.

Courtney brushed her teeth, prayed, and went to bed. She lay under the blanket and thought about her church, and the upcoming event, until she passed into sleep. A door opened at dusk. A little girl stood on the threshold and watched the last rays of the setting sun in semi-darkness. A woman sat on an inky floor. The floor wavered. She was surrounded by three other women. They beckoned the little girl to come inside; she did. A gale came right through the open window and shut the door. The women smiled and asked the little girl to massage the shoulders of a woman sitting in the middle, while the others watched. All these women sat on a dusky floor, which was slowly warping. They sat on a pool of water. The little girl stood over them and complied. She bent her knees on the woman's shoulders and rubbed them while standing on water. The silk-water overwhelmed her. The women spoke amongst themselves. They said, "Only the firstborn could heal this pain. Where no doctors succeeded, she, this little girl, could." Then it was over.

Courtney screamed and woke up. Her sweat dripped down. She lit the bedside table lamp and got out of bed. The sun had not come up, yet. Just like her dream, she sat in the fluid darkness and waited for its full bright light. Let there be light, so she could see better. Untested virtue, what was it? What was good without any tests and trials? Good for the sake of being good? Courtney never cared for any living creatures, great or small. However, she waited patiently. She wanted to go to church and pray. As soon as the sun rose, she put on her clothes and set off for the train station.

117

Out on the street, she thought, she saw the boy from last night disappear around the corner. "They wake up early, those crazy urchins," she mumbled.

The train was late. A pedlar's song drifted through the silent morning. She felt refreshed in the first air. Alone on the platform, this early, she waited for the train. Then it came. It was an empty phantom train. While she waited on the platform, the pedlar vanished. The singing stopped. Ghastly haunting, she was surprised that there wasn't even a train operator. When it took off, it gradually picked up speed; it went too fast; way too fast. She was on her way to church. Then the train stopped. She saw Sara Knightly again. She stood in white, on an empty platform, a picnic basket in her hand, with the little urchin. Sara held a newspaper; she let go of it. It blew in the hard wind. Courtney got off the train. The newspaper landed at her feet. She picked it up; it was an old newspaper from two years ago. Why would Sara carry an old newspaper? It had a picture of a derailed train and a few scattered bodies. Those were Sara Knightly and the urchin. When she looked up, they had disappeared. But a drift of winds, imbued in the true scent of goodness, awakened her to a path of righteousness, she had not known.

Juliet's Song

Juliet worked in a café up the road. Her pretty smile was something to see first thing in the morning. But she didn't know that. She worked her shifts around the clock, being nice to the lovers of coffee, serving them, and taking orders. Juliet was stringent with her time. However, occasionally, she would generously spare a few moments to chat at the till. No one knew what went on in her head. Nobody cared to find out what her thoughts were. And that was how it was; strictly professional.

One morning a lady by the name of Rita Chowder, a regular at the café, came in and sat down at a corner. It was a quiet day. In fact, Rita was the only customer at the time. She finished her first cup of coffee. Then she waved at Juliet. And when she came by, Rita asked her for another shot. Juliet brought it over to her. As she took a sip, Juliet noticed tears.

"What's wrong?" she asked, frowning.

"What do you mean?" Rita asked.

"Are you crying?" Julia asked.

"Yes."

Juliet asked, "Why?"

"Oh, it is a long, long story. I think I am about to lose my house to the bank," she answered.

"That's no good."

"I have been frugal all my life. Worked hard and drove second-hand beat-up cars. I always dreamt of buying a new car one day, but that never happened. I just couldn't save up enough, always behind, no matter how hard I worked."

"Oh, no."

"Turns out, that's the way it was all going to be," Rita concluded.

Juliet wanted to help, but what could she do? How was

119

Rita to fight the big banks and the hiking interest rates? Juliet moved away from her to serve another customer. By the time she came back, Rita was gone. But she noticed, she'd left something on the table. It was a card, with her phone number written on it. Juliet picked it up. She gazed outside through the café gates and saw Rita walking away. Should she keep the card? Clients came and went every day, but who cared about their stories? Something told her to keep it. She tucked it away in her apron pocket. When she looked again, she saw the last of Rita's floral dress at the vanishing point, behind the garden's neat hedges.

After work, that night Juliet returned to her two-bed apartment. She shared it with another girl named Kate. Juliet showered, then wrapped herself in a dressing gown. They ate some pasta together, which her roommate had cooked, as they watched television. Over dinner, they had a conversation.

"I was speaking to a customer this morning and she was saying that she may lose her house to the bank."

"Really? Can she not pay her mortgage anymore?" Kate asked.

"Yeah, something like that," Juliet answered.

"That would be really awful."

"Yeah, wouldn't it?

"Do you want to buy a house someday?" Kate asked.

"Me? Ha! Funny you ask. I'm even lucky to pay my rent." Juliet smiled.

They both laughed and finished dinner. They watched the news and discussed what the banks were doing and have been doing to their clients. After the news finished, they rose from their chairs and dumped their plates in the sink. Juliet said goodnight and went to bed. She had an early shift the next day. She didn't go to sleep right away. It bothered her that people like Rita had to suffer. She thought only people in the developing world suffered like this. She didn't understand the economics of it at all. However, she took her diary out of the bedside table drawer and began to write. Most were her own ramblings, but she also penned down Rita's predicament. It hadn't dawned upon her entirely, until now, how many people were out there, who tirelessly put uncountable hours into work, for negligible returns. What was it in the end, if they couldn't even own one house in retirement or drive a brand-new car? What was it? Was anything worth it? That people had to pay back double, even triple, with interest on the principle they borrowed from the banks? That it would take four generations, if not more, to pay back. Was it even fair? Juliet had no answers.

In the morning, she had a new resolution. She wanted to smell the sweetness of spring in all its freshness. She wanted to make money, travel, purchase a house, drive brand new cars. Live it up! After all, she lived in a first world country, and she should be entitled to those world-class benefits. On her way to the café, she went to the newsagents to buy a copy of the Sydney Herald. She turned to shares and bonds.

Investing in shares and bonds was the way to go. At twenty-five, she'd figured it out. She must tell Rita, too, if she were to save her house. Juliet thought of investing her small savings. She was going to buy blue chips. On lunch-break, she researched long-term investments; the rises and the falls of share markets. Windfalls, making quick money, while improbable, was not impossible. She called her brokers and invested all her savings into a diversified portfolio. She was not going to end up like Rita. Where was Rita anyway? She didn't come today. Juliet was distracted; she expected Rita to walk in through those gates.

After work, Juliet thought about Rita. She was just a client in the café, who'd come for a regular caffeine shot.

Juliet didn't even know where she lived or anything about her, but she wanted her to know that there was a way out. If Juliet could sell and buy shares wisely, she could end up with a little pot of gold. That night, she came back from work. It was her turn to cook dinner. She turned on the TV and took an onion to slice. She must follow the market closely. On the news, an accident was reported. A body was found washed up by the local riverbank. Most likely, it was suicide. A name was also released: Rita Chowder. The knife fell from Juliet's hand, and the onion rolled off the cutting board. Rita was no relative, hardly even a friend, but Juliet felt she was so much more.

This was puzzling. Her breathing was short and shallow, as she struggled to accept this. She had to sit down. She didn't realise she would miss Rita that much. She tried to imagine Rita's dreams. It appeared like a jagged rainbow under wrinkled water. That night she could not eat dinner but went to bed straight away.

A fresh start in the morning, this new day, should bring a refreshing new perspective, she hoped, and coffee shots gave her those false moods. But she felt that something positive may happen. And it did. In the winter months of the coming year, Juliet made some money in the stock market and was able to travel.

The Blue Butterflies

The war ate the fourteen-year-olds. Such were the days, when young boys wielded swords and died in this dust. Politicians, drunk in the revelry of power and greed, sent the elderly and the young to join the army to fight senseless battles in the name of the king. Not knowing whose wars they fought, these soldiers were perfect cannon fodder. Wars, which took place many years ago, under hot suns and rising sands of the desert Gulaag.

The Gulaag was vast and dry. It was hard to spot an oasis anywhere. This was an empty space made up of rippled sand dunes and sporadic barrel cacti. Kings thought this arid land was ideal for battle.

At a time like this, a baby boy was born. His name was Hajji. His mother named him in his father's absence because the father was taken by the imperial force long before his birth. He grew up without opulence with his mother in this small town in eastern Gulaag, on the border between two warring kingdoms.

The wars were far from over. This godforsaken land, Gulaag, couldn't be appeased any time soon. Royal armies fed on the vulnerable, as did their sinful paymasters. It was an ever-hungry beast; no number of humans, camels, or horses was enough to satisfy this desert.

Hajji's mother, Jainab, had no other place to go. This was where she must stay, on this little patch of land her husband had left for her. Her fate was tied up with the Gulaag. But she lived in constant fear, like every other mother on the land, that the army would come after their sons. Hajji had just turned twelve. Jainab watched him around the clock and kept him close. Sometimes she would send him to tend the sheep far out into the desert.

Today, in the first light of morning, Hajji took off at

dawn. He took his flock from the shed at the back of their mud house and headed towards the Gulaag. Those were the quietest moments, when the army slept. When he had walked nearly a quarter of a mile into the desert, he saw a great number of tents, strewn across the sands, in which soldiers rested after their long night's shift. The Gulaag slept like a giant at their feet. Hajji walked over the placid sands ahead of his herd. Then he heard a small cry beyond one of the rippled dunes. Hajji stopped. It was a feeble cry, almost a whimper. It didn't sound like a human voice, at first. He followed the sound. It was a human voice after all. It came from a boy, about his age, crawling over slithering sand. His little body was cut and bruised. Hajji ran over and sat down by his side.

"You are hurt!" Hajji said.

The boy looked at him wide-eyed and nodded.

"Who did this to you?" Hajji asked.

"Enemy," he said. "Water, water, may I have some?"

Hajji looked around. He found some prickly pears by the dunes and then searched for something sharp. He found a flat pebble.

"Hang in there, okay?"

Hajji cut some pulp with the sharp edge of the pebble. He took the prickles out carefully, pouched the pear pulp into the corner of his long shirt and came back to the boy. Hajji asked him to open his mouth. As he did so, Hajji squeezed the pulp into it.

"I'll have to piggyback you home with me if I can't find a camel," Hajji told the boy.

The boy was weak. His wounds were fresh. He said nothing but waited for Hajji to make arrangements. Hajji walked across the wide dune and found a camel near the army tents. The beast of the desert stood aloof, tied to a tent's hook. When Hajji peeked through one of the tent's

124

opening, his sharp eyes fell on several men sleeping. They were too close and huddled together. Some were child warriors.

Hajji walked behind a tent. A few guards were drowning in sleep. He walked past them unnoticed and went up to the camel. Hajji hid behind its rear and moved his lithe body between the camel's four lanky legs, until he reached the hook, where the camel was tied with a rope. He untied it, held it by its rein and brought it over.

Jainab sat on the threshold of her house. Hajji was late today. She boiled some chickpeas over a clay stove. "Where is my boy? I hope soldiers haven't taken him!" This brought her memory back to when her husband lived with her. Some were happy memories; others were not, but unforgettable all the same.

This was not where she had met him, not in this house, but someplace else on the Gulaag. She had been travelling with her nomadic tribe for days on end. One day, when evening fell, the cavalcade stopped to camp in the desert. They had anchored tents into the sand when a cold blast blew. Men and women lit a fire and sat around it. A man took a fiddle out and played a moon song, while the others rose to perform a dance. In this mesmerising song and the fire dance, the moonlight appeared to slide on the open desert; they gushed out like a silver stream of frozen waterfalls.

There he was: a stranger. Who knew, where he had come from? He was a lad of twenty; she, barely eighteen. They had sat across the desert fire. She thought of him as a rare breed. He was taller than any man she knew and wore a horseshoe moustache which suited his long chiselled, jawline. He rose and began to dance with her folks, who he'd barely known, looking at her, smiling and nodding as

125

though he did this to impress her. As though, he wanted to know if she'd approved of it. When she smiled and nodded back, he'd winked. Impressive as he was, she had gazed at him by the campfire. Caught off-guard in enchantment, she couldn't take her eyes off him, as one couldn't, if struck by a host of blue butterflies resting on the trunk of giant kapok in the sun.

He had smiled and she had shot him a shy glance. After that, they both knew that there were no retreats. At midnight, when the tribe went to bed, she had come out to wait under a starry sky. He was there. His long shadow loomed on the calm sand by a pile of dying firewood. She saw a shadow move, towering over her. He held her hand and pulled her towards him, away from the stationary convoy. They stumbled on the sand and rolled over, in the silver light.

The next day the sun had risen over the dunes. He walked over to Jainab's father with a marriage proposal. Jainab's father liked him too, but he had questions. Where was he from? What did he do? He said he was a farmer. Jainab didn't care what he did or where he lived. She was just happy to be with him. A wedding soon ensued and it took place in the desert. The man gave Jainab a gold coin. The short ceremony concluded in the presence of the tribe.

That night, there was a feast in the open-air of buttered rice and eggplant casserole, cooked over a big spitting fire. There was also some lamb dish cooked in a sauce of fermented dried yogurt, served with bulgur, and prickly pear cactus. There were wild dances and songs of the heart. A sandstorm was unleashed towards the late night. It blew russet particles everywhere, darkening the world to blindness. Everyone took cover within their own tents. While people lay low, only the stoic camels stood their ground. A new tent was set up for the newlyweds.

The storm yielded. It took some time. People came out of their tents. They sat down in the same place and began to sing again, while the newlywed remained indoors. In the morning, the couple decided to leave. Jainab and her man packed their luggage as they said farewell to the tribe. Tears were unnecessary because they believed that on life's journey, people were bound to meet again.

Her husband's name was Hashimuddin. Jainab softly asked where they were going. He told her they were going east. There was a desert tavern along the way, where she could rest if she needed to, but she said she was okay. Uncertainty didn't bother her; that was her nomadic upbringing. In the evening, they arrived at the destination. A mellowed sun had been hurled over to the western sky. Jainab could see a border between this kingdom and the enemy territory, with whom they were perpetually at war. Along the border, she also saw a big patch of greenery and a row of red mud houses. Hashimuddin veered the camel towards one and pulled its reins to a stop in front of a house. He helped Jainab to get off.

After Jainab and Hashimuddin had departed, the nomads sat around. They were enjoying a cup of tea and preparing to get the cavalcade back on the road. Just as well they heard horses. The Gulaag was a hostile place. Sporadic wars often broke out. Not surprisingly, a situation emerged suddenly. The tribe found themselves amidst a volatile army, who held them captive at razor's edge. Sharp blades pierced their hearts and slashed their necks like butchered chickens. The gold sand dunes turned scarlet with slain heads scattered all over. Their camels were taken. Children and women became spoils of war to be turned into murderous soldiers and sex slaves overnight.

Hashimuddin and Jainab had escaped just by a few hours. They were on the edge of the eastern Gulaag when it happened; cries couldn't be heard from there. Jainab reached her new home feeling safe and warm in love, without any knowledge of the massacre.

Such horrendous breakouts were common, as though God had singled out this land for such human misery to occur. Religion, morality, philosophy, or any known wisdom, proved to be futile – a place riddled with greed, corruption, and a complete disregard for life, human or animal.

Jainab's son was still not home. It was evening. She sat by the fire and kindled it to cook a meal. She looked out intermittently and saw a mirage, visions of indecipherable outlines across space; they had become more defined. They were small but clearer. She saw them walking through the mirage and stood in excitement: it was her son, Hajji. But Hajji was not alone. There was a camel with a body lying over it. She rushed out to meet them.

It was the day when the soldiers had come to take Hashimuddin. That morning, the sun had streamed low through the cracks of the mud house windows, and Hashimuddin and Jainab were deep in an embrace on the threshold of the door. She had been on her way to the kitchen. Hashimuddin held her back. He'd grabbed her right arm and pulled her towards his chest.

"Where do you think you're going?"

Oh, those sweet, sweet words. "To make breakfast."

"No. I have to tie you to my long shirt to stop you from running away."

She had laughed. Hashim gazed at her beautiful smile. "If you keep smiling like that, I may never be able to let you go."

He whispered and kissed her henna-fragrant hair, losing his face in its mass. She laughed again. Hashim held her steady.

"C'mon, you have to let me go sometime."

"And do you think it's fair to ask me to let you go? Hmm?" he asked.

"Gosh, you're crazy, you know that?"

"Am I crazy? If you say so, then I am. Completely nuts, because I'm in love with you, my pretty one," he said.

Jainab could smell the hukkah in his breath.

He whispered, "Oh, I could never, ever let you go."

He pressed her softness with his gentle hands. She lay on his chest and he caressed her like a match striking a flame to a candle wick. He was her Hashimuddin, who had crossed her path on an evening of munificence.

A few days on, she had realised that she was with child. She hadn't told him yet. She didn't have to, because her soft blushes and smiles revealed the secrets of her heart. She resided in the reverie of her own coloured world. As each day went by, Hashim watched her across the courtyard and wondered. Then one morning, she took a bath and stood on the doorway of the red mud house, where Hashim could see her. Her wet hair cascaded down to her waist. Hashim couldn't resist. He walked over and picked her up. A tremor ran right through her.

"What's up? Why do you look so radiant?" he asked.

"Do you want to know? Do you really, really want to know?"

The shy smiles, the sidelong glances. "You're doing it again," he said.

"What? What am I doing?"

"Crazy, you're making me crazy again."

He took a sharp breath. And then held her narrow waist to lift her. He looked into her kohl-black eyes. At this moment, his pretty Jainab was the dark-kohl enchantress.

"You're going to be a daddy soon," she announced, gently.

"What? Oh, dear God, when did you find out?"

He didn't even wait for an answer but had carried her straight into the bedroom and had laid her down on the bed. Her eyes danced like sparkles in the dark. He closed his eyes and kissed her forehead; he kissed each piece of her body, like pieces of a jigsaw puzzle, one at a time, savouring, lingering, locking his wet lips onto hers, then unlocking them soundingly, smooching, to move on to her neck and down.

She felt euphoric. She had a vision: millions of blue butterflies pasted on a tree trunk in the depths of the Amazon. A noise broke her spell. She heard hooves near her doorstep. They had come closer. They were the army. The soldiers barged into the house through the flimsy door. The army of death wielded sharp swords. Hashim had already seen them through the window. He picked her up and said, "Run, run to the neighbours."

"What? What about you? Aren't you coming?"

"No. God willing, I'll see you again one day. No goodbyes. Run along, now."

Fear had paralysed her. She shook like a frightened rabbit at midnight before bright lights on a mountain pass. Hashim screamed. He backed off from her. She hid there on the outside, nailed to the wall. She heard scuffles inside the room. Then the noises of the hooves faded. She saw across the desert, Hashim's back on a horse. He had been taken. That was the last of it. The end of her blue butterfly, which had flown into the dusk in a flicker.

Hajji and the boy were much closer. But dust rose and covered them. The obedient herd was right behind. Jainab ran towards them. She fell on the shifty sands and waited.

Her baby, Hajji, was born nine months after her husband had been taken. Hajji came at the stroke of midnight. Neighbours

130

had assisted in the delivery. Her neighbours were like siblings, who tilled her land and helped her out. They sold her chickpeas in the market and brought money home to Jainab. Jainab paid them their dues. The day Hashim was taken, other men in the neighbourhood were out to the market. The soldiers had found Hashim at home and had taken him. It was her fault that her kohl beauty, this dark spell, kept him indoors. She blamed no one but herself. Twelve years now, Hashim had been missing.

Jainab sat, a nervous wreck, on the sand. Hajji and his companion were home at last. He ran up to her and picked her up. She kissed and hugged him.

"Oh! Why were you so late? I thought they'd taken you."

"No, but I found someone on the edge of the Gulaag. He's a wounded child soldier."

"Right. Let's bring him in, then, shall we?"

Jainab and Hajji slid the boy off the camel's back. They carried him into the house, just the way Hashimuddin had carried her, like a bride over the threshold of the mud house. The boy had many injuries, she noted, as she laid him down in bed. It was a huge task fixing his wounds. A cog in their home, another mouth to feed, but her motherly instincts couldn't let him go. She nursed him and protected this child as her own.

Jainab knelt before him and rubbed off his blood with a loincloth soaked in warm water. His wounds were deep. She applied herbal medicines and put a bandage across his arms and waist. Towards dawn, the boy opened his eyes and said he was thirsty. Hajji ran into the kitchen area and took a pouring pitcher. He came back into the room and walked through the backdoor. A house-well was in the back yard. Walking up to it, he dropped a broad-based bucket

131

into the well. It was hanging on rope down a pole over the well. He pulled up some water, poured it into the pitcher, and brought it back to Jainab. Through its spout, she poured a few drops onto the boy's dry lips. She dressed the wounds and thought that they would take some time to recover. As a nomad, she had some ancestral knowledge about ancient medicine, thankfully, they came handy.

Jainab rose to brew some tea and organise breakfast in the kitchen. She made falafel. She asked Hajji to come outside. His eyes were bloodshot from sleeplessness. She gave him red tea in a glass and some falafel with dry dates on a platter.

"These are really nice," he said. "I have been so hungry and tired since last night. I don't think I can tend the sheep today."

"That's okay. You don't need to go anywhere. After breakfast, go sleep, with the boy. Do you know his name?" Jainab asked.

"No, he was too weak to talk. I was lucky to bring him home. I don't even know if he's a friend or an enemy."

"Don't worry about that. It's not our place to judge the wounded. We do our best to heal them so he can go back to his parents. You took a great risk stealing that camel from the soldiers' camp, though. Where was the herd?"

"Oh! They were around, chewing cactus flowers," Hajji said, with a smile, and rose to go into his room.

Jainab had just finished in the kitchen when she heard the familiar sound, the sound of hooves. The horses were back. The soldiers were back. She rushed into the room and carried the boy, asking Hajji to come with her. She went through the backdoor into the desert, straight to the well. She grabbed the bucket sitting on the well's periphery, and put it on the ground by the well. Its rope noosed on the ground.

132

She lay down behind it crouched on her side with Hajji and the boy, right against the well, pinned to its wall, stuck like a wallflower, not even daring to breathe. She couldn't see any of the men from this angle and decided that perhaps, the men couldn't see them either. However, there was the shed further away from the house and the well; she thought maybe the shed would have been a better hiding place, because the bucket, although tall and broad was flimsy protection. But she sensed the men must be there by now. And they must have turned it upside down.

She assumed correctly; men were here and rummaging through her things, inside the house. They came out of the open back door, and went straight into the shed. Her neighbour had left piles of shearers' sheepskin a couple of weeks ago. They took a pitchfork and poked at the edge and around the shearer's pile, in a corner. They even forked out some from the pile's depth. Further away, the well was within the line of vision from here. They gazed at it but couldn't see anything from this angle, except for a tall, broad-based bucket and some rope. They thought nothing of it and left, after a while.

Dust rose from the horses' gallops. She tried to hear if the winds carried any sounds, at all. There was silence, then some fading talks drifted. She figured, they must have left. She felt relieved. She raised her head first and scanned the area over the bucket. It was now safe. She came out of hiding and she stood up. Sweat beads on her forehead, she wiped them off on the palm. She carried the boy, and nudged at Hajji to rise. As they walked back to the house, she glanced at the open desert, and saw hoof marks on the sand's outbound trail. She peeked into the shed too, and saw it in a state she might have imagined it to be in, after the men were done with it.

She brought the boys inside, and laid them down on

133

the kilim, spread out on the floor. She grabbed a hand fan, fanning them until Hajji and the boy fell asleep. The wounded boy opened his eyes a fraction to take a slit-look at Jainab. After that, he lost consciousness. Jainab sprinkled water on his little pale face. He opened his eyes again. He smiled and went back to sleep. Jainab lay down by her children. She fidgeted for a while and then fell fast asleep.

The sands of the hourglass slid as time passed. It had been nearly seven days since Hajji brought the boy home. On the morning of the seventh day, she woke up next to Hajji and the boy. The boy showed clear signs of improvement. He curled up in bed and ate for the first time. He didn't feel hot or cold. The sounds of the hooves had not returned. They left them in peace today, perhaps to fight. The boys sat together outside in the yard, drinking red hot tea, which Jainab poured out of a vaporous kettle. She placed it back on the hot clay stove. A neighbour pushed in through the doors.

"I came for my wool," he said.

"Sure, pick em' up from the shed," she said.

"Who is this?" he asked, looking at the new boy.

"Oh! This is Hajji's cousin, come here to spend a few days with us."

"I didn't know you had any relatives left."

"Why would you think that?"

"Didn't your tribe get wiped out on the Gulaag some twelve years ago?"

"Did they? What are you saying?" she asked.

"Twelve years had passed and you didn't know?"

"Know what? Why would you think it was us?"

"Because I was there, at your wedding."

"What? And it took you twelve years to tell me this?"

134

"I'm sorry. So, so sorry. Please understand, the day the army had butchered your tribe, they also took me. But I proved not much of a soldier. One dark night, when they lay drunk in the arms of women from your tribe, I took a camel and escaped. It took me days to get home, but when I did, I saw you with Hashimuddin in this house..."

"Stop! Please stop. Say no more!" Jainab began to cry.

In her heart, she had cherished the idea that her tribe was safe somewhere within the four corners of the world. Nomads never exchanged news or met for many years. But this, this distressing news; she wished these ill tidings had never reached her doors. She wished this quiet neighbour had remained so. Her grief swelled like a dust cloud. Moments of unsettled thoughts and opaque visions. Grief would settle down surely one day, as the dust often did. But now it lumped a corner of her stricken heart.

Days went by; Jainab grew paler. She took to bed. Hajji and the boy did what they could to nurse her, but Jainab didn't improve. One day, the boy, now strong enough to move, suggested to Hajji, "Why don't I go home and bring my parents here, so they could take care of your mother?"

"What? Are you crazy? The army will take you back if they find you," Hajji said.

"Well, I'll just have to take my chances. If we don't take care of your mother, she will die," he said. "I shall go tonight."

"Where do you even live?" Hajji asked.

"Across the border. However, I am from the enemy camp, so you know. But we are brothers now, so it doesn't matter. You've saved me, Hajji."

"Can you go alone? Because I can't leave my mother like this in her present condition. I wish that neighbour had never opened his mouth."

"I know. I also wish that he hadn't," the boy said.

135

"It's good, though, that mother told him you were my cousin, but I don't think he believed her," Hajji said.

"No." The boy nodded. "Your mother is really good."

"Yeah, she's good," Hajji agreed.

"Okay, then, I'll set out tonight and bring my father back."

"You don't need to, because our neighbours will help my mother get better," said Hajji.

"Still, I need to go now. I miss my parents. And the border is just here; I can even see it."

"Well, okay, if you want to, you can go. I hope I won't see you in the Gulaag again."

"Me too."

That night, Hajji and the boy sneaked out. They ran over dense sand; the little footsteps etched on it. Hajji took him as far as the border. The boys hugged each other and kissed on the cheeks. Just when they turned to go, they saw men marching straight towards them. The captors ambushed them under their naked sword, which glimmered in the moonlight. The desert air reeked of blood and sweat. The boys were in shock. It didn't matter whether these were foes or friends. In the end, all became decomposed bodies dumped on Gulaag's tail-road.

Jainab, delirious from grief, called out, "Hajji! Hajji!"

But Hajji was nowhere. She forced herself to get out of bed to search for him. There were little footprints on the sand in the direction of the border. Jainab feared the worst. She dragged herself to her quiet neighbour's house and told him what had happened.

"I may have a clue as to where they have been taken," he said.

"Can you help, brother? As you know, I have no one but Hajji."

"I know, sister, Jainab. I am sorry I brought you such ill

136

tidings. But I thought in twelve years you may have heard something. If I had known…"

"These twelve years have passed like a dream. I don't even think I saw the rising of the moons or the setting of the suns. My days have been long, as have been my nights. Now, I'm really afraid."

"Please, do not worry. Although I have never had enough courage to face up to the army, I must own up to you, for putting you through this. I am not bad, but I'm also not brave."

Jainab left. She went back to her house while her neighbour figured out what to do. He knew how soldiers behaved and knew their routine well – he had to be strong. No matter, he pulled himself up and decided to look for the Hajji. At night, he set out with a torch in the direction of the footprints. They led to army tents, tethered along the western front. He even stumbled a few times on the sand. His breathing short and shallow, he approached the army tents. He heard the obnoxious clamour of drunkenness. Stealthily, he continued on his track, to look for the boys. On the southern point, suppressed cries wafted through the air. He opened a tent and heard them clearly. Looking around in the dark, he followed the cries, and flashed his torch on something. He found them; the boys were perched upon tenterhooks. They didn't see him at first.

He walked towards them and whispered, "I am your Uncle Abdallah, your neighbour, I've come to rescue you."

The boys were silent for some time. They couldn't believe that their neighbour had actually come to their rescue. Then one said, "I saw them put a sword, there, in that corner."

"Is that Hajji?" Abdallah asked.

"Yes."

"I'm here too," whispered the other.

137

"What's your name, boy?" Abdallah asked.

"Hussain."

"I'm going to unhook you both and get you out of here, okay?"

Then they heard someone cough outside the tent. Abdallah hid away in a dark corner. A man peeked through and saw the boys' straight faces. He went away. Abdallah crawled towards the boys and brought them down to the floor. The suspension caused some trepidation. They sat on the floor to catch a breath and then tiptoed to egress. Once they were out, they ran in the opposite direction from the tents in which they'd been held captive. The sands slowed them down, but resilience saved them in the end. They crossed the border into the next kingdom.

Hajji's enemy kingdom was Hussain's homeland. But Hussain couldn't remember the long way to his village. He knew a name: Kundi. They stopped by and asked for directions. It took them another full day. By the time they had arrived there, they were famished. They found a tea stall on the outskirts of a lush village. An errand boy served them a platter of yoghurt sauce with dried fruits, falafel, wild chickpea salad, flatbreads, and fried eggs. They could see Kundi from there. The manager of the restaurant had his back towards them. Hajji peeked and saw that he was pouring himself a glass of piping red tea. He turned around. Hussain saw him first. He screamed, "Father, Father."

The manager heard Hussain and ran towards him. Abdallah saw him, too, and froze for a second.

"Hashimuddin?" Abdallah cried.

"Who's that?" the manager asked and came running to pick up his Hussain. "My name is Hassan Karemi, not Hashimuddin."

"But that's impossible. I was at your wedding. I am

138

your neighbour. I saw you and sister Jainab together before our army took you," Abdallah said.

"Shush! Speak softly." He looked around timidly. "What are you saying? Anyway, you brought my son back. I would like to welcome you to my house as my guest tonight."

Abdallah couldn't believe this. He accepted the invitation. He had to find out more for sister Jainab. This betrayal was far too much to bear. Hashimuddin was living a dual life under a different name with a wife present.

At night, a party was held at Hashimuddin's place. Among others, there were his in-laws: his father and uncles-in-law, the entire clan. Abdallah sat down with the father-in-law. They exchanged greetings, then talks turned to politics and war. He told Abdallah how Hussain was abducted while playing with friends.

Abdallah asked, "How did you meet Hussain's father?"

"Oh! That is another long story. We found him at Gulaag's edge. He was unconscious and wounded. My brother was passing through one midnight. He found him under the lantern and brought him home. We revived him. But he couldn't remember anything. He was as good as dead. After six months, when he was well again, he started to go out, but he was very weak. He still walks with a limp, as you can see. He is only fit to do desk work. The army lost interest in him, but they took his son instead. We're grateful to you for bringing him back. We could never have found him alive in these difficult times."

Abdallah didn't say much after that. He watched Hajji playing with the kid. Technically, they were in the enemy camp, but they were able to blend in so that no one noticed. The party ended. Everyone went to bed.

At daybreak, Abdallah woke. He saw the white crack of light run through the sky. When he came out, he saw Hashimuddin at the gate. They exchanged greetings.

139

"What my father-in-law told you is incorrect. My memory had always been intact. I always remembered Jainab. My name is not Hashimuddin but Hassan Karemi. As much as I wanted to tell Jainab the truth, I couldn't. I couldn't tell her that I was from across the border, Kundi. Because I was afraid to lose her. Here, I could not tell anyone about her because of severe punishments for marrying an enemy." He stopped. "If I had told them the entire truth, I would be hanging low from the spikes by now, like many in the market square." After a pause, he said, "My Jainab was with child. Have you seen it?"

"Yes, little Hajji there. That's him, your little boy. Why do you not leave, leave now with us? People leave all the time, no?" Abdallah asked.

"They do. War is crazy. It does crazy things to people. I do believe that my in-laws would send an army after me if I'd left. There's Hussain now as well as Hajji, my two boys. The hunt for me would go on. They'd take my sons," he said. "Where could I hide them on the open Gulaag? Anyhow, to go back to my story. When I got better, my in-laws forced me into this marriage with their daughter, a girl whom no man would have because of her scarred face from fire burns. They had already shackled me, made me a prisoner of their whim. They reminded me of how I owed them my life."

"That's nonsense, you could've tried to leave. Did you at least try? Your sons could be taken anytime, regardless," Abdallah persisted.

"No, I couldn't. They kept a close watch. This place is full of spies. No one trusts anyone."

"What do you want me to tell sister Jainab, then?"

"It's complicated. The war is upon us. Hussain here, Hajji over in the enemy land, this fractured life. Jainab my love, my magic…" he murmured.

140

Hashimuddin went to Hajji and picked him up. He gave him a tight hug and a kiss. He gave them a camel to cross the formidable border and saw them get reduced to a dot, an apparition along the far side of the horizon. The days of the hummingbirds and the blue butterflies were numbered; the fire-dances and the full moon songs.

Autumn in a Coffee Cup

Minah and Sidu reached puberty more or less together. Short for Siddhartha, Sidu was Minah's best friend. Their favourite pastime was hanging out in their old haunt, the mango grove by the village pond. Here, they laughed, skipped around, climbed trees, larked about. Minah danced insanely with the accompaniment of the bamboo flute which Sidu often played.

This bonding sealed itself with the promise that they would always be there for each other; not knowing, however, that in the cosmic scheme, they had already been set apart for their inherent beliefs, and gender. For Minah was a girl and Sidu a boy. While Minah's Muslim family had great wealth, Sidu's family was orthodox Brahmins of the highest caste. Any misgiving was like a feather in a storm, swept away by their carefree sense of youth. Fatalistic or not, changes did occur, emerging incognito.

One day, Sidu was waiting for Minah in their usual place. She'd arrived late. By then, Minah had turned eighteen and Sidu twenty. When Minah showed up, Sidu scrutinised her from head to toe. Something was wrong.

"About time. You took forever to get here today, didn't you?" he asked her. "You look, hmm, different. And, why are you dressed like that?"

"Why? Because people came to see me today."

She sat down on a grassy patch under the mango tree near Sidu.

"Who? Who came to see you?"

"People."

"What people?"

"How would I know? I guess I am getting married soon."

"And, when did you buy this sari? You never told me."

142

"No, Amma bought it. What do you think of the colour?" Minah asked.

"It's nice, nice, just that… that, I'm not used to seeing you in a sari. By the way, that red, it really suits you. When's the occasion?"

"I don't know, silly."

"You look pretty, like a grown woman."

Minah stood and pulled him up by the hand.

"Come, let's do something."

"You could wear this for the Durga Puja though, couldn't you? I could buy you matching bangles. Do you think you might be married off by then?"

He rambled on, walking the mango grove, holding her hand, unaware how much things were going to change. Something suddenly dropped from the tree and landed before their feet on soft mud.

"It's an egg. We need to put it back," Sidu said.

A couple of cuckoo birds had nested, in one of the mango trees. He picked up the egg, but the nest being too high, he needed Minah's help.

"I'll put it back. I'm sure I'd be able to reach the branch if I stood on your shoulders," she said.

It seemed like a good plan. Minah took the little egg from his hand. With her feet firmly pressed on Sidu's shoulders, she stood up shakily and caught the broad branch above. While she set the egg gently back into the nest, her sari buffered Sidu's head against the woody trunk. He looked up. No sooner was the job done than she'd lost balance, and they tumbled down to the lowland near a pond.

The highly respected school pundit, Mr Mukherjee, was passing by. He was Sidu's father. Being out of school since graduation, it had slipped Sidu's mind that it was lunchtime and his father would come home for the lunch break. Mr

143

Mukherjee was also Minah's teacher at school. He bent his head slightly down and looked at them over his spectacles which had slipped to the end of his nose. They stood up in the meantime, arranging their dishevelled clothes. Minah's sari was now well up above her knees, which she pulled down to her ankles. The pundit ran towards them.

"Are you hurt?" he asked.

"We're fine," Sidu said.

"What's up?"

"We just fell down."

"Oh, I can see that," he said, and then laughed. "You're going to be married soon, my dear. It's not good to be seen out with him anymore,"

"What of it?" Minah hissed.

The pundit looked sharply at Minah. He invited them to join him for lunch.

Sidu lived with his mother, father and a younger sister, Moushumi, in a small, two-bedroom brick house with a verandah in the front. Seeing them approach, Nondini, Sidu's mother, who was cooking in the verandah greeted them with and smile. A pot of hot rice boiled on a kerosene stove at the far end. She had just finished stirring the rice with a wooden spoon when they stepped inside. She put the lid back on the pot and put the spoon away.

"Hello, Minah, how are you, love?" she asked. "Why? How lucky are we today! Our guest is a bride-to-be." She smiled.

"Umm. What have you been cookin', mashima?" Minah asked, lowering her eyes. Her cheeks had a faint brush of red.

"A blushing bride already, eh? All your favourite dishes, dear; fried Hilsa, Daal, and fried potatoes in tomato sauce."

"Yummy." Minah chuckled.

144

"Sidu, help Minah wash her hands. Lunch is ready."

Mrs Mukherjee rolled out a mat sitting in a corner, and laid down five copper plates and glasses. Sidu poured a mug full of water down Minah's hands from a bucket, placed on the edge of the open verandah. Their hands touched. On the mat afterwards, Sidu sat with his legs crossed into each other in a yoga position, between Minah and his sister Moushumi. Mr and Mrs Mukherjee sat opposite them.

Minah's father was one of the village's wealthiest rice farmers, who owned much fertile land. He sold rice to the big superstores and village markets around the country. This gave him a powerful station in the hierarchical social order. Her home just next door, was a two-storied rendered, brick house with a large balcony. It was secured by a gated wall. On the balcony, hurricane lanterns were hung from a curved iron dowel on a horizontal cane pole. Minah lit the lanterns every evening.

Mr Mukherjee served Minah spoonfuls of rice that afternoon. Minah laughed saying that she could not eat anymore, but that did not deter him.

"We have to get you something nice for the wedding, don't we?" Mrs Mukherjee said.

She turned her gaze away from Minah to scan Mr Mukherjee's placid face. She saw the pundit smile at her ruefully. It had not escaped their eyes that whenever the 'w' word was spoken, Sidu moved his fingers either too fast through the rice or gulped water so hurriedly that he nearly choked.

"Go easy on the fish. Don't forget it is Hilsa. Those razor-sharp bones could cause havoc if they were to get caught up in your throat, Sidu," the pundit cautioned.

"Yes, if we could only change the subject," Sidu answered,

145

chewing a mouthful of rice. "I don't think Minah wants to talk about her wedding plans right now."

He glanced at her, and she lowered her head.

"I haven't seen your amma lately," said Mrs Mukherjee.

"Haven't you? She did mention you last night, said she would drop in soon, if not today then tomorrow, perhaps?" she said.

"Yeah, she probably would."

"Minah, are you going to move out, once you're married?" Moushumi asked.

"Most likely," said the pundit.

There was no getting away from this topic, Sidu regretted. He took his drinking glass and washed his soiled hand on his plate of half-eaten food. Then he stood up and left the mat, to everybody's uneasiness. He waited for Minah, in the front yard.

Lunch was over soon. Mrs Mukherjee collected the plates and took them out to the well, where Sidu had been standing in the front yard. While she scraped his soiled dishes, a tired, malnourished dog came by and licked up the food, at the well. Sidu took Minah home. Minah said good-bye to everyone and squeezed Moushumi's chubby cheeks. Not participating in the good-bye ceremony, the pundit stepped inside, for he gauged life's many complexities.

Sidu and Minah were at the gate of her big house. Minah's mother, Mrs Ruby Rahman, stood on the balcony upstairs, looking at them. When Sidu saw her, he conjoined hands to greet her nomoskar. She nodded with a smile. Sidu left Minah at the gates. Minah ran up the stairs.

Mrs Rahman sat erectly on an easy chair made of cane. She leaned forward to pick up the knitting from the basket by her side. Minah came around to stand by the railing of the balcony.

"I've already had lunch at mashima's," she said.

"Yeah, I figured that. What did you have at your aunty's?"

"Oh, the usual, but it was tasty."

"How's she? Haven't seen her in a while."

"Cheerful, as always," Minah said.

"Yeah, well, now that you're about to get married, you need to stay home. The jeweller will come this afternoon to take orders. I want you to be here with me; don't just take off."

The lady of the house was a woman of few words, but she was usually clear on what she wanted. Despite all her wealth, she was a plain-looking character who seldom interfered in other people's affairs.

"The matchmaker was here a little while ago. A wedding date has been fixed."

Minah's mind was racing. Who was he? What did he do for a living? Where would they live? This whole affair was daunting. She continued to look ahead at the rice fields, while her heart pounded away. A maid beckoned Mrs Rahman inside. The fish seller, the vendor, had come to collect his money.

Minah gazed at the tall, green grass swaying in the late autumnal winds. She visualised an uncertain future, bleak with apprehensions. Her thin, determined lips looked sallow without lipstick on an expressionless fair, small face; her untidy, curly hair brushed against her cheeks. The sun had dipped into the blushing western sky, a blush that matched hers. It was time to light the lanterns.

She had bent down to pick up the matchbox, stashed in a blind corner behind a balcony pillar. Pushing the glass over on its bracket, she'd held the first lantern at an angle to light the wick. Suddenly, she became aware that there was an audience. She turned around to look at her neighbour's house. Sidu was there. He'd locked his gaze into hers. Smiling wanly, she extricated herself from the gaze, lit up all of the lanterns and went inside the house.

The wedding preparations were well underway. Minah heard people come and go downstairs every day. More maids, and page boys were employed. Relatives came from afar to stay with them. As soon as the jewellers left, tailors came in to take measurements. There were endless supplies of Sweets, Shingaras, and Pithas; oodles of lunches and dinners. The spread consisted of many items of fish, meat, and vegetables. Men mostly ate downstairs and women upstairs. The house smelled festive for many days. Minah saw Mrs Mukherjee but was not sure if Sidu had also come. She did not go out anymore but saw his dark, eager looks from the other side of the fence every evening from the balcony in the glow of the lanterns.

A few days before the wedding, Minah heard noises coming from Sidu's house. She looked through the window. There was a cry. Sidu stalked out of the house, followed by Mrs Mukherjee's frantic appeals. Minah was curious. After dinner, when her parents chatted in the main bedroom, she slipped out of the house. She heard faded conversations from her parent's bedroom, but she ran down the stairs, across the hall, into the yard, and out of the gate.

Moushumi sat dourly, on the verandah steps. Minah pushed herself in through their cane-fenced door.

"Moushumi, what has happened here?" Minah asked.

Moushumi hesitated, while Minah looked at her in a silent query.

"It's Sidu," Moushumi said.

"Well?"

"He asked baba if he could marry you."

148

"What? And, then?"

"Baba said no."

Neither of them had realised though that Sidu's parents had appeared and overheard them. The pundit ushered Minah into the lounge room. They sat on short bamboo stools facing each other. While Mrs Mukherjee and Moushumi hovered in the doorway, unbearable silence thickened the air.

"And, we love you very much," he said. "But, I am bound by the tenets of our religion. I can't permit Sidu to marry you. Please forgive me. We would become ostracised; no one would marry Moushumi. These are ancient traditions and customs which are very hard to break."

Through the dim light of a wick lantern on the edge of the verandah, Minah saw his deep scowls, the stress marks, on his narrow forehead. His voice trailed off. She looked around and saw a big pile of fat books on a corner table of the room. She felt dejected that there was no place for her and Sidu in them.

"I must go then, mustn't I?" she asked.

"Yes, you must," he paused. "I'll pray for your happiness, always. I wish you only the best. May Bhagwan bless you, dear child."

Minah could not sleep that night. She listened to the creaky noises in the wooden window shutters. She heard them slam in the hollow winds. She kept her ears open, even craned her neck to check if Sidu was in. Apart from the murmur of dry leaves of autumn, there was nothing; nothing to console her fretful soul, not even a shadow under the full, yellow moon of that night.

In the last few days, she seemed to care more for Sidu. She had tremors and her lips quivered as she craved his company, his soft touches. They gazed at each other over the fence in the evenings; she felt a desire to be with him.

Is this love? she asked herself. *I must, oh, I must meet him at least once. This will be the last, I promise. I promise.*

The next morning, a maid entered her room. Minah wasn't there. The maid thought she may have gone out for a walk, but this early?

"Sister Minah, sister Minah, where're you?" she called out.

But she was nowhere in her room. The maid's cries aroused everyone in the house to the knowledge that Minah had gone missing.

Not fully awake yet, Mr Rahman squinted. He got out of bed, yawning, and went to the balcony but saw nothing. Servants were sent all around. This stirred up the entire village, including Sidu and his parents. When he heard, Sidu took off. He knew exactly where to find her. And, he did. He carried Minah back through the gates of the big house.

They met a clearly distressed Ruby Rahman at the entrance. "Where did you find her?"

Sidu staggered, then moved towards her room. He laid her down on the bed. Mr Rahman quickly sent a pageboy to scurry along the jagged dirt paths to find a doctor.

"Under the mango tree by the pond, but she's okay," Sidu gasped.

When the doctor arrived, he asked everyone else, apart from Ruby Rahman, to leave the room. He turned Minah over and found a tiny bit of blood clot on the back of her head. There was a fracture. Minah woke up disoriented.

"What's wrong?" she asked.

"That's what we'd also like to know. How? Why?"

Ruby's bitter tirades shook Minah. Afterwards, the doctor sat with them on the balcony. He told Mr and Mrs

150

Rahman, over a cup of tea, that Minah may have been sleepwalking. She may have fallen and injured herself on the tree's knotty roots.

"If this is what you say, can she do this again?" Mr Rahman enquired.

"It's possible," the doctor replied.

Mr and Mrs Rahman sat thinking of how this might affect the wedding. In the meantime, one of the pageboys burst in holding a lantern.

"What is it?" Mrs Ruby Rahman cried.

"I found this lantern by the pond."

Ruby looked up and saw an empty spot on the cane pole that held all the lanterns together.

"Indeed."

The boy hung it back and left. The doctor had left too. But by now the entire village knew that she had slept under the mango tree and that Sidu had brought her home. This was just what the gossip required. The maids and housewives talked at every corner, in the market, on the street, and in their homes. Some said she was jinxed. Others thought she might be possessed. Some women questioned her honour. They whispered that Sidu and Minah might have spent the night together, or else how would he know where to find her?

The wedding was just ten days away. This shameful news had travelled all the way to Minah's in-law's house. Barely three days had passed when the matchmaker was back at Mr Rahman's place. Mr Rahman greeted the matchmaker, while Ruby quickly draped her head with the sari's loose end, the Anchal.

"Asslaam-u-alaikum," said Mr Rahman.

"O-laikum-us-salaam," the matchmaker replied.

"Please have a seat," said Mr Rahman.

151

They sat down on high-backed chairs. Ruby excused herself. She sent out refreshments for the guest, which a pageboy carried on a tray. They were homemade cakes, Bhapa Pitha, with tea. Mr Rahman placed one such Pitha on a plate and offered it to the matchmaker.

"There have been issues lately," he said. "It's bothering many people."

The viscous molasses oozed out of the coconut covering, at his first bite into the Pitha. The molasses drooled out like saliva slinging on his lower lip, which he swiped off with his tongue.

"What do you mean?" Mr Rahman asked.

"Well, they want to break up the wedding over this incident. They think Minah might be possessed."

"Oh! No, no! She was sleepwalking."

"Look, they don't want to know this mumbo jumbo, okay? She needs to be exorcised and that's that. You would have to put a ritual in place to expel that devil from her head."

"And, then? Then, would they rethink?"

"Yes."

The slick mercenary, pinching his prickly moustache on his nondescript, grubby face, studied Mr Rahman's sullen expression. He observed his keenness, which clued him in on a shrewd plan. He thought there was a potential bargaining position here, more money into his own coffers.

"They might, for a price. Pay me fifty-thousand cash; let me try and negotiate a deal with them.

"Fifty-thousand!"

"Take it or leave it; there are other more pertinent issues as well."

"What other issues?" Mr Rahman asked.

The matchmaker gave him a shrewd smile. "You know what I mean. The gossip around Sidu and Minah could tarnish her reputation in the village."

"Okay, okay. I'll do it, but I'll need more time. As soon as I have the money, I'll let you know."

"Let me know soon."

Mr Rahman sat mulling over this matter. His daughter would be stigmatised forever if this wedding did not go ahead. No honourable boy would marry her. That would be a great loss, which he couldn't afford. For a respectable life in the village, he was prepared to make any sacrifices, any rewarding concessions. If he had to sell land to raise money, so be it, get Minah exorcised, so be it, but the scandal, oh, the horror!

Minah hardly came out of her room now. She became forlorn and began to wear this loneliness on her face; her eyes were increasingly cheerless, and vacuous. She grew thinner by the day. Her appetite dissipated. Time seemed to have come to a halt, but it could not end her furtive longings for Sidu. Each day her affection for him grew more than ever. She felt an uncontrollable desire to meet him under the mango tree by the pond.

Minah planned to sneak out of her house, yet again, one dark, cool autumn night. On her way to the pond, she peered in the direction of Sidu's verandah. Other than the slight radiance from the wick lantern ponding on the floor, there was nothing. Drawing nearer to the mango grove, the usual meeting place, she chanted his name, Sidu, Sidu. She knew Sidu would be there. In a moment, she saw a figure in white. She saw Sidu's Dhoti and the top. Sidu saw her too, as well as heard her footsteps over the fallen autumn leaves. He extended his arms, and she ran straight into them. Minah was not sleepwalking tonight.

Sidu held Minah in a tight embrace. She rested her head on his heaving chest.

"I missed you," he said, heavily.

"I missed you more."

Sidu took Minah's chin. He tilted it with his index finger and kissed her. A touch at first, then the kisses became more and more insistent, the embrace tighter. Sidu held her by her waist; Minah held on to his shoulders. Minah sat down on the stump of the tree. Sidu, sat beside her and caressed her shoulders. He gently touched the soft skin of her willowy arms, moved it down to the elbow, and then back up to her lips. They made love and lay contented beside each other; an occasional owl hooted at a distance in the murky night. The mango tree, the lover's den, witnessed it all.

"When's the wedding?"

"Don't know, don't want to know," Minah said, with eyes still closed. "Say no more."

"We shall meet, no matter what," Sidu said.

"We're already together. Do you not understand, Sidu? I want to be with you, near you, always."

Minah looked into the depths of his dark, troubled eyes. But they had also twinkled as though he had a plan. It was a celestial union, which none of the world's social or religious laws could alter. They stood before the heavens and chose each other as partners. The gentle sound of the azan shortly drifted through the silence of the night, proclaiming the Morning Prayer, the Fajr.

"I need to go," Minah said.

Sidu grabbed her hand. "No. Don't go. Not just yet. Stay, stay a bit."

"I'll come back tonight, same time, I promise," Minah said.

He let her go. He kept looking at her with a strong nudge within him to be near her. She headed down the narrow dirt road, disappearing into the tender night that broke into dawn. Its sporadic, dark patches were visible in a pale sky.

Back into the house, she locked the front gate and hung the key beside it on a nail, then darted up the few steps into the safety of her room.

Warily she went into the bathroom to take off her sweaty clothes. She took several mugs of water from a bucket set in the bathroom and poured it over her head. She changed into fresh clothes and dried her wet body with a red gamcha. She saw bloodstains on the sari. She hid it under the bed.

Mr Rahman was able to sell some land eventually. But Minah did not need to get exorcized. She had stopped sleepwalking for a while. A wedding date was fixed again and the wedding was due to take place within seven days, once the money had been paid to the matchmaker. The deal had closed. Minah knew she had been taken as a hostage to preserve the family honour. Therefore, she said nothing. On the day of the wedding, she thought of only Sidu. She was sure that he would not be present among the large crowd of invitees.

The day before the wedding, they had met again at midnight for the last time. Intertwined in spirit and in body, they knew that they were one; they knew in this great oneness, they would always communicate, even if they may not meet physically again.

Next day, the wedding was held, on a late-autumn afternoon of the 15th of October. Minah's in-laws were another traditional family, who lived about five miles away from her village. They had arrived by train around mid-morning. The ceremony took place in the bride's house as per tradition, before hundreds of invitees. Kalema, had sanctioned the wedding legally and socially. This was followed by a grand lunch of sumptuous mutton Biryani,

155

yoghurt drink, beef kabab and spicy fish drowned in thick masala gravy. Laughter and talks, filled up the atmosphere, as the wedding guests ate and drank.

After the wedding, it was time to say goodbye. Minah was sitting by her groom, when her mother had come around and had whispered into her ears that she needed to stand up with her husband. She did as she had been told. She stood up as did the groom. She hugged her mother and cried on her shoulder, saying goodbye, which brides usually did. Surrounded by their many guests, her father had then walked her slowly outside the house to her palanquin. It had been decorated with fresh flowers for the occasion, unlike the plain ones used by other female guests-in-law.

The guests had now jostled outside Minah's house and were saying goodbyes, ready to leave for the train station. They were going back by train, the same way they had arrived. All the women sat in their respective palanquins. A procession soon ensued towards the station. The men walked alongside the cavalcade. Minah sat quietly and looked out through the small draped palanquin window. There was something that caught her attention. She thought, she saw Sidu. She thought, he'd appeared and disappeared over the horizon.

When they'd arrived at the train station and the palanquins were parked on the platform, the groom walked over to the wedding palanquin in which Minah was sitting. He looked inside and asked her get off. She did; then he carried her into the train and callously put her down on a window seat of an empty carriage; he left her without a word.

She sat alone. One short moment, her life had turned. She waited. She looked out occasionally in anticipation, not for the man she had just married, but for Sidu, the man she loved. She could not, rather would not, say goodbye to him. In desperation, she cried out, "Sidu!"

The train hadn't departed yet. The wedding party, her in-laws were still chatting on the platform and slowly getting on the train, one by one. Minah stared out blankly; then suddenly, she glimpsed a man's shape in the carriage doorway, a vision blurred and vaguely recognisable. Two strong arms seized her and took her out. In one long stride, they dismounted from the quieter end of the train and she was put back in the same palanquin. The bearers lifted it; in light, hasty pace, dashed out of the station. Her in-laws climbed up the train from the other end, at about the same time.

The train slugged away. All Minah could see was a number of passing faces looking incredulously through the carriage windows. Next was pure enchantment. Sidu had entered through the small opening, when bearers put the palanquin down.

"I couldn't let you go. You do understand that, right?" he asked.

Minah stared at him, with her mouth wide open. How extraordinary for this to be really happening! Sidu was quite an adventurous man.

"I bribed the bearers. I told my parents that I was adopting celibacy to hone my skills by going away on a pilgrimage. I would study religion to become a better teacher, never to return," Sidu explained.

"Did they believe you?"

"Yes, they did. They said it was an acceptable proposition."

"Where to now?" Minah asked.

"Don't know."

He brought his head to her parted lips and kissed her. One of the bearers knocked on the wobbly little door of

157

the palanquin, saying that they needed to leave before dark. Sidu asked him to carry them to the outskirts of the village.

Minah was declared missing. The police had searched everywhere. They carried on an investigation and questioned the bearers. All the bearers could say was that Minah was last seen with a tall and dark man, but they couldn't tell the police the whereabouts. Given the scanty nature of the evidence, the police gave up a month later.

Soon the others gave up too. Life moved on as the gossip and the moaning ended. The story that spread through the village was that Minah was kidnapped from the train for jewellery and was left to die alone in a distant place. Her body was never found. Ruby Rahman, who had entered Minah's room when they'd left for the station, checked if her trousseau was all taken. As she looked under her bed, she saw a sari and pulled it out. Seeing the dry bloodstains, she washed it with her own hands and put it away in her closet. This would be her best-kept secret, for she feared the worst. What if this was hymen, torn by another man?

Since the day they had gone missing, the pundit guessed wisely. Only Moushumi knew for certain. Because, Sidu wrote letters to her from anonymous addresses and asked her to bury them in their legendary secret garden, under the desolate mango tree. In her diary, nevertheless, Moushumi wrote this narrative without ever exposing their identity: *The autumn leaves had once brewed a romance, under a perfect autumn sun.*

The Flower Girl

"Push, push," the midwife screamed as I bawled to get the baby out. My hands were tired from grasping the hospital bed, my head was thrown up, and sweat dripped down my forehead. It felt like I was going to die. This baby, this poor baby, would have to be given up. The more I thought, the more agonising each effort became.

The midwife did not give up.

"One last push, with all your strength. C'mon girl, you can do it."

I did just that and the baby slithered out.

"Wonderful," she said, hugely satisfied and grinning widely. "Well, you did it. It's a boy."

I peeked at the creature, through half-opened eyelids. Weary from my labour, I forgot to smile. I kept looking at this miracle, this thing, this marvel that had grown within my womb. Often I imagined its face, as I sat alone after a terrible bout with my partner. And now, now that I saw him, his little face all wrinkled and fresh, I just stared.

My heart felt nothing when the nurse placed the baby in my arms. His face was barely visible from all that wrapping about him; deep furrows appeared on his forehead and his eyes were all swollen like a soaked-up sponge. I wondered what to do, love him, or despise him? The nurses kept telling me about bonding, how it should be fed straight away, or else the food wouldn't be ready. I, however, deliberated. This was the sleepy and confused face of a new-born. It yawned and stretched in my arms. I held it close, then closer, smiling tenderly until I began to feel that this baby was mine, my possession, only mine to keep. I jolted back to reality when unexpectedly the nurse said that she needed to take him away to the nursery.

"Why? Where would you take him?"

"He needs to be in the nursery," the nurse replied. "This is not where he belongs, of course. You, of all people, should know that."

"No, I don't know. Tell me about it."

"My, my, how quickly we forget, eh?

"Forget what?"

"Never mind. If you're not going to feed it, I'll have to get a wet nurse to do it."

The baby was snatched from my bosom and it had disappeared in the nurse's muscular arms. They left through the back door.

"No. Wait, please, someone, I need to know what's going on. You can't take my baby away. I need to speak to my partner."

No one paid attention. The staff who walked the dimly-lit corridors were like apparitions, moving deftly through the stark walls just like their uniforms. They were surreal. No one knew where they went.

The psychiatrist looked at me solemnly, while I sat up on the divan. I opened my eyes to look at him, Dr Bringwell.

"Terrible nightmares, hey Mary?" he asked.

"Yes, Dr Bringwell. I also hear whispers that tell me to be good, not to get angry, to eat, to sleep, to pray. What's wrong with me?"

"Not sure yet," he said, looking at the notes he took. "What you have described just now were your nightmares, hallucinations, and psychotic episodes. But we're only at the tip of the iceberg. We'll have to work through your problems. For now, I'll give you a prescription. Take one tablet every day with food."

"Am I ever going to get better? My nightmares are so real. I see the same baby. His face is always the same. People disappear into walls. I wake up every night feeling dizzy, sweaty, and panicky that I might have the same fate one day and just vanish into walls. What's on the other side though? You do believe me, yeah?"

"Of course, I believe you. It's awful. But you'll be fine. We'll make sure that you are," he said.

"Thanks."

Dr Bringwell wrote a prescription. "I'll see you in three weeks. In the meantime, feel free to call us if you need to."

I stepped out of the surgery onto the crowded street, which was full of slush from the melted snow. A car honked and sent a shudder through me. I walked across nervously on to the narrow alley and over to the other side, hopping quickly up on the pavement. I stopped at the corner store to buy a packet of cigarettes. I slid my fingers into the black coat pocket and took a cigarette out of the box along with the lighter. I pressed the butt between my lips and lit it. I inhaled a slow puff and smoked out rings in the air. My lips were pouted and my head thrown backwards. Glancing at the yellow marks on the tip of my right hand, I bit the inner skin of my index finger and rubbed it against the roughness of the coat sleeve.

Under the lamppost, with my arms crossed over my chest, I bent down to do up the boot laces. I side-glanced at a pair of pointy black shiny shoes on a person. I liked them. I continued to look at the shoes until I stood up abreast with the person. It was a middle-aged gentleman, waiting for the bus just like me.

"The bus is late," I said.

He looked at me grimly and nodded. He had a black overcoat on with a red striped silk tie peeking out and held a briefcase in his hand. I looked at it briefly and wondered what was in it. The man looked sideways at me, then moved his head left, then right, to check if anyone was coming. I was observing him with much interest and wondered what

161

he might do next. The man turned around and looked at me squarely.

"I'm new here," he said. "Do you know if buses come this late?"

"No. I wonder what's wrong."

"Well, why don't we sit down on that bench while we wait?"

"Sure, why not?"

We made our way towards the bench, which was slightly behind the pole where we initially stood. I took out another cigarette and the lighter from my pocket.

"Do you smoke?" I asked.

"No. Not much."

"Would you like one?"

"Hmm, okay, I'll have one today."

I lit it for him and lit my own. The man coughed a little as he blew out a tiny round of smoke into the air.

"What do you do?" he asked.

"Me?"

"Who else?"

"Yeah, I sell flowers."

"Oh, that's nice? Do you have a flower shop?"

"I work in a flower shop."

"Oh, I see."

"Although, I do believe that I'll own it one day, or partially at least."

I did not say much after that but looked up at the grey sky on the eastern corner. It was a harsh, Canadian winter that was drawing towards an end. The man was looking at me. I noted his gaze travelling all over my face.

"I don't think any bus is coming this way today," I said.

"Maybe not."

I looked away and added, "There's a storm coming on. I got to go."

"How?" he asked. "I mean, do you mean to call a cab?"

"Not sure. I think I'll start walking. Cabs are expensive in Halifax, so you know."

"Expensive, really? Won't you get caught in the storm?"

"Maybe, but what else is there to do?"

A menacing storm brewed. I rose suddenly and started to walk. I saw through the corner of my eyes that the man looked at me. I was going away without saying goodbye. He was not a friend we both knew, but I also felt what he may be thinking. What kind of an odd person was this who shared a moment and would walk away like that?

"Don't leave me in the storm."

"I'm not your keeper. I fly, like a free albatross. Don't hold me back,"

I turned around to tell him. My voice faded as I took off.

"I'll tell you all about the shop one day if we meet again."

"I wouldn't know where to find you."

"Flower shop on the corner of Barrington Street."

At that, I ran away and disappeared around the corner.

A few days had passed since the storm. The man sat at the desk editing his book. He looked out of the window. Broken branches lay across the road and loose electric wires leftover from the havoc of the stormy day. He wondered how the girl was; he wondered if any flying debris hurt her. The unnamed girl aroused sympathy.

He had a desire to see her, a desire, strong enough to see her now. She did mention that she worked at a flower shop on the corner of Barrington Street. He rose from his chair and picked up his hat and the black briefcase.

What a long winter it was, he thought, as he walked

towards the bus stop. The bus arrived. He hailed it and asked the driver if it went to Barrington Street. The driver nodded and said, yes, it did.

His chest distended, he thought of the girl. The more he thought, the more restless he became. There was something about her which pulled him. The age difference was large, but he could not disregard her. He reckoned he ought to know her a bit better. Before he could finish his thoughts, the bus reached its destination.

He disembarked at the corner of Barrington Street and looked for the flower shop. There were several. He walked towards the first one but realised that they never really introduced themselves to each other. He did not know how to find her. His grip on the briefcase tightened and his jaw muscles clamped. He entered the first visible shop. There were several girls working here. They gathered garlands and bouquets of scarlet, crimson, and russet into brilliantly vibrant arrays.

"May I help you, Sir?" one asked.

"Yeah, I'm looking for a young girl of about medium height."

"Do you have a name?"

"Not really she had to go before I could ask. But, she smokes. She smokes, quite a bit, in fact."

"Lots of girls smoke here, sir. Can you describe her?"

"Hmm, greyish blue eyes, dark hair, coffee-coloured skin."

"Like you, sir? Did she look a bit like you?"

"No, no, I don't think so."

"Well, I've seen a girl that matches your description, but she has a mole right under her nose. She works in the next shop. Could it be her?"

"Thank you. You've been very helpful."

The girls at the flower shops smiled and squinted at him.

The man stumbled. Awkwardly, he rushed out of the shop. He proceeded next door.

I was arranging a huge bouquet of flowers, at the entrance of my shop where I worked. When I saw him, I looked at him briefly. Over the multi-coloured flowers, I smiled and put the bouquet down behind on a stool. I turned around to give him my full attention.

"Hi!"

"Hi," he said. "I, umm, came by to see if you were hurt in that storm."

"No, I wasn't. I got in just in time," I said simply. "But, it's awfully nice of you to check on me. No one else did."

"I'm sorry to hear that."

"That's okay, was there something you wanted?"

"Yeah, I was thinking that maybe…" He paused. "Could we have a private chat somewhere?"

"Okay, may I know what it is that you wish to speak to me about?"

"I'll tell you later."

"That's a strange request."

"I know, it may sound a bit strange, now."

"I'm curious."

"Can we meet then?"

"Look, I'm on my lunch break now. Could we perhaps go to that café across the road?" I suggested.

"That would be lovely."

"Can you give me a minute? I need to finish up something first," I said.

"Certainly, I'll wait for you outside."

The man walked out of the store. I picked up the bouquet from the stool, away from the afternoon light, and went inside through the curtains behind the door. The parted

165

curtains had faded almost into white. I waited there and looked at him through the glass door, as I put the bouquet in a huge jar, which was partially filled with water. The man standing outside seemed kind, but also too keen.

"Who are you looking at?"

I jerked around and looked at the speaker standing in the shadow of the foliage.

"No, no one just thinking of lunch, I guess. You gave me such a fright," I said.

I averted my eyes and looked around. This room was filled with a huge pile of green leaves, flowers, and scissors as well as velvety papers of multi-coloured cuttings.

"Don't get funny ideas, okay?" he said.

"Of course not, Mark, why should I?"

"You never know who you might meet these days? You can't be too careful."

"Of course. When's your meeting?" I asked.

"In about half an hour," he said, looking suspiciously at me.

"Well, I'll go now and see you after lunch then?"

"Yeah," he said.

Mark was the owner of this shop and he was also going out with me. In fact, I moved in with him. I worked in his shop five days a week, kept his bed warm at night, and in return I got the minimum wage, which had come with the promise that one day, I could own a share of the shop. I was happy with this agreement and thought that I had done well at nineteen. I had a decent life apart from those nightmares.

I should not keep the gentleman waiting. I quickly washed my hands and wiped them clean before opening the glass door. I made my way out and met him up-front under the awning.

"Sorry to have kept you waiting. I got held up in the back room there."

166

"That's fine, Which way do we go? You lead the way."

"There's a crossing at the lights on our left."

"Sure."

We walked together towards the lights, waiting with a crowd of people. The lights turned. We stepped out on the crossing together. The café was just around the corner of North Street. I was in the lead. A waiter took us to a nice table. We sat down in some privacy. I only had about half an hour to spare. We sat down opposite to each other in the dimly-lit room across the tiny round table. I noted quite a few grey hairs and a receding forehead. "What could this man possibly want from me?"

"What are we ordering?" he asked.

He placed the briefcase on the empty chair next to him. And we looked through the menu together. While he ordered the soup of the day with a slice of buttered rye, I ordered a vegetable pizza.

"My name is Anthony, Anthony Chang. But, people call me Tony. I should have introduced myself sooner, sorry."

"That's okay, I didn't think we would meet again. Our meeting has been pretty strange too."

"What's yours?" he asked me.

"Mary."

"Mary?"

"Yes just Mary."

"No surname?"

"No."

"How come?"

"I don't know who my parents were."

"I'm sorry. Why do you say, *were*?"

"Don't be," I said, politely. "I was raised in a church as an orphan."

"Oh, for how long?"

167

"Eighteen years."

"Eighteen years?"

"Yes I didn't want to be a nun, so I left. I was lucky to have found work here at the flower shop."

Tony did not say anything for a while. Our food had arrived. Tony took the white napkin off the table, unfolded it, and spread it on his lap, just as I did the same. We both ate quietly.

"You look pretty thin. Did they not feed you properly?" he asked, eventually. "What's the name of the church?"

"Why do you want to know?" I asked.

"I'm just curious, that's all."

I was a bit unenthusiastic this time. Okay, I was having a good time and enjoying my pizza with this man who calls himself Tony, or Anthony, whatever. But, he was also years older than I. I was suddenly reminded of Mark's cautionary words. Perhaps it was not a good idea to tell a stranger everything. Perhaps, noticing my reluctance, Tony kept quiet, but he must have seen how fast I had finished my pizza. I said I had to leave because my lunchtime was over.

"Maybe I'll see you again. Life's full of surprises, isn't it?" I said.

"It is. Maybe I'll see you sooner than you think. Oh, one other thing, you don't have to tell me, if you don't want to. Do you live alone?" Tony asked.

"Look, I'd rather not, if you don't mind."

"That's okay, run along then. You don't want to get into trouble with your boss."

"Thanks for understanding, bye."

"Bye."

I ran outside, merging with the crowd.

Tony was still in the café. I looked over my shoulder and saw that he had taken a notebook out of his jacket pocket and scribbled a few words. He put it back in, and was ordering with the waiter. He could still see me, through the long and curtained French windows. My hair and a bit of that pink floral skirt that danced in the air, until I was gone out of his line of vision.

The order had arrived. It was a short black. Tony took a sip and looked at the briefcase. He even touched it tentatively. What was he going to do about this girl? Should he let her slide? He picked up the briefcase and paid the waiter a tip on his way out. The girl had left money for the pizza under the drinking glass. Tony smiled and put the money in his wallet. He wanted to see her again, to return it, but the thought crossed his mind that he might not be welcome just yet. He might have to pay her a visit later in the week.

Tony sat down in his room. The room had an open plan. It was spacious with a kitchenette, a bed, an easy chair and a writing desk. It also had an old-fashioned log fireplace made of bricks and a chimney. The bricks had become slightly charred.

He started a new story:

The boat suddenly found itself in the middle of this raging storm as the ocean rocked it violently. A young man woke up and looked for his wife beside him. Along with ten dozen other refugees on the boat, they were destined for Canada. It was a long voyage from the orient, and they were on this boat for days with people starving, vomiting, leering, and in the end stages of death. Not everyone died; some survived; those who did, survived through the hottest days, the hungriest hours, and the most perilous of times.

Tonight, he could not find her. The young man went outside and looked. As he stood on the deck, a cry came from behind. He looked back and found his wife struggling to crawl towards him, clinging to the steel boat rail. Her hands slipped. She receded. The boat swayed and tipped sideways; the tempest was tumultuous. He hurried towards her and hoped to save her from this. Before he could do so, the strong winds swept her away, nearly to the rear of the boat. But the man did not give up. He went after her and grabbed her arms.

Tony read out loud what he had just written, took a printout, and edited it again and again until he deemed it perfect. Then he put it away on his desk and stood up to pace the room. He stood behind the easy chair. Sitting down, not thinking of anything particularly, a slight restlessness rose within him. Like a cat-and-mouse loop chase, he resumed his pacing, up and down.

Thinking of the mole under her nose, he reflected on her appearance, her simplicity. He thought of her almond grey-green eyes. He went back to his desk and took out his briefcase from under the table. With trembling fingers, he pressed a metal button and it opened with a click. It contained many odd papers and books, but it also held passports. He took two passports out and opened them one after the other. By now, he had begun to take deep breaths to calm down. The pictures on the passport were those of a young man and a woman. Not a spitting image as such, but the woman had a mole exactly in the same place and just the right size as the girl he met; they had the same eyes, too. Tony sat down on the high-backed chair at the writing desk. "Oh, God! Could this be true?"

A lot more evidence was required. He would have to be fully convinced before he could believe what he wanted to believe. He put the two passports back in the briefcase along with the printouts of the manuscript, and walked towards the bed, but checking the door first before climbing into bed. Still holding the briefcase, he put it down on the pillow next to him. As though it were a child, he covered it and laid a protective arm over it.

I was at the flower shop, early in the morning. It was just a few mornings after I'd met with Tony. Although nothing significant had happened between us, I felt an uncanny desire to be near him. Come on, I told myself, he was old enough to be my dad, and that was something he couldn't be, because I was an orphan. Besides, even if I were not an orphan, it was just too much of a coincidence to have met my dad at the bus-stop. It sounded like a contrived plot.

I hadn't realised that Mark had come in and was watching me.

"Mary, what's wrong?"

"Nothing," I said.

"Something is not right."

"Like what?"

"How should I know? You tell me."

"I'm fine! Leave me alone!"

"You weren't the same last night. You were obviously distracted."

"What do you want from me? Go away!"

"Are you asking me to go away?" he sneered.

I kept quiet. I wanted to tell him that I felt like pouring hot oil over him while I cooked. I felt like telling him that I wanted to block such thoughts, such harmful thoughts, and get them out of my mind. It was awful that I could not. However, I would not tell him any of this, for I was afraid that he would want to get out of the relationship, leaving me out in the cold. No way, Mark must never know that I have a mental illness and had been to a psychiatrist.

Mark went away. I saw his anger seething through his gait. His gold chain jiggled around his neck between the buttons of his tight fitted, floral shirt. His ugly buttocks protruded and swayed through his tight, patchy jeans. I was frightened. What if he hit me tonight or fired me and did not give me the promised share of the shop? Could I go back to the church? Did I want to? I could run away though. Get another job, but this uncertainty frightened me. What if I didn't get another job? There was always that possibility. A known devil was better than... No. I was tied to Mark, not only because he was a meal ticket, but also because I loved him, he was my protector. Of course, he would give me a share of the shop, one day.

The next morning was bright, quiet. The shops had opened, one by one. A few people stopped by to either collect pre-ordered bouquets, or to put new orders in for various occasions. There was one for a wedding, one for a funeral, and several others for lovers' birthdays, Valentine's Day, and so on. The delivery truck dropped off more flowers and the delivery boy winked at me. He expressed at some point that he wanted to have tête-à-têtes. Oh, how insufferable! Issues were on my mind today. Lunch with Mark was really important as I needed to ask him about the shop. When was he going to transfer the partial ownership, find out about proper documents and all that? Then, I would be set for life. The sky could not have looked bluer, not a single patch of clouds anywhere.

I felt a sudden boost when I went in to check Mark's diary for the day. He was free at lunchtime. But, as I closed the diary, there was a strange noise coming from the back room. I stumbled on the door's threshold and fell. I felt a presence in the room. I looked up immediately. Someone was standing there, in the dark. Was Mark spying on me? I felt frightened. When I looked again, the person had left.

Could it be the delivery boy? But what would he do here? He'd already delivered the day's flowers up in the

172

front. I came out of the room and asked one of the girls if they'd heard anything. They said no, they had heard nothing. Distractedly, I went about my business, tidying flowers and answering phones. Soon, I forgot about the intruder.

Mark suddenly appeared out of nowhere, startling me again.

"Why don't we have lunch today?" I asked.

"Yeah, we'll leave in half an hour."

"Sure."

Mark looked at me, seemingly trying to comprehend my expression. I was happy now. Our need for each other was mutual. He needed me, just as I needed him for the promised share of the shop. I believed that he would hand it over because of my loyalty, for the services that I'd given him freely over the one year since I had met him. Today, however, the matter just needed to be finalised, brought into the open, and completed. I felt confident that this could be the day. It would not take too long to resolve. Mark went to the back room. He said he would be out here soon and I needed to wait. Half an hour passed, but no sign of him yet. I began to twist my fingers and press my lips unnecessarily and wondered why he was late.

I went to the back room and looked for Mark, but he was not there. I would have to go on my own and postpone the discussion, or bring up the matter at night, which was going to be difficult. He would be in no mood to talk business at home. My mobile suddenly rang and it was Mark. He said that he would not be able to make it today and that something had come up. I would have to go on my own. This news and Mark's tone upset me. He had stood me up. I thought about what I could do for lunch and decided to hop on the next bus and take off for an hour.

I did not feel like coming back to the store but wanted

to go to the hospital instead, to meet Dr Bringwell. My next appointment was a few days away, however.

A few minutes into the ride, Tony sat down beside me.

"Hi there," he said.

"Are you stalking me or something? I've already told you I'm not interested."

"I suppose you're interested in that jerk. He's just using you. You should know that."

"How do you know? You don't know that. On the contrary, he loves me."

"Ha! You really believe that? He gets what he wants from you. And you give it to him free. It's not costing him, anything."

"Look, I don't want to talk to you," I said, pulling the chain.

The bus stopped. I got off in a real hurry and stepped onto a pavement. But I saw from there that Tony was looking at me through the double-glazed window. It had fogged up in no time from his heavy breathing.

A bittersweet aftertaste remained as we parted in this manner. However, I had an occasional inkling something was wrong. I had the same sense, when I had left him at the café. I felt that the force of the inkling was in him as well. The bus rolled on and we lost each other.

After dinner that evening, Tony sat down at his writing desk. He wrote:

The young man pulled his wife back into the cabin. The leaky boat went adrift and it started leaking even more. People jumped into the high seas. Poseidon's wrath surged and the ocean darkened to a terrifying menace. Absolute mayhem of dunking heads of men, women, and children on the waves. They gurgled and screamed in desperation. There

174

were no lifeboats to be lowered, only a few life vests. Luckily, there was another boat nearby, a bigger one that came to people's rescue.

People cried to stay afloat on the ghastly big waves. These screams were carried through the gale of the night and were heard by the soul, seizing sirens, who'd responded unequivocally until they'd become a mélange of cries in the darkness. They appeared from nowhere and took what they had desired. Before they plummeted, they performed a light-footed ritual of synchronised summersaults. Then, they swiftly disappeared into the depths of the blue seas; no Mariner's vision could be compared to this, no rime was sung, although all the boards did shrink.

They were taken on board. The young man and his wife were amongst the lucky ones who made it to the new boat. The others were not so lucky. Luck began to dwindle for this young couple too. The pregnant wife went into early labour the moment they were taken aboard. The turbulent waves were relentless and people threw up everywhere on the swelling seas.

The wife howled in pain, but no one paid attention. The young husband sat by her and the birth of a beautiful baby girl soon followed. The umbilical cord was cut with the Swiss army knife that he had in his zippered shirt pocket. The wife smiled, and immediately fed the baby. Later that evening, a terrible infection and a high fever ravaged the wife. The pain and desperation were too much to bear. She had died, leaving the young man to take care of the baby. On the boat, the wretched travellers gaped at them. The storm went down and the ocean had

175

quieted. The serenity was restored just as the boat reached the shores of Halifax in Nova Scotia.

Tony stopped typing. It was a silent room. He had become the quintessential 'hollow man', even though his sins were purged and atonement made. He took the printouts and put them inside his briefcase along with the rest of his manuscript.

I slept alone in my bed that evening. Mark had not come home. He called to say that he was travelling interstate on business. He would not return until the weekend. The next morning, I dressed to go to work. I wore a pale grey skirt and did not really care whether or not the shocking pink top matched. I ran a comb through my hair and attempted to get out the knots which hung like a tangled web.

I sat down for breakfast. Not having much appetite was the least of my problems. Last night's nightmare, the same recurring dream, had kept me awake. I was fearful. The lights were on all night and still I heard voices and saw thousands of crawling spiders on the ceiling above. Shop or no shop, I could not wait for Mark to return. I was a prisoner of my own shortcomings and I wanted a transformed life, free from drudgery, voices, and shadows. I didn't know if Mark loved me, but he certainly seemed to enjoy my company. That was enough for me, for now.

I was just about to go out when I noticed Tony, standing across from my apartment on the street near the bus stop. No, not again! But, it was too late. Tony saw me and signalled that he was coming upstairs.

"What do you want from me?" I asked.

"Which church took you in?"

The words flew out of our mouths simultaneously as Tony reached the threshold, panting.

"Why do you want to know?"

176

"I'll tell you later."

"Why won't you tell me now? I'll have to tell Mark about you."

"You think that he can protect you? You're just a flower girl in a flower shop, eating him out of house and home. That's all you are to him? Anyway, watch the news, okay?"

I kept quiet and I allowed him to continue.

"Do you think that he'll ever give it to you? How could he give you something that he didn't even own in the first place? He belongs to the underworld, my dear. And, that shop is just a front."

"What? What do you mean? How do you know? Get out of here."

"Never mind how, but that's the truth. Now tell me the name of the church and I'll go," he insisted.

"Protestant Orphan's Home on North Park Street."

"Thanks and goodbye. I'll see you soon. Don't be afraid. You might not be alone after all."

Tony had left.

What did he mean by that? I needed to find out more. Watch news.

I could not concentrate that morning. Where had Mark gone? As I stood outside under the awning, a BMW stopped at my shop. A beautifully-dressed lady stepped out of the driver's seat. She was dressed in an Emerald silk skirt and a floral green matching top. The air thickened with her expensive perfume. As she walked through, it reeked, mingled with the fragrances of the flowers around.

"Good morning," she said.

I looked up at her curiously.

"I'm Margaret. Margaret Deshong. I'm the new owner of this shop. I have come to introduce myself. Mark won't be the manager anymore. You'll have a new manager."

Mark was the manager? Not the owner? I was dizzy. I sat down on the pavement under the awning and suddenly felt sick. Margaret went inside and began to give new inventory instructions to everyone. I needed confirmation. Where was Mark now? What else did he do? I dared not ask any of this to my "new" employer. When I went inside to get my bag, I found the two other girls whispering in the shade of the foliage of the back room. I walked in and they stopped talking.

I swung the bag on my shoulder and left without a word. I saw Margaret on my way out, driving away in her flashy car. When I returned home, I found letters in my mailbox. I took them out and balanced my bag on my shoulder. As I sorted through them, I found one addressed to Mark. I ran upstairs and opened my door. I flopped on the sofa in the living room. Then I took a bold step and opened them. There was no letter, just pictures.

These were pictures of guns and bullets that I had seen on television. I didn't know what to make of it and thought about what to do next. I'd turned on the television for news and waited impatiently.

The news started and the first footage was on arms smuggling. That some smugglers had been apprehended by the police. Then there was Mark's picture on television! He was in handcuffs with two other people. They were arrested in the morning and charged with smuggling arms to terrorists. The police had been onto them for quite some time.

The news did not make much sense. It was complete gibberish, 'words, words, words'. I sat awkwardly on the sofa with legs joined together and arms crossed over my chest. My shallow breathing and twitchy movements started almost immediately. I slouched and held on to my clothes. I looked at my feet and kept looking at them until I began to shake uncontrollably. This was followed by the tapping of my feet. I lay down on the sofa, trying to breathe normally. I had nowhere to go, nowhere at all.

Tony went to the church and spoke to the clerk. He asked him about a baby girl, who should be nineteen years of age now. After searching for a while, they confirmed that maybe an orphaned baby was left in their care around that time. Could they call him later in the day? Tony agreed and took a cab home.

Once it reached his apartment, he entered his room and sat down in the easy chair by the bed. Then he stood up and poured himself a glass of water before sitting down at his writing desk.

He jotted something down with pen and paper:

As soon as the rescue boat arrived on the shore, the refugees were processed. The young man had nothing on him except for the baby in his arms. He stood in the queue with the others, even though he needed emergency help for the baby. Famished and dehydrated, the baby had become lethargic by now. She continued to cry from hunger and exhaustion. Soon a nurse came and took them out of the queue. The other refugees eyed him enviously. They went to a detention centre and the nurse asked his name.

"Anthony, Anthony Chang," he replied.

The nurse wrote down his name on a form she was filling out. In her clinical professionalism, she made no mistakes; no loose ends were left untied, and no amendments to be made later.

"What do you intend to do with the baby?"

"I want to give her up for adoption."

He winced in pain and his face became distorted, but he forced the words out of his mouth. Inwardly

179

though, he knew that she would surely die if she was left with him. He did not think he could give her the proper care.

"Okay," said the nurse. "I'll ask the sisters at the church to take her away. You need to sign these papers."

"Also, could I give you this? The one thing I have to pass on." He paused. "Let her have it when she is older."

He signed the papers without any hesitation but as though he was signing his soul away to Mephistopheles. The baby was gone. Many years had passed by the time he was released from detention. But, this release came with a price. Once he was out, he went knocking on every door, looking for her in every church. He had come here too, in search of her.

After all these years, Tony thought that he might have found her at last, on that lucky break at the bus-stop. What were the chances of this meeting, but a miracle? He needed to get her away from that crook. He had heard Mark speak to a fellow the other day, when Tony had stood hidden in the flower shop's backroom. He'd figured that Mark was involved in a smuggling deal. Tony was behind the sofa when Mary had barged in and barely escaped being noticed.

He realised that the frightened girl had been out of her wits. But papers, evidence, anything, and everything regarding Mary, needed to be researched. The girl had already left the room. Tony was within earshot to Mark's conversation.

"The flower shop is nothing to me. I am going to get out sooner than you think. My cover may already have blown by now..." Mark spoke on the mobile outside the back room. The window behind the

curtains was open and nobody else noticed that Tony was there.

Tony had followed him in a cab all the way to their apartment. He drove out later in the afternoon while Mary waited in the front. He left the cab once he saw where Mark had lived and hopped on the next bus to get back to Mary with the dreadful news. Mary, however, never gave him a chance when they fortuitously met on the bus.

Now that he was almost certain that Mary was his forsaken daughter, he decided to see her at once. It could not wait. He called a cab off the street outside his apartment and asked the driver to take him to Barrington Street. The cab arrived and parked outside the shop. He did not pay the driver but asked him to wait while he went fervently in to look for her. Then they would both go to the café for lunch to celebrate.

Mary had left by then and the girls could not give him any information about her plans for the day. Tony thought he would stop by her apartment next, and leave a note in her mailbox. He had waited nineteen years and each moment was agonisingly precious now. The note said:

Mary, I have something very important to tell you. Please meet me tomorrow at the same café for lunch. It's urgent. I've waited a long time to see my daughter again.

There was an ambulance parked on the street in front of the apartment building. Tony got out of the cab quickly and paid the driver. A body, a body covered in white from head to toe was being carried into the ambulance on a stretcher trolley. Tony mumbled something to the ambulance driver. He looked at him blankly, not fully grasping his question. The police had found her this morning when they broke into

181

the apartment with a search warrant. They found the body of a girl lying on the sofa. She had died from an overdose of sleeping pills. They found the empty bottle by her side.

The letter had arrived. But too late that Tony had now held in his hand, looked at it, and looking still, gave it to the ambulance man. The man read it. Tony stood paralysed. He saw how the body was slowly being taken into the ambulance in a mechanical perfection. The clicks, clacks, and the clangs of the stretcher moved the body onto a bed, neatly into position.

Nothing moved him. No sense could knock him into a reaction; no tears of regret flowed from those weary eyes. This seemingly innocuous episode had transpired into such a great tragedy, but it left him vaguely disengaged. He did what he was told. Gazing vacuously, he climbed into the ambulance beside the body and sat in silence.

The grieving period slowly passed. And one night, when he sat down at his desk by the fireplace to write the rest of his story, he opened the briefcase and took out his manuscript. He wrote:

The Church authorities wrote him an official letter with a little parcel in it, confirming that Mary was indeed the baby girl he had given up nineteen years ago. The parcel contained the Swiss army knife he had given to the nurse at the time for safekeeping. Mary did not want it, which was why it was never given to her. It had always been in the custody of the Church.

Most untimely, a death so poignant and if ripeness was all, then, Ophelia's tragedy perhaps would have fared better, who at least entered heaven with a soul full of Hamlet's love, amounting to forty-thousand brothers. This anonymous flower girl had

182

none. She lived to die unseen, nipped in the first blush of blossoming. The unloved bud lay inert under winter's callous frost. The tragedy compounded as both shared the same fate in not knowing how much love there was, one by her lover, the other by her father.

Tony's breathing intensified and his heart ached in a dull, spun out pain. No matter how much he lamented, the unassailable facts remained that he had given her up, found her, and had lost her again.

He put the manuscript back in the briefcase. With both hands, he pressed the lid down. It closed with a click. While staring at the red, hot flame in the fireplace, he glanced at the briefcase. This briefcase was his life. He could neither keep it, nor destroy. It held him under a spell that he couldn't break. He made a decision. He couldn't publish the story. This would remain untold, for his exclusive readership only. It was not a fable entirely, but a text of confession, of endurance, and of resilience.

Spring River

On an idyllic spring morning, Mila woke up with a yawn. Gibberish talks had drifted from uncertain directions. She squinted to check the time. It was hardly ten o'clock, a lazy Sunday. But people had already dropped in. She got out of bed, walked up to the window, and gazed downstairs. She saw men jostle in the orchard, in the back yard of the house. These were her uncles and their friends, coming over for a Sunday morning tea. She heard them talk, often breaking into passionate outbursts, but could not understand the reason for clamour.

Mila's sixteenth birthday was last month. This tender age rendered her vulnerable. But she grew up feeling privileged at home. The House of Chowdhury was where she had lived with a family of at least ten people – her grandparents, Mr and Mrs Chowdhury, her aunt Lutfun, her two uncles, Ashik and Sheri, her mother Nazmun Banu, and her father, Ekram. She reckoned, out of all her relatives, her grandmother, Mrs Chowdhury, loved her the most.

Her bedroom window lent a view of the orchard. The wooden, green, shutters of the window splayed wide this morning; she didn't close them the night before, to let some spring breeze seep through. She fell asleep in the wafted air of citrus fruit profusion. Standing by the window, a few words that she overheard from the heated debate eluded her. These were big words, such as revolution, change of government, etc, etc. Whatever those words meant, Mila had to run along. But her friends were coming over. They had planned a picnic under an Indian jujube tree at the far end of the orchard.

Mila saw their black bobbing heads through the window. She got dressed, picked up a matchbox from an ornate dresser-drawer, and ran downstairs. Pots and pans lay haphazard on the grassy patch. One friend picked up a rock and hurled it at a bunch of russet jujubes, hanging down its stringy bark. A few luscious fruits plopped on the ground. They bent over to pick a small handful each. They giggled without a reason, as they chewed them, casually spitting the pits around.

Most of them lived locally. Her closest was, Shreya Mukherjee. When Shreya saw Mila come through the orchard, she went halfway to meet her. They greeted and hugged. Rabeya smiled and sat down by the pots and Lima dug a hole in the ground to make a stove bowered by the tall orchard trees. They were beautiful teenagers. Wrapped in curvy, silky scarves around their chests, they frolicked in their short, floral frocks, worn over long, stripe pants. They planned on making long Khichuri this afternoon, a sumptuous gruel of rice, daal, salt, a pinch of turmeric, and oil, cooked in a pot of water.

They shoved twigs and dry leaves into the stove-hole. Mila took a stick out of the matchbox and struck a flame. She held it to the stuffings of dry, leafy twigs in the stove-hole to light a fire. A pot of Khichuri mixture was hauled and put over it. Luminous embers emanated like fireflies around the orchard.

The girls cut a long plantain leaf and spread it along, next to the jujube tree, to use as a shared plate. In about half an hour, the Khichuri was ready and the remaining fire dwindled. Lima opened the pot's lid. Charcoal smell pervaded the air.

Shreya and Lima pulled the heavy pot of the gruel off the stove and used the momentum to bring it over to the leaf, where the girls had sat. They scooped up and splashed it along on each plate. Their laughter said it all. Whether or not it was tasty with a tinge of a smokey BBQ flavour, they couldn't care less, but they ate it up with gusto. The twigs in the stove-hole burnt gradually to a cinder. The picnic was over.

"Where do we dispose of the banana leaf?" Shreya asked.

Hmm, good question, I guess just leave it here under the tree," Mila answered.

"Under the tree? Just like that?" Shreya asked.

"Yeah."

"Okay. But it's hardly a clean leaf."

"Doesn't matter. It would eventually go into the soil. Where do you think all the fallen leaves go?" asked Mila.

"Into the soil, but…"

"Well?" Rabeya asked, eagerly.

"You know, how the leaf is all dirty and all. Besides, it would take some time for this to mix with the soil, too. It's still so green," said Shreya.

"Don't worry, just leave it. It will all be okay, trust me," Mila said.

"Okay, if you say so."

Even for a fifteen year old, Shreya was matured enough to know that something was awry. The soiled plantation leaf shouldn't be exposed to the elements like this.

"Why do you care so much about being tidy?" Mila asked, suddenly.

"Why not? What a crazy question is that? Why? You don't care about it at all?"

"No need, because nature takes care of it for us."

"Still, you just don't keep things lying around, because it is going to biodegrade 'eventually'."

Mila kept quiet but Shreya discerned, a dark, new dimension in Mila's character. She had a point though. However, sloth seemed more like a reason to Shreya. Mila went up to the main gate with her friends and saw them out. As she walked back, she saw Mrs Chowdhury's retinue of maids cleaning up the orchard. They shovelled dirt into the pit and levelled it up along with all the other litter. The orchard was back to its pristine, most magical state, in no time.

Mila and Shreya had a special bond. Mrs Chowdhury knew that. A while back, she had discovered a secret hideout, a cubby house in the orchard under an old jackfruit tree. Inside the little cubby house, there were copies of English romance books, Mills and Boons, and a carom board, biscuit crumbs, and pieces of torn chapati. She had also found a few cigarette butts on the floor next to an old blanket, which Mila had taken from a rusty, antique trunk in the attic. But how did these cigarette butts get here? Surely, it must be Shreya's idea. Her own granddaughter wouldn't dare.

Perhaps it was Shreya who coughed the first smoke, Mrs Chowdhury imagined. It had to be her, that Shreya, who planted this in her granddaughter's head to pinch a cigarette packet from her uncles, which Mila did surreptitiously one afternoon when everyone had gone for a siesta. At least, they were careful not to burn this blanket. But a maid knew. She was nearby, doing laundry by the pond. She had overheard Mila propose that they smoked and that she would snitch a packet of cigarettes from her uncles. Shreya had opposed the idea; it was Mila's idea all along.

Mila sat on the old blanket and looked for the hidden, cigarette pack under it. She pulled it out; it had dented by then. She drew a cigarette and ignited it. She took a couple of easy puffs; just then, she heard a sound. It distracted her. It was a sound of a rally passing through her alley. She stood up on her toes and looked through the cubby window. Over the short, orchard fence, she saw a massive demonstration. Her cigarette burnt out; the heat touched the tip on her index finger. She'd dropped it and crushed the smoking butt with her heels. She jumped on her red bike, which had been leaning against the cubby house, and rode it to the rally. She read slogans written largely in black on white placards. They demanded equality. Equal pay; freedom from oppression and exploitation. The rally went as far as the mosque at the end of the alley and had stopped near to a slum.

Mila turned her bike around to get home. Revolution sounded all very romantic, but notional to her. The likelihood of her participating in the protests was nearly nil. She would sit in the orchard a few evenings by herself. Its enchantment inspired her to think big. She thought of the words she had eavesdropped on her uncles' conversations with friends. She could even get Shreya dragged into it. She was going to hide it from her relatives. Every evening when this rally passed through, it aroused her revolutionary curiosity. She rode out to the meetings at the mosque square. It had become a hotbed for free speeches. Mila listened to them mesmerised. She began to attend them regularly. Her mother and Mrs Chowdhury had noted her absence; they thought she was with friends.

However, one spring night of 1971, the alley was unnaturally calm. None of the demands had been met. Exploitation was at its peak. Leaders of this movement had declared war against the government and proposed that every household became a fortress. The government was given an ultimatum to resign, to make way for new leadership.

On such a night, Mila was returning from the mosque square. In the passing, she heard a terrible wail from Shreya's house. She saw Shreya, running haphazardly into the open street, followed by soldiers in Khaki uniforms. These were soldiers cracking down, not only on protestors but civilians as well. Mila hid behind a streetlamp and saw those hyenas chasing her.

An army truck stood at the entrance of the alley, and Mila heard girls and women crying. A truckload of women was picked up. Mila blinked a few times. A cold sweat ran down her spine. She saw the truck drive away. Shreya had disappeared into the darkness of the road too. Mila rode home and entered the room of her grandparents, who sat grimly at the dining table listening to radio news.

Mrs Chowdhury looked up and said, "From now on, you're not allowed to go anywhere, except school. Do you understand?"

Mila nodded, with a frown. She told them what she had seen on the road. And then Shreya, where was Shreya, anyway? She asked herself. Mrs Chowdhury sat Mila down. She explained to her that they were at war. The government had declared war on its own citizens. The military ruthlessly tried to squash this rebellion. These absurdities, shameful, and merciless crimes against humanity broke out like blisters, Mr and Mrs Chowdhury said.

Suddenly, Shreya burst into the room. Her long hair was untied and dishevelled, a mass of netted bird's nest. She flopped down on the floor.

"Shreya? What happened?" Mila asked. "I saw you running on the street a while back."

"They took boro didi!"

"They did what?" Mila asked.

"They took her."

Mila tried to understand the situation. Shreya's elder sister, Krishna, was on that truck. Why though? Mila was young, but in her heart she felt ominous suspicions of why the military had taken young girls and women. This was how they were going to squash the movement, by taking the women away and making them pay for it. Mrs Chowdhury asked Shreya to sit on a chair at the table. She tried to calm her.

"If your mother is still at home, go now, go already to help her find out where the army may have taken your sister," Mrs Chowdhury said, urgently.

"But that's nearly impossible; Baba could never find out."

"Why not?" Mrs Chowdhury asked.

"Because he doesn't know anyone in the army who could tell him."

"Could she stay the night here?" asked Mila.

"Yes, she could, but you must ask her mother."

Shreya rose to leave. She had a sense of foreboding that perhaps she would never see Mila again. She walked under the pale lamps; desultory darkness enveloped the lane. Just two houses away from Mila's house. She reached home. She walked through the open door and saw her father and her twin brother, Shuvo, sitting glumly in the drawing-room. Her mother performed puja at the altar of Vishnu, the great god of preserver, in a corner carved out for prayers. Shreya stood at the door, feeling restive. She saw her mother was in deep meditation. This unparalleled devotion – could this change the course of history? What was it? What gave her this strength to be so calm at a moment like this? To be able to give Lord Vishnu her undivided attention. Even Vishnu himself would be perturbed. Or perhaps not, or else, he would have descended from heaven to rescue the drowning world. But he remained cold like this marble statue at the altar, as someone who only watched moving cinemas of human dramas, played out on earth on its axis of destruction and preservation. It was hard to know his hand in this. Shuvo came and stood beside her. She looked at his tear-stained eyes.

"I need to tell you something," he said.

"What?" Shreya asked.

"I am leaving home."

"Leaving home? At a time like this? What do you mean?"

"Yes, leaving. Now or never. Just tell them. Tell Maa and Baba that I have joined the revolution."

"Are you crazy? At sixteen, you want to be a revolutionary? You have not even seen a gun yet, let alone used one."

"Don't be silly, Shreya. It has been going on for a while. Most young boys, my friends, have already joined. I have even seen Mila at the mosque square. Why do you think the military was here? Why do you think they came to our house?"

"Why?

"Because they want to arrest boys and men. They think they're the ones fanning the movement. And they are. Do you understand now? Young boys, men, are leaving in droves to join this fight."

"That is so foolish."

"Foolish? What's foolish is your naivety! The army is targeting every young person they can lay their hands on. They think other countries may be behind this too. This army will find us and kill us one by one. Today, they couldn't. But they will come back looking for me since I am one of the eligible 'young boys'. Also, to take you and didi to their pleasure house. You were lucky, you got away. I was at the corner shop lighting a cigarette. By the time I came home, it was too late. They had already taken didi. They kept Maa and baba alive because of me. The military is using them as bait to catch me. Someone must have tipped them off."

"Oh no! Even if all this were true, how were we going to win this? Our boys are no match for them."

"That may be. But our enemy is clueless. They have no

191

idea, and neither do you. Anyway, I've got to go. Tell Maa to pray for me."

"Wait, Shuvo."

But Shuvo had walked away, Shreya went after him to the door. He closed it behind him to brave a revolution. All this was so quick. What could have happened overnight to bring this on? It happened, all too bitter a revelation, at least for Shreya. Mila had known for a while now, sneaking out to attend those rallies at the mosque square. But Shreya had no idea. She was not political, nor an activist. She returned to the puja corner. It smelled of burned incense. At the altar, Vishnu stood with a conch shell amongst all its fruit offerings and sweets in return to the third eye that he had bestowed to its devotees. Except for the flicker of candles in the wind, there were no lights.

Lord Vishu's imposing presence, created a strange aura. Shreya felt that the Lord would keep his promise, and save the world for his devotees who prayed in such elaborate pujas. He would blow into the conch shell any time now to summon his demi-gods to carry out the commands. While her mother continued, Shreya felt she actually heard the ancient callings of preservation.

A desperate knock on the front door broke her spell. She saw Mila push herself in.

"What's up?" Shreya asked.

"We need to go."

"What do you mean?"

"I said we need to go. Where's Aunty?" Mila asked.

"She's in puja."

"Pack a suitcase and come to our house with your baba and Maa, as soon as you can."

"Why?"

"Seriously? Don't you listen to the BBC?"

Shreya kept quiet. Mila could be irritating sometimes.

"Tell me, do you or do you not know that there's a war going on?" Mila asked.

"I didn't until didi was abducted and Shuvo left home."

"Just as well, I heard that our place was going to be attacked soon. They're coming after us. They'll soon start a door-to-door search for every young boy and man in the vicinity, without fail. Our house is next. They will kill, plunder and rape any way they can. We are planning to flee to our ancestral home in the village. Grandma said to get you, so you could escape with us."

"Okay, okay. Enough said. I'll see you at your place soon. Go now. It's not safe for you to be out and about either."

Shreya saw Mila to the door. Mila mounted her bike and peddled it along into the night. The suddenness of it all made her dizzy; she began to throw up. The revolution had been brewing for a while yet. It just hadn't descended on her until now.

It was decided then. The two families would leave town and move to the village. Maids had whispered something in the orchard earlier, which had alerted Mrs Chowdhury.

"What is it?" she had asked them.

A maid looked at her. She was so pale that she startled her. "Well, when I took Shreya didi to the gate this evening, I saw things and overheard something."

"What did you hear and what did you see?"

"That two men, street dwellers were whispering in the alley, talking about the Imam of the mosque," she said.

"What were they saying?" Mrs Chowdhury asked.

"That the Imam is a military spy. He often tells the military about our neighbourhood kids, about how many young people live on this block; which homes have young girls, boys, and revolutionaries. He also tells them which house belongs to whom."

193

"The Imam is a collaborator? An informant?" Mrs Chowdhury asked. "Quickly pack your bags and tell the other maids to do the same. We're leaving town."

The maids left. Meanwhile, she shouted out to Mila to gather Shreya and her family. The Imam must have collaborated. He was the one to tip off the military about Shuvo, Krishna, and Shreya. How else would they know about these young people living in that house? This house was next. The military had found out about The House of Chowdhury, by now, she was certain of it.

She had two sons of her own and lots of young girls in the house. The Imam knew this neighbourhood better than any residents living here. They must leave at once. The Chowdhury family began packing little suitcases with clothes, hard molasses, and dried rice. It took them until midnight to finish. Mila's uncles and aunties were ready. They waited for Shreya and her family. As soon as they appeared in the doorway, they rose to leave. There would be at least twenty of them including the maids. The one car in the garage would not be nearly enough. Shreya's father also brought his own car.

The two cars set off in the cover of darkness towards the river, where they had planned to take boats across to their village. On the road, there was the reek of decomposed flesh; mangled distorted bodies, dumped callously in the drains. The killers, the army, called themselves humans but even the dead seemed more human. Expressions of horror and confusion were frozen on their cold faces. The soldiers had nothing. They were robotic creatures of the night.

The two cars sped through the graveyard shift. Mila, sitting in one of them, saw abandoned rickshaws lined up on the lane. The bodies of the drivers were still, like statues – inert arms and legs flung outside. The mosque square was ground zero. Only vultures and crows flew at night in the

194

full moon that shed light in the crematorium of this desolated place. This had become a wasteland of stark trees, tall and short pointy branches. They had stood out like crooked, uneven fingers of a banshee, posed for a ritualistic dance of death and doom. Mila rolled up the car window and covered her ears and eyes. Shreya who sat next to her, held her close.

The army had looted every house and had ransacked the fruit-laden orchard of The House of Chowdhury. It was spring, but the deathly shadow was cast over the season's new bloom. They went after almost every citizen; murdered them and took them away at gunpoint; relentlessly, not sparing any young boys or girls. Children witnessed horrendous murders of parents. Their sharp cries rang through caged ribs within their bodies. Shuvo and his friends had already fled and joined the movement. The streets and dirt paths were packed with never-ending processions of men, women, children, and babies in their mothers' laps; babies never stopped crying. Hunger pains were greatest at a time like this, but they must all make it to the river.

Mila and Shreya's family cars were full. One of Mila's uncles even had to sit in a half-opened boot. Closer to the river, Mila peered through the darkness. She could see boats in the offing. They would be needing a few of them at least. Mrs Chowdhury did not leave anyone behind. Everyone in the house came with them, including the orphan twins that her adopted daughter, Lutfun, had picked up from the dustbin two years ago.

They queued up to step into the boats. Mila stood last, just behind Shreya. The cars were left behind. An uncertain journey of refugee life began. A new day would begin surely, but slowly, when the revolution ended. The vast river before them had answers to the beginnings and the endings of time; the boats sailed unhindered in the soft, night breeze. The river spoke to them of journeys and destinations; it gurgled a tale of mystery. That life floated aimlessly from one impermanent place to another. Wisdom came only when people learned to communicate with the river.

The boat moved quietly. The distant gunshots reminded them of the orchard. Only birds pecked at its sullied fruits. Shreya mused, no one knew where her sister was, and Shuvo? Would he come home any time soon?

However, when Mrs Chowdhury and Shreya looked for Mila on the boat, she was gone. She had heard too much, and she had seen far too much. She felt an incandescent love for the revolution. The breathing orchard awaited, as did the hummingbirds.

Mother of March

A cuckoo bird's intermittent whistle on this silent afternoon was a telltale sign. Taramon, a motherless farmer's daughter of twenty-four, wouldn't bet on an imminent danger, but she felt uneasy from this quietude. Through the breezy bamboo bush, the bird tried to whisper a trepidation, but it eluded her; she was still inclined to have lunch with her siblings, as it was lunchtime in Madhupur.

Heaviness in the air, her family of four siblings sat down around a mat rolled out in the middle of their thatched mud floor, like an island. Taramon brought the food out. Red clay bowls, grooved around the rim: rice, daal, and curried fish. Except for her, the family helped themselves to scoops of this delightful meal. Taramon looked at them. She was jittery; they must hurry; time was in a scurry; the bird's signal, a kind of lurry.

Hush! Hush! A gunshot, grave, and almost guttural, blasted through the skies. It shook them to the core. Aves took off. Flights of sweeping wings inverted like flying buttresses. The aves chirruped on the fence. A boy ran in, amok. Taramon stood up and looked at this befuddled boy, as did her siblings.

"What's this sound?" Taramon asked.

Her question perplexed the boy.

"Don't you know?" he asked.

"Know what?"

"That the army has just marched into our village."

"The enemy is here already?" she asked.

"Yes, and rounding up every girl and woman, killing husbands, fathers, mothers, and children. People, fleeing like crazy."

"Why are you still here, then?" she asked.

"Because I've lost them. I was in the field when I saw a

gunboat upstream. I ran as fast as I could, to come home to my parents. They were gone by then."

"Gone? Where to?"

"I don't know."

The boy broke down in tears; the bird launched into a piercing trill; a moth hovered over them. Taramon looked at her siblings and the boy and told them to follow her. They ran out of the house. On the road, they saw denizens of the fields and the forests; they ran in a frenzy as a mad rush of adrenaline propelled them; the mud huts fell into decrepit pits; the bird piped in. Taramon found their hapless neighbours, her own father, and friends in frenzy in this hellish situation. Some people carried crying babies. Others carried elderly parents. They were leaving home, headed to the border, to cross into the neighbouring country. Overnight turned into refugees, this nightmare, too real to encapsulate. Amid this, one young mother stalled, not because she was tired, but because of something else, something on her mind; she took a step backward to return to the village. Taramon stood in her way. The woman howled, like the monsoon wild winds over the swollen, serpentine river stream.

She said, "Don't. Don't. My... Mm little baby... there... She was fast asleep. She, in the house. I... in the field, when they chased me out. Bewildered. I ran. I didn't know where I was going. I just did... I left her. Oh! I left her in the house. She sleeps alone. My baby... my baby. I must return. Let me go... Let me go...'

Taramon would not let her go. No way. She embraced her tightly. Others helped Taramon to get the woman back in this panic-stricken procession line. She looked at nothing. Silent like a broken clock, she had stopped ticking. They lifted her up like a body bag. This woman, a wreck, frightened them.

198

Then they approached the border, the haven. Taramon was placid. She had made up her mind to fight, to be a freedom fighter. The enemy had come to take their land but hadn't seen the ferocity of a tiger. That was her resolve.

Taramon stood at the forefront of a winning line. A guerrilla fight ensued. Regardless of storms, rains, and floods, on rickety boats, the fighters battled a formidable army. Harder and harder, each step became, they kept coming back and on to them. The green blades of grass, now the soil soaked up much of the scarlet blood; unmarked in death, foe or friend.

Young Taramon never gave up. She defended her land, valiantly. In the cover of darkness, she took her rifle, hidden under her clothes, and set off across the border. At the checkpoint, she lay low under the barbed wires to drag herself through, away from the guards. She was an invisible speck in a coal-spattered night. She chose this spot where security was slack. For the guards were drunk in the whorehouse; this shit-hole of a shack. This was her ruse. Once across, she hid amongst the heap of the carcasses, covered in filth, dirt, and blood. When she spotted one or two uniformed soldiers in her gun's crosshair, they had no chance of living.

However, something happened a week before independence. Taramon was out on one of her errands, under the barbed wire, when she felt someone's breath right over her head. She was compromised but not caught out; the bird tweeted loudly. That moment, lying flat on the ground, she pointed her gun at no assailant. It was the young mother from the procession.

"You?" Taramon cried. "Do you know how dangerous this is?"

"All missions are dangerous," she said. "I want to be your bodyguard, Taramon."

"Are you sure? I thought you were too fragile to fight."

Taramon had undermined the mother's courage. Sure enough, she took a bullet for Taramon one Sunday, when the duo walked straight into an enemy ambush to pounce on prey. Freedom was gained; Taramon lived. Perched on the fence the bird's old tweets, told of the mother's feat, glad tidings, and her warranted legacy.

Scroll of the Turul

Down by the River Danube, a hooded man in a long, black cape ran to get away from the biting, winter winds. This was the worst winter in Etelköz, in many years. He didn't want to be late for the secret blood oath ceremony of the lords of the seven Magyar tribes, in the city hall of Kecskemét. He felt fear. When he entered the hall, the evening had fallen over the Carpathian Mountains. The ceremony hadn't started yet.

The seven lords from Jenő, Kér, Keszi, Kürt-Gyarmat, Megyer, Nyék, and the Tarjá tribes had arrived at this city hall. Lord Álmos was also amongst them. Something big was going to take place here, this evening. They jostled in the middle of the hall. A conference ensued. A pagan priest presided. They sat in high thrones around a bucket of spitting fire.

"The rulers of Pannonia will push us farther if we don't do something," said Lord Keszi.

Lord Megyer nodded. "They've gained massive strength, since their invasion of Pannonia."

They nodded in agreement, as Lord Kér added, "The Bavarians must be avenged, no matter how long it may take. Be it a bloodthirsty battle, bring them to their knees on the Great Plains. Pannonia will be ours."

"Yes, those traitors must pay for what they did. How they had invited Prince Kurszán, our Magyar kündü kagán, and ruthlessly butchered them at the dining table. But we need to be careful and gain enough strength to match theirs. Let's not forget the Bulgars, the Moravians, and the Frankish of the plains that we are up against. We must stand united. We must form a confederation to that effect," said Lord Jenő.

They sat rummaging for a while and then Lord Kürt-Gyarmat spoke, breaking the cold silence. "Ah! But who could forget the bloody banquet of Fischa? Who could forget how they ambushed and killed our lord, Prince Kurszán? We also need to appoint one of us to head this confederacy."

"This war, even if we can pull it off in the end, will be long and bloody. Are we up to it?" asked Lord Nyék.

"It will undoubtedly be difficult, spanning over many years, I'm sure, but I have someone in mind who could be our supreme leader of this confederacy, if we are to go ahead with it till the end, that is," said Lord Tarjá.

"Who do you have in mind?" asked Lord Keszi.

All the lords looked at Lord Tarjá in anticipation.

"Our Lord Álmos, Duke of Onoğur," he declared, looking at Lord Álmos. "Why not appoint him?"

"But, I'm on my last leg already. Age breaks me even as we speak," said Lord Álmos.

"You may be old, but not still so old," said Lord Tarjá. "However, you're also wise. Politics play, making negotiations, are your forte. Besides, you're the great Álmos. Remember your mother's dreams? It was a powerful prophesy. That the Princess Emese, consort of the Scythian king had dreamt. A turul had impregnated her by divine decree. You were born to be our leader, Lord Álmos. I believe we can put our trust in you."

"Hmm, also, let's not forget, young Árpád, your son," said Lord Keszi. "Should anything happen to you, Duke, Álmos, we could always appoint him as commander-in-chief of the army confederation. It is time that Magyars came out of Pontic Steppes and Etelköz. The Moravians and The Bulgars have used our horsemen, time and time again, to fight their own battles. Everyone has had a piece of Pannonia. Just name it, the Scythians, the Slavs, the Lombards, the Nomadic Avars, the Huns, the Romans, the Bulgars, and the Frankish. Our turn awaits on the plains."

"Yes, indeed. We have descended to hateful, barbaric raiders. The bloodthirsty hordes that gorge on blood, a nation of pillagers, plundering and torching villages," said Lord Tarjá.

The man in the long black cape held a scroll in his hand. He hid behind a thick stone pillar and listened. He saw a table in the middle of the vast room. The seven lords talked and shaped a destiny.

"What should we do then?" asked Lord Kürt-Gyarmat. "In the name of our great ancestors, Attila, an expedition must be led into Pannonia. Our experience with the vassal Svatopluk says that the rulers of Pannonia are weak. However, we must not underestimate their powers. If we do win, we will change everything. We will make history."

"Unitedly, I believe, we can do this. A bloody long war, maybe, but we will make an ingress in small migration into the plains. And I also believe it to be a huge responsibility we are about to undertake, and put on your shoulders, Lord Álmos," Lord Keszi commented.

They sat pondering for a few minutes, around the crackling fire in the aluminium bucket that made its presence known by spitting occasional flying cinders around. The lords looked at the mesmerising fire until fire rose within their hearts.

Then Lord Nyék cried out, "Now or never, before it is too late. As we stand together today, we must make an oath, and seal this fellowship of brotherhood in blood."

His passionate outburst stirred the other lords. All seven cried out unanimously. "Bonded by a blood oath. History is in the making."

The seven noble lords then stood up and walked to the table in the middle of the room. They queued behind one another along the table in their ceremonial attires of long robes. The pagan priest placed a chalice in the middle with the face of a deadly viper engraved on it. Dim lights were shed from the fire torches on the hall's cold stone walls.

The pagan rites began. In the slight light, the man saw the seven lords drawing black stonewash knives from their sheaths slinging down the slick long shirts. With the knife, the knafa, they lacerated a tiny fraction of skin on their wrists. The lords stepped towards the bowl, one after another, and squeezed some blood into the chalice. Soon the chalice contained enough for everyone to drink.

The master of ceremony, the pagan priest, then announced, "Following this sacred ritual held in secrecy, within the walls of the town hall, as of today we elect Duke Álmos of the Danubian Onoğur the leader of this confederation. His son, Árpád, is the appointed commander-in-chief."

The lords conceded by a war cry which sounded off a grim message through the dark hall. The ceremony ended. The lords gathered in a corner of the hall and made their exits. The hooded man saw the Magyar lords and the three Pechenegs leave the city hall one by one. They had mounted their horses and rode off. He sat down on the floor of the city hall and wrote his scroll:

This decisive moment for the Magyars, of the lowland was a promise to oust all of its ruling powers, the Bulgars, the Frankish, the Bavarians, and the Moravians forever from Pannonia. Ironically, the Magyars and Turkic Pechenegs were united in this. The Magyars spoke their language too, although Pechenegs were once a foe. This pact of the confederation promised a future annexation of a Magyar homeland on the Carpathian Basin by gradual and hostile land-taking.

When the man came out of the hall, he looked up at the stars. Dots were formed in the shape of a horse with a rider at helm. He shot an arrow from a terse bow into the future. The arrow had flung far. The man took his cape off and walked along the Danube. At the far end of the river, he had stopped to take a breath as he came up to the entrance of a village outside the citadel of Etelköz.

Around 895-96

The Carpathian Basin

Árpád, son of Duke Álmos, had to stop several times on the grassy steppes of the Carpathian Mountain. He led an army of the seven Magyar clans for a battle, a battle which would mark a victory for Hungary of the Magyars, in the settlement of a homeland. This was not the first battle here. The Carpathian Basin saw many warring nations. Nomads and Semi-Nomads had fought relentlessly before them for the control of the Basin: the Slavs, the Huns, the Tartars, the Vlachs, the Bulgars, the Pechenegs, the Moravians, the Byzantines, Bavarians, and the Romans over several centuries. The rains fell yet again to prepare the field for another imminent battle, now underway.

Prince Árpád thought of his father, Álmos, who was now frail but accompanied them anyway. A bucket of tame fire burned in the far end of the tent. They'd stopped here to rest, at the entrance of the Great Hungarian Plains.

The journey over the mountain terrain was arduous. Árpád chose this strip of land by the Danube for a few days of the army camp. This was a dangerous mission. The fire in the tent flickered at a sudden cold gust of the northerly wind. Goulash was being stewed outside in large cast-iron pots, over the fresh fire, to feed the army. The vapour from the stew rose high like dark mist, clouding much of this area by the Danube. The vastness of the Ural

205

region had buffered the army from the battlefield, not far from here.

As Árpád and Álmos pored over the maps in the tent that afternoon, they heard distant cries. The cries hollered through the winds into the camp. These didn't sound like ordinary war cries or war drums. Prince Árpád came out of the tent. He took his tethered horse and untied it swiftly. He had to find out about the cries. He mounted the horse decisively and followed them. His horse was fast. Árpád rode it like a winged chariot. It stopped at the entrance of a village. Males, females and families were in total disarray as they fled. Armed fighters on horses plunged swords into the men and took their young daughters and wives. Then the looting and the torching of the village had begun. Raiders went into their little huts and took whatever they found here. Amid this chaos a young maiden ran up to Árpád.

"Please, please save me."

Árpád picked her up in one sway and then rode away into the dusk. He stopped on the grassy steppes and dismounted. She was still on the horse, trembling like a new leaf in a storm. Prince Árpád looked at her, exquisite in a red gown and a bejewelled headgear. He commanded her to get off the horse and she obeyed. He asked her to take her headgear off so he could take a better look at her. She took off the Hun style decorative headgear. Árpád stepped closer, took her by the arm and pulled her nearer. He liked what he saw – her young, dark, almond eyes and fair skin.

"My name is Prince Árpád. Son of Duke Álmos," he said.

She stepped back at the name like a frightened gazelle. "I am the village chieftain's daughter," she replied. "My name is Pirosko."

"What happened here? Tell me. Do not fear, dear Pirosko."

"They, they said, those plunderers, that they are The Vlachs, but I'm not sure, they could also be Magyars," she stammered.

He frowned. He was silent and serious. Then he said, "Are you sure?"

"I could be wrong, but I thought that's what I heard from villagers."

"No matter. No harm will come to you, I promise. Tomorrow we lead an army to the plains. You will stay here in my tent. Do you understand?"

"They took my brother and killed my father. They slashed their swords through the necks of many. And you think I'll be safe in your tent?"

"You don't have a choice, Pirosko. This, our promised homeland, and war is the only way. A win would surely bring peace in the region. A Magyar kingdom needs to be established to put a stop to raiders and invaders coming like this in waves."

"But the Magyars, are they any different from other plunderers?" she snarled.

"I promise you, this will end here," Árpád said, then pulled her in his arms.

Pirosko began to cry. She must stand up to this man, Avar-Onogurs, his ancestors were no better when it came to plundering. The raiders took everyone she ever loved. She looked up to him and placed a tight slap across his face. Árpád wasn't ready for this. But he didn't fight back. He disengaged himself from her, returned her bejewelled gear, and walked up to climb back on his horse. He mounted his horse and waited for Pirosko.

Pirosko looked around her and only saw dark clouds descending over the steppes. There was no other way but to go with him. She would have to think of something to avenge what was taken from her.

They both headed towards the army camp. It was evening by the time they'd arrived. Árpád's men came forward to hold the horse's rein as he dismounted. He helped Pirosko to dismount. He told his men to take Pirosko to a tent, where she could spend the night safely. In the morning, she could decide what she wanted to do. He was this young girl's saviour. She was his responsibility. She had to be saved from the raiders at any cost.

The army sat down for yet another night of Hungarian Goulash under the starry night. They sat in separate groups, as they ate spoonfuls from the wooden bowls. This dinner was also served to Álmos and Árpád in their tents. Pirosko entered the king's tent followed by a slave. Pirosko bowed before old Álmos. He sat on his high throne, the lord of lords of the seven clans, with Árpád sitting next to him.

"Speak up, my child. Do not be afraid," said the old Lord.

"My ancestors were the great Attila," she said.

"I see. You are a descendant of no other. No matter, we are related then. I am also a descendant of Attila. My son is leading the Magyars to a war on the plains."

"Yes, my Lord, I understand. But a group of Vlachs raiders has ransacked my home, killed my family, and torched the villages like the raiders before them."

"What do you seek?"

Pirosko was quiet. She held her head high and stood tall, said loud and clear, "Justice."

"I may be able to give you justice. But you must wait until we win this land to ensure security."

"That may be, but I have my own ways of getting it, my Lord."

"I see it in your eyes that you seek justice through revenge."

"Allow me this little secret," she said.

"Why must I keep you alive then? My people have done nothing to harm you."

"Because I can give you valuable information. That is why you will need to keep me alive until I get my revenge."

"Valuable information? What valuable information could you possibly give us?"

"You will be surprised, my Lord, how much I know. I was in charge of my father's scrolls. I'm also a scroll writer myself."

"So, you tell me that your scrolls can be trusted?"

"Yes, my father's scrolls taught me about your old enemies, when the allied Bulgars and the Pechenegs raided your land. These are recent histories when allied forces of the Magyar and the Byzantine attacked Bulgar. The Pechenegs were your enemy who at the behest of the Bulgars killed your men at the time. They plundered your land and took your women and children. Now, the Pechenegs are your allies. You even speak a Turkic language. I also read the scrolls on the blood oath. My father had witnessed and written it in the city hall.

"Your father was at a secret meeting? How did he get in?" Lord Álmos asked.

Pirosko was silent.

"You may go now," Álmos said.

After she had left, Lord Álmos looked at Prince Árpád and said, "Be careful of that girl. You never know whose side she is on. You cannot trust anyone."

"As you say, my Lord." Árpád bowed deeply and left Álmos alone to go towards his own tent. On his way, he looked at Pirosko's tent just two tents away and saw that she stood outside in the dark. Árpád looked at her curiously. She didn't see him. Árpád saw that she spoke to a man in a foreign language. The conversation became heated; it was

209

evident, even though they tried to suppress the angry tone. The man drew a sword and attacked the girl. Árpád jumped in like an agile leopard. The man saw him and tried to fight him too. There was a fierce duel, but the man fell panting eventually. He suddenly got up and fled from the scene, only to be captured by Árpád's soldiers.

Árpád saved Pirosko's life again, from clear and present danger. This softened her heart towards him.

"Who was he?" Árpád demanded.

"A Bulgar spy."

"What did you tell him?"

"The truth."

"The truth?"

"Yes, the truth that you have saved my life."

"And then?"

"When he knew he couldn't get anything out, he wanted to kill me, when you saved me again."

"If I'm your saviour, why're you then so angry with me? Because of what my people may have done?"

"Yes. I read much about Magyars' raids and plunders, one too many on the plains. How can I trust you?"

"Well, you just have to."

Árpád picked her up and carried her into his tent. Her head inclined towards his broad shielded chest like a shy bride.

"What else can you tell me?"

Árpád cajoled Pirosko, who now lay by his side under the same sheepskin blanket.

"He told me that Bulgar is now an ally of the king of Eastern Francia. Your army may have to face the allied forces."

"What did he trade that information for? Certainly not with the 'truth' you told him. Tell me, what else did you say?" he demanded.

210

"I told him about the legend, the turul."

"The turul? What about it?"

"The legend of turul, that it would lead you to victory, according to the scrolls of your grandmother, Princess Emese's, dream," she said.

"I see. Well, hopefully, we'll have the once enemy, the Moravian leader, Rastislav, on our side by then. With his help, we will invade all of Pannonia soon. But before that, we must win some lowland of the plains."

"Will this be a long bloody battle then?"

"We'll have to wait and see but hopefully not the one today. This will be short and easy. This war, we must win, and all of the land taken from our enemy before they grow too strong and formidable."

As they lay engaged in pillow talk, they heard a horse stop, before the tent. Prince Árpád got out of bed. He looked at her and said, "Stay there."

Then he came out of the tent in the pitch dark. There was an informant.

"It'd better be good," Árpád said.

"Bulgaria and the Pechenegs, our old enemies, have resurfaced and have attacked the Magyars in Etelköz."

"Hmm, have they now? Okay, you may go."

Árpád called the seven lords to another tent for an emergency meeting. This was the eve of the battle; in a few hours, the army would enter the Carpathian Basin. Árpád showed the land on the map that they could easily capture for the moment. It was a sparsely-populated area, located in the northeast of the Danube, around the Tisza River. This was an easy target without encountering much resistance. This would pave a stepping stone.

When the sun finally rose, the confederation of the Magyar entered the basin, encountering shepherds and a weak army. This was a clear win for Árpád and his soldiers.

This battle took them the same time as it might have taken a turul to scour across the plain. The victory was gained in just minutes within the short, sweet hour. It was a strategic and impressive move. When the enemy retreated, this became the Magyar's first territory, with more dangerous wars in the offing. The army returned practically intact to the campground. But as Árpád entered Álmos's tent with the news, he found Pirosko seated by his bed. The Duke had passed away.

Author's Note: This is a work of fiction and fantasy. However, some Magyar accounts have been gleaned from the following book:

PAUL, LENDVAI. The Hungarians: A Thousand Years of Victory in Defeat, Translated by Ann Major: Princeton University Press, Princeton, New Jersey, 2003

Sweet Calling

I wrote as I looked out at a collage of zebras and giraffes farther out on the open Savannah. There they were standing listlessly on this hot day.

Another hot day in the Savannah, the young man, barely twenty-four, wouldn't take his eyes off her picture on Facebook. This man would do anything for the woman on whose profile he doted.

That was odd, but I wrote:

The man wrote secret messages to her, saying he wanted to know her better; he wanted to speak to her. He even called her a few times, only to be disappointed. They chatted on Facebook, using first names as an endearment. But in the indomitable spirit of youth, the man demanded more. Her profile looked pretty. He wanted to know where she lived, what she ate for breakfast. He wanted to hear her voice on the phone.

One day, he asked her what she did. She told him singing was her hobby and writing her passion. She even got awards. She asked herself, was she trying to sell him her books? Was she treating him like a potential client? She allowed this relationship to grow.

I put my laptop down and went into the kitchen to make some tea. I thought she knew what he ate for breakfast every day, eggs, bread, and tea. He also knew what she ate for breakfast every day, coffee. Now, those were some intimate details about each other. Should she tell him more? Egg him on? After all, it was all virtual. No one had to come upfront or needed to become personal. This was intriguing. I had finished my tea and went back to my computer.

In the meantime, a strong storm rose. The sky was shaded in grey patches of ink smudges. She could hear the wind rage outside the closed window. Lyre of unbroken strings, a rhythm trying to push through. This pensive, pale day of mourning for labour's lost love. How would this story transpire? A comedy, a tragedy, humour? Where was morality in all this? Should morality even have a place? No. No. She must not indulge in this. She must tell him at once that she couldn't go any further, prepare him for a romantic interlude. Why did it matter? Love of the heart, love of the mind, all was fair and square in affairs of love. No? A soulmate, perhaps, across long distance and time. Both a virtual and a virtuous relationship – that he was young, but he was also mature. She liked him. She liked him a lot. Wait! Should she block him? He was calling again. Her impulsive fingers, like bare brown winter twigs, teetered on the brink of this fantasy/reality button. She went to the edit option on WhatsApp. She blocked him. She quickly rushed to block him on Facebook and deleted all the messages on Facebook and WhatsApp. There, all gone, a clean slate.

She sat down quietly listening to the winds. There was a song in her heart too. She looked out at the night and saw two shadows mating on the opposite balcony. She ran out to see more, but saw two potted palm fronds rubbing each other in the dark. She took her phone absent-mindedly and went back to their chat. Had she not blocked this man?. There were no new messages about how her mornings had been, whether or not she had her breakfasts, if she was taking care of herself. This intimacy, she had deleted, murdered at a brute press of a fingertip. But there were no restraint buttons on her emotion. She began to miss him.

214

Which way was it all going? She was going to engage him in interesting conversations. She was going to unblock him. Before she unblocked him, she tried to remember his last messages. How he asked her every day what she did, and she had said, she wrote all day. Then he said, how come you never rest? She had allayed her fears. She felt this man had something that pulled her. He had a sensitive heart and wanted to learn about life. He had even told her that he wanted to listen to her songs. So, should he call her? She had said no, no, never. He demanded why not, ever. She had said, she had her reasons, her vulnerabilities. She was going to unblock him today. It was really mean of her to do what she had done to this man. He had not done anything even remotely bad to deserve this. On the contrary, he had said he could give her a few lessons on his culture, the country he grew up in. It was rude to have blocked him.

As soon as she had unblocked him, she asked why he had called? He apologised and told her that he didn't mean to; it was an accident. She took him back. The usual chatting began all over. But she knew this was a caprice, for her at least. What should she do? Play with his emotions a bit, feather them, and brush them up in pale pink and blue with romance? The romantic flutters, the aahs, and the oohs. Open up, let yourself go, revel in the warmth of young love, imagine yourself in his deep embraces, and hot sighs on your hair. He, inhaling the fragrances of your hair; lips connected. Loves entwined! Let go! Let go!

Stop! Stop right there. I took my fingers off the computer. By now the sizzling heat had mellowed on the far Savannah. The giraffe and the zebra had left. I looked out at the stifling sun. It dipped down the horizon. The Savannah stood aloof in the backdrop of a scarred night of pimpled feral hyenas, and wild spotted dalmatians.

She was going to wreck him. She was going to woo him to a disaster with her words, so he'd be glued to his phone. She was going to wrap him up in the powers of her poetry and beguile him so that he'd forget to eat his breakfasts; his sleep would be wet awakenings, night sweats in the early hours. She was going to push him to the cliff where she would rule supreme like Venus, drive him to his fantasies and lock him in this gilded cage of her fling, her own little toy bird. Those sweet nothings, her magic potions, her fluttering joys. Could she be this heartless? Could she crush a half-fledged man to his emotional demise? After all, what was in it for her? An escape from this remarkable drudgery of boredom? It couldn't be love. No. She couldn't be that person. No matter how lonely, how bored she was.

I took a break again. I walked to the balcony. The heavy clouds glided across the sky in spectacular elegance; the wind bit my face. Fly, fly away, the wings of poesy declared, a steamy romance in the air.

"Tell me, tell me, why do you not want me to call you?" he wrote.

"Because I have problems."

"Like what? You can tell me, yeah? Are you married? What is it?"

"No, I can't. Forgive me, please forgive," she pleaded. "Stop this. Does it matter if I'm married?"

"No, not at all, but I cannot stop now. I like you. I like you a lot. You cannot ask me to stop. I think I'm in love."

216

"In love with whom? Do you have a beautiful girlfriend?" her fingers trembled.

"Girlfriend? Must you ask? How did your breakfast taste this morning?"

"Good and you?" she asked.

"You had me for breakfast? How did I taste, my love, my sweetheart?"

"What? I have to go. Bye."

She quickly logged out. She felt agitated. Next, he would want to know where she lived and try to come over. And then, and then... But she went back to the chats immediately, anyway.

His messages lay in the chat box. "You work too hard. You should rest from your writings sometimes."

"Thank you for your concern," she had replied.

"You're bored and lonely, and that's the plain truth. But you must learn to enjoy life too. Life is for enjoyment. Let me call, let me hear your voice, I'm dying to hear it. Let me hear your songs, I'm dying to hear them. How else could I listen to your songs, if I couldn't call you?"

"No. No. No. Never, you must never ask for more than what I can give you. I don't have time to talk," she fired.

"Make time then. I'm going to die if you won't let me." He was unstoppable.

"Love me all you like but only in your fantasy. We must never meet," she replied, with loud clicks.

She logged out. She was sitting in her bed. She slipped solidly under the quilt and covered her head. She panted awhile. This gave her a thrill, this cyber romance, as much as it thrilled him. Both waited eagerly for the next text.

"It's raining here, today. I love rain," she wrote.

"Are you taking care of yourself? Or drinking just

coffee? Why? Are you on a diet or something?" he
replied.

   "Why do you care so much?"
   "I don't know. I just do."
   "You do realise that we would never meet? And
that this has to be a long-distance relationship, pure
and sweet?"
   "That is true. You're right. But I just need to
write, and write to you."
   "I understand. But I've to go now, bye."

   I paused. These short bursts of texts had an exultant
effect on the man. He thought she was playing hard to get.
I thought it was time to end this charade. I thought, she must
tell him.

   The next morning, she woke up and found the
phone right next to her bed. She went straight to
WhatsApp. There were no new messages.
   She wrote, "How old are you?"
   Instantly, he replied, "Twenty-four, and you?"
   She thought for a while; this restless lad kept
shooting the same message at least five times.
   "Sixty."
   "Seriously? Are you kidding me? You don't look
your age at all in your profile. Tell me you're joking."
   "No, I'm not joking. Time you found a girlfriend
your age," she said.
   "Haha, girlfriend? You search for one, okay?"
   "Oh! I can't."
   "Just joking."
   "I guess, this is it then? Goodbye," she said.
   "Girlfriends are mostly bimbos. I'd rather have
one true friend, and that would be you."
   "You really are good, you know. Honest. I

wondered why I continued. Now I know why. It was your purity that attracted me."

"I know," he said. "But you know what, I also care about you, far too much."

After that day, the texting stopped. She repeatedly went to WhatsApp. But there were no new texts. She looked at herself in the mirror and the deep wrinkles mortified her, as did her wrinkly fingers, her sagging skin, the drooping lips; the ephemera reared its ugly head.

A new text arrived. "Hello, how're you?"

"I'm good, and you?"

Then the woman sat back and thought about his parents. What would they say? Yet, she couldn't bring herself to end this relationship, either. There was a picture on his profile. But who knew if this was his real face?

Another message. "I feel like talking to you all day."

"Oh, no, you must go to work, not waste time on me."

She thought she needed to change her role from a potential lover to a mentor, to guide the young man who was so obviously smitten by her.

"Yes, yes, I know. You're still the most beautiful woman. You get more and more beautiful with age."

"But I can never be yours."

"I love, I love your beautiful mind."

"You must go to college."

"I love you."

"As a friend?"

Communications stopped.

The End

That Rain, When the Peacock Danced

Days of the month had slipped. This monsoon morning, a wedding preparation was well underway in The House of Chowdhury. Mila Chowdhury, the granddaughter of Mr and Mrs Chowdhury, was to be betrothed to her boyfriend of three years, Irfaan Khan this evening.

For the wedding, Mr Chowdhury had engaged decorators. They provided the essentials, such as chairs, tables, tarp, fairy lights, and a recorder/speakers. Today, the decorators came early, to put the finishing touches. They brought in multi-coloured fairy lights and soft coverings, linen for chairs and tables, and streamers. The chairs and the tables had already been laid earlier in the week.

The wires of the fairy lights lay in a braided jumble all over the grounds. While some men untied the jumble, others used a ladder to haul the wires to hang the lights across the entrance gate and over the big house. The House of Chowdhury, would stand in the backdrop of a massive illumination in the evening. A wooden gate was temporarily erected in front of the fixed gated entrance. The double gates were framed within multi-coloured lights. This artificial gate too was wrapped, crisscrossed, and scissored in rainbow-coloured cotton streamers.

A tarpaulin was hoisted to cover the entire front yard over the wooden chairs. The chairs were placed next to each other. In the orchard, makeshift clay stove were carved out. The wedding feast was to be cooked on them. The menu was Biriyani, Mutton Kabab, and Murag Musallam and a yoghurt drink called the Lassi. A chef was appointed along with a retinue of assistants; a DJ, to play continuous recorded songs, befitting to the occasion.

The rain dripped through the cracks and crevices, of the tarp all day long. Wet chairs sat on wet grounds. There was nothing much anyone could do to keep the rain away. Except, perhaps hire more people to keep the chairs plastic-covered, then uncover just before the guests arrived. Or hire more expensive tarp. But the bride, Mila, knew how difficult it was for her mother, Nazmun, to fight funds out of her father. Had it not been for her uncles, Sheri and Ashik, who chipped in and supported this wedding, it would not have come even this far. The bride's aunts, Uncle Ashik's wife Prema, and Uncle Sheri's wife Lutfun, went out shopping each Sunday morning with her mother Nazmun Banu for two entire weeks. They bought wedding sarees, and gold jewellery. The jewellery was studded with semi-precious stones of red ruby, green emerald, and white sapphire of cloudy hue. The old family jeweller was summoned, who was only too eager to help. He had found the best craftsmen in town; the family pride must be held up.

Mila's father, Dr Ekram Chowdhury, had a flourishing medical practice in town. The only time he had appeared, was on the morning of the wedding day. Mila had come out of the bath and was getting dressed in an everyday cotton saree, to go to the hairdresser, just when she saw him enter, through her bedroom's window. He had sauntered through the outer gate. Mila rushed out of her room to greet him. Instead, she saw her grandmother sitting at the dining table; Mila calmed down, and sat next to her, waiting for him. In a moment, Ekram breezed in through the door, humming a little tune. The sky was overcast as usual. Yet again, another monsoon pouring began.

"Where are you these days?" Mrs Chowdhury asked. "Am I glad to see you, today?"

"Sorry, amma. I'm sorry to disappoint you."

"Regardless, and thank God for your brothers, this wedding would have been a disaster."

221

"My brothers have saved yet another day, then?" he asked.

"Again, as usual," Mila chimed in.

"Anyway, I'm here now and that makes a difference, no?" he said.

"Should it?" A shrill voice wavered through the doorway. Nazmun and Prema walked in with jewellery boxes and sarees.

"Typical! How typical of you to disappear like this. Days on end you were gone. Not involved in anything. Then you appear suddenly, like a rare comet. Are you the father or what? A guest, come by to sneak a peek?"

"Mum, please," Mila said. "Not today."

"No? What is he going to do? Walk out? Has he even paid a dime?" Nazmun Banu spat out.

"How much? How much do you need? Here, take it. There's all the money, right here."

He pushed a large A4 size brown envelope before them on the table.

"Huh? Stuff you."

Nazmun Banu turned on her heels and walked away.

"Here, amma, you keep the money, then."

He insisted that his mother take the envelope. In fact, he forced it into her hand. Mrs Chowdhury took it. But she scowled deeply. She looked at Mila and gave it to her. Mila's father stood up and walked towards the orchard where her uncles were seated with a large pot of chai under the tarp. As soon as he appeared, they greeted him and asked him to sit down, but soon had to run inside because of the rain.

The day advanced. Lutfun asked a pageboy to call a rickshaw. She was taking Mila to the hairdresser. The boy did as he was told. The vehicle arrived, and waited for them

222

outside the decorative gates. Lutfun and Mila came out of the house and walked through the front yard's turmoil, somehow to the vehicle. They embarked. The afternoon was quiet and grey. The rickshaw puller cycled slowly down the narrow alley and headed off for the salon down by the mosque square. Mila put her head on Lutfun's shoulder. Lutfun crooked it into her elbow, caressing it with her idle palm.

"Everything will be fine," Lutfun said, smoothly. "I'm going to get my hair done too. I'm doing a French Knot."

"Yeah, you'll look really good. What're you wearing?" Mila asked.

"Glad that you sound a little upbeat now. It's your wedding for God's sake. Cheer up, girl! Yes, I'll wear my pink Kathan with my old diamonds. But we did discuss it the other day, remember?"

"Oh, yeah. I remember now."

The slow-paced rickshaw reached the salon. The puller's hard-pressed hand brakes stopped the vehicle. They disembarked awkwardly from its caddy seat and stepped onto a sodden path. Mila followed Lutfun, tiptoeing through a rainwater puddle into a shop that had Salon written large on a billboard down the parapet. The outer wall looked mouldy. It had peeled-off paint in various places, through which a set of horizontal bare bricks grinned like a Cheshire cat. The parlour was upstairs. After climbing two flights, Lutfun and Mila entered a crowded parlour. There was only one empty, corner chair left. Lutfun egged Mila to take it, as Mila did the same to Lutfun. She pushed Mila right up to the chair and sat her down.

While Lutfun stood by Mila, they watched the other young brides-to-be, sitting in a row before their respective mirrors; still little dolls in the process of a full bridal makeover. Mila's turn came as soon as one finished. She sat down before a mirror; her reflection was clear. Lutfun was next when another chair became available. Mila and Lutfun sat close by, but they didn't speak much during the session. Only occasionally, they made eye contact through the mirror. Mila sat straight-faced like a dummy. She looked at her cobweb mass of long hair arranged by the expert hands of the hairdresser. It took a while to get it right. Lutfun's French Knot was done before Mila had finished. She waited, as the dresser fine-tuned Mila's bridal bun. Pleased, Lutfun walked over and paid at the counter by the entrance. As soon as Mila finished, both left through the nearby front door.

The rain had not abated. They stood under the shop's roof parapet wall, looking for a rickshaw to take them home. One came along while they waited there. They hailed it and dashed in the blinding rain in its direction, pulling the saree's fallen drape as half a veil, to cover the hair arrangements. Getting up on its slippery footboard was challenging; once they stepped on, they dropped themselves on the seat immediately, with a sigh, and rushed to pull the collapsible hood over their heads. The rickshaw puller gave them a long plastic sheet to cover them. They pulled it up to the chin, trying to hold it tightly about them, which would not stay still anyway, in these blustery winds.

"I hope you won't get a chill today," Lutfun said.

"I hope not. I think I'll be fine," Mila answered.

After a pause, Mila asked, "Are you happy, Aunty Lutfun?"

Lutfun inclined her head towards her, and said, "Yes, of course, I'm happy, dear. Do you not see it?"

"I do, but who knows what's going on deep down inside your heart?" Mila asked, then regretted it. "Never mind. You don't need to answer that."

"No, I will, since you asked. Happiness is elusive.

224

Money can't always make people happy. Material objects can't either. Even if they did, it would be short-lived. Happiness is something else. It's much more complex. It's almost like a shooting star which we see, but we cannot really house it."

"I don't understand. When you feel happy that usually means you have housed the emotion in your heart. Although, I do agree, material objects cannot always make one happy. Those who are happy, they're happy regardless. If one really searched for it, they could find it among slum-dwellers, even."

"Yes, I meant, it's not a steady emotion. One cannot be consistently happy. It can pass, but can also come back, you know what I mean? An interplay, of sorrow and happiness, if you like."

"Yes, like the flashing lights of a shooting star in the night's sky. They cannot be pinned down."

They were quiet after that. The rickshaw soon stopped at the entrance of The House of Chowdhury. The puller got off his seat in the front and stood on a puddle. He removed the plastic sheet with one hand and took the fare in the other. Lutfun had opened her purse, she had been carrying within her palm all this while and placed the money on his open palm. Mila sprang out of the vehicle from her side; Lutfun followed. They ran indoors in the bucketing rain. They pulled the anchals by the corners, over their heads in veils, to protect the expensive buns until they were in.

"Now, go to your room and get some rest, dear, I'll bring you lunch in a bit."

Having said so, Lutfun walked towards her mother-in-law, Mrs Chowdhury's room, and disappeared in the passageway. Mila entered her bedroom through the open door. It was empty. Through the windows she saw her mother, her aunts and uncles outside under the umbrella of a neem tree, giving instructions to the decorators and supervising the wedding dinner. Just this once, her father was also with them, jostled in the front yard.

Her eyes fell on a rotund, mosaic table by the window in her room. It stood on curved antique legs by an easy chair, set at an angle. A radio sat on the table. She reached out for the radio and peered through the long, horizontal window grills. A dense rain splattered over trembling leaves outside. She picked up the radio, and tuned it to Dhaka station, popular movie songs; Abdul Jabbar singing, *Ore neel doriya*, from the movie *Sareng Bou*. She spaced out for a while into the dazzling rain; it charmed her. She turned around with the radio in her hand and walked towards her bed. She climbed it and sat on its edge.

Oddly enough, she thought of her old fling. He had become a relic by now, who remotely reminded her of a lost relationship. Rahim Ali had married Papri. Were they happy? Oh! Stop! Stop it! She screamed in her head. Not now, not ever. She could still hear her relatives. Their faint air-borne waves of laughter sounded like a tinkle off a Morano glass. She lay down on one side of the bed, listening to the song. An ephemera. How fragile was this existence? Her journey had only just begun, and a sense of an ending was already closing in. This house, her relatives, where they would all be in fifty years' time? Where would she be on this bumpy road to posterity? Her eyes were closed. She opened them and saw that Lutfun had entered with a meal. She stood before her, smiling. She coughed lightly to awaken her from a reverie.

"Oh! It's you?" Mila said, opening her eyes.

"I hope you haven't ruined your hair," Lutfun said. "No, it's okay, I think. Here take this and eat up. You'll need a lot of energy today."

"I don't think I have much appetite."

"Eat just a little, still," Lutfun insisted.

Mila took the plate and ate a few mouthfuls of rice and fried fish. Then she gave the plate back to her.

"Are you okay? What's bothering you, if I may ask?" Lutfun asked, touching her forehead.

"No, it's just, just that I'm suddenly all philosophical today, thinking of life and death and the journey itself."

"Oh! This is no time to have such profound thoughts, is it?" Lutfun said.

"I know, I know," Mila said.

"Don't think of these things. Where is your trousseau, now?"

Lutfun looked under the bed and pulled out a heavy trunk. She opened it and found a few sarees, bed linens, and blankets. She took them out and glanced over them. Decidedly, more clothes needed to be trunked. Rising up, Lutfun zipped out of the room into her own and opened her wardrobe to find some new sarees sitting in their virgin folds. She pulled out the bunch and retraced her steps to Mila's room.

Mila looked at her surprised. "But these are all yours."

"So? They're yours now. What would your in-laws think if they knew you have a near-empty trousseau?"

"Who cares?" Mila pounced. "I don't want your sarees, Aunty Lutfun."

"Don't worry, you can buy me heaps later," she said, smiling, as she dropped them in the trunk and ironed the creases with her palm, levelling the clothes neatly. She closed the metal lid with both hands.

"Are you sure?" Mila asked.

"A hundred percent."

Lutfun reached for the lunch plate. As she exited, she crossed her path with Mila's other aunt, Prema on the threshold. Prema entered with a cosmetic case. She was doing the bridal makeup. She'd left the case on Mila's bed and sped out of the room, saying that she'd forgotten something. She closed the bedroom door behind her and caught up with Lutfun in the passage.

Mila reached for the radio. She turned it off. She climbed down her bed and sat on an easy chair, by the window. She felt trepidation. An ink doused, monsoon afternoon; viewing it through the window, she couldn't tell if it was evening already because the sky had never cleared. She sat on the easy chair, absorbed, listening to the rain's sound. She heard a knock. The door opened and in came her friends, Shreya and Shuvo with their mother, Shri Devi Mukherjee. Mila called her mashima. Shri Devi came straight up and pulled her out of the easy chair. She gave Mila a tight hug and a deep kiss on her smooth forehead.

"Why do you look so grim, dear?" she asked.

Mila smiled and stood aside. She offered her the chair. Shuvo and Shreya smiled back at her, who had by now settled themselves cosily on the edge of the bed. Mila walked across and sat alongside them, facing Shri Devi. Their feet dangled off the cold floor. Mila's bed was a highly fashionable antique with an ornate headrest, back in the day.

"How's everything coming along?" asked Shri Devi.

"So far so good, I guess. But the rain could spoil it," Mila said.

"You know what? There's a saying that wedding rains are not a harbinger of bad luck. On the contrary, they bring peace into the house."

"I hope so," Mila mumbled, thinking of her rather angst-ridden childhood with her parents. Had it not been for her grandparents, uncles, and aunts, a street life was a near possibility. Where would her mother and she be today, if kicked-out? Shreya looked at her metal trousseau peeking under the bed.

228

"Are you taking that with you?" she asked.

"Yes, that's my bridal trousseau," Mila said. "It has some sarees and bed linen."

"Well, it's all in the stars, I believe," Shuvo began, suddenly.

"What do you mean? Don't you start already?" Shreya snapped.

"Start? What have I said? All I wanted to say is this, that we were born from elements of the stars which, when showered upon us, made us. Humans are borne out of stars. They give us the essential building blocks, but in unique sort of ways, not make clones out of us, but like the many Rubik's Cube patterns. Stars govern us. They give us our individual characteristics. Our destinies are made in Heaven, including marriages."

"How astonishing! I wonder which star made you. Must be something totally out of our orbit. However, I do know which star governs you for talking nonsense! Saturn!"

"Hmm! You're insanely critical," Shuvo reflected, calmly.

They all laughed. Mila laughed the most. Shuvo sure brightened up this dull day for her.

The evening had now well and truly set in. The ceremony would start soon. Prema and Lutfun flitted in and out of the room. Cars' incessant honking at the entrance had begun. Chatter rose and became louder; peals of laughter and greetings enlivened the house, awakening it from a hundred years of hibernation, as it were. Shri Devi rose from the easy chair and excused herself, saying that she must meet with Mila's mother and grandmother. She'd stepped out just when Prema also returned, gasping, nearly colliding with Shri Devi at the door. She entered the room and stood before Mila and the company under the ceiling fan. She gauged the situation for a few seconds and asked

229

Mila to move to the middle of the bed. In the meantime, more people poured in, causing a jam almost in the doorway. Decked in expensive sarees and glittering jewellery, her friends entered, crowding into the room. Some sat around Mila, on the bed. Prema walked up to bolt the doors. It was now time to begin the bridal make-up.

Prema was a natural. She knew exactly what to do. She started with a facial foundation, then rubbed some of it down her neck and then to her arms and forearms. Her kit was fully equipped and she, a skilful makeup artist, applied the rouge, the powder, lipsticks diligently – a detailed makeup was underway, the eye makeup was performed with great precision, with eyeliner, eyeshade, and long brushes of mascara strokes. Not until each nail was painted and perfected painstakingly with nail polish, did Prema stop. The bed was strewn with stained cotton buds, ripped clothes, little pieces of chucks to wipe off the extra colours. By the time Prema had finished, Mila had transformed into this beauty. All that was left now was to put her bridal attire on.

A ruckus outside alerted Prema. Someone just screamed that the groom's party had arrived. Mila's friends who were seated calmly over the make-up session rose with sudden alacrity. They rushed towards the door to greet the groom; a perfumed trail of sweetness lingered in the air, as they left. Mila felt her heartbeat increase; it was stifling hot on this muggy evening. The ceiling fan was in full swing, but the steaminess wouldn't dissipate.

Shouts and cheers at the gate, the groom's party had been held up here by a queue of pretty girls. They'd barred them from entering unless he paid a certain amount of toll.

"How much?" the groom's party shouted.

"Not less than a thousand rupees," one of Mila's cousins screamed back.

"Wow! That's too much."

"No, it isn't. Our sister doesn't come cheap."

"How about five hundred?" a friend negotiated on behalf of the groom.

"No. Eight hundred," the girls cried.

"Deal."

A clear win for the girls; the deal closed after about fifteen minutes of haggling. They let them in. Some of the groom's friends winked at them, too; eligible bachelors tried to gate crash, pushing through the young beauties. The girls led the groom and his friends to the bridal podium.

The podium, built out of wide, wooden floor plank, was decorated with the same multi-coloured streamers as the outer gates were. It had a supporting back wall and was covered with a thick Persian rug. Rolled bolsters of glittery velvet were thrown over the rug as soft cushioning. Irfaan Khan, the groom, climbed up with his friends and sat on the rugged plank. He looked handsome in his new white sequined Sherwani suit and plain russet turban. Irfaan sat in the middle of the podium, flanked by his friends. They leaned against the bolsters like a king with his knights in a king's court. He cracked jokes and laughed with friends tonight. One night's king; Mila, his queen would soon be by his side.

"There's still time to escape, before signing on the dotted line," a friend joked. They laughed and they knew that this was it. Irfaan's bachelor days were over.

Prema thickened the bride's lashes with an extra layer of mascara, as she polished the make-up before finishing it. The room had quietened because the girls had gone to greet the groom's party. She put her index finger under Mila's chin to lift her face to a small mirror that she held in front of her. Mila looked into the mirror. She sure looked pretty. It was time to put on the wedding saree. Prema and Mila both climbed down the bed.

Prema asked Mila to wear the matching blouse and the petticoat. Mila obeyed. The saree was expensive. It was a red sequined Kathan, heavy with gold-threaded gems. In her slim fitted blouse and the petticoat, Mila stood in the middle of the room. Prema took the saree and unfolded the nine-metre drape to wrap around Mila. Not a rushed job, slowly, and artfully making sure that every single pleat of the unstitched drape fell evenly in place. She secured the pleats midway down the fall with a safety pin which had pierced through a small piece of paper to protect the fabric. The pleats had fallen uniformly at Mila's feet. Prema drew the rest of the drape to wrap it around her tender, curved waist and threw it over her full breasts. She pleated it again over the left shoulder and pinned the pleats through the blouse on that shoulder. A trail dangled elegantly at the hip.

Prema stepped back and assessed Mila. She thought the saree looked tight and tucked around Mila's taut body. Prema now turned her attention to jewellery. They were in boxes inside a tall, ornate Almirah in one corner of the room. She opened the Almirah with a key, kept in the drawer of the mosaic table by the window. She pulled a few crisp, new boxes out of a hidden safe in the Almirah. A diamond necklace and several other semi-precious gilded necklaces studded in stone. She helped Mila wear them one after another. They adorned her long, unwrinkled neck. Prema took Chanel No.9 out of her make-up box and sprayed some, lightly, over Mila's sari. Prema thought, Mila looked delicate like a fawn.

"How do you feel?" Prema asked.

"Nervous."

"You'll be fine. Before going to bed, take off your jewellery and put them in the box. If he'll give you the time, that is."

Prema smiled slyly, giving her a slight nudge.

Mila nodded and lowered her eyes with a slight cunning smile on her painted lips.

"It will hurt the first time," Aunt Prema continued, oblivious that her niece wasn't little anymore, and that she was a doctor. That's what elders did, Mila thought. Love had blinded them in a way that they didn't see the obvious. That was how her family was. Love was paramount over hardships. Whatever had happened in their lives, nothing came between relationships. Credit be to Mr and Mrs Chowdhury for raising such a devoted family, where love burst at the seams; the same love to blanket distant relatives too, as far back as it could go, in a close-knit family.

The door burst open. The girls came giggling in, pushing through the doorway. Mila, a demure bride, sat in the easy chair under the full speed of a ceiling fan. Prema left her to the girls. Their oos and aahs put a delicate smile on Mila's lips. The room had now begun to reek of light sweat, mingled with perfume. In a bit, there was a knock on the door, the Moulavi seeking permission to come inside. He had brought with him two elders, her two uncles, Sheri and Ashik, as witnesses, to ask for Mila's permission to this wedding. If she said no, then the groom's party must depart without a marriage.

He recited, while her uncles gave a patient hearing.

"Mila Chowdhury, do you of your own accord take Irfaan Khan to be your wedded husband?"

Mila was silent the first time. This silence, however, wasn't construed as anything foreboding; it was uncivil and too forward to reply straight away. She said "yes", "yes" and "yes" to the questions asked three times but paused a few seconds between each. A contract was now handed to her with a pen. She held it tightly between her sweaty fingers, while her uncles held the contract paper on her lap to keep it steady. She signed. The most important moment

233

of her life, her maiden life given away; this free life she'd had until now was over. An ugly cramp slowly rose in her lower belly. The Moulavi and her uncles departed.

The same happened outside on the podium too. Irfaan Khan signed the same contract. The wedding was now properly sealed and declared official. The guests held their hands up, like half-opened Pistachio shells, to pray. When prayers finished, they vocalised, an Ameen together in sombre and a befitting manner.

The pageboys served the food. They spread it out on dining tables, in the makeshift dining area, not far from the guests, where they had been seated on the semi wet chairs, all this time and praying before the bridal podium. Those boys also poured Lassi in each glass. However, the Lassi drink had turned into cocktail mix of leaking rain water.; sloppy management as no one oversaw that the Lassi jugs were uncovered under a thick tarp tear over the table. A special banquet was prepared for the groom and his friends. The groom's table was served with several whole chickens, roasted in almond and ghee; whole smoked Hilsa fish on silver platters.

The formalities out of the way, Nazmun Banu could relax. She was still worried about the Lassi being too watery from rain water, but the constant presence of her two brothers-in-law by her side gave her some courage. They made sure that the food did not fall short in supply. The guests enjoyed the meal. In the end, they were rather entertained by the Lassi fiasco, rather than offended.

Prema and Lutfun each ate fast. They hurried back to Mila's bedroom. Mila sat, looking sedated in a queen's attire and full jewellery. Her silken veil trembled under the ceiling fan. It was time. She had to be moved to the bridal podium outside. The guests had by now sat down and settled in their chairs after dinner. The rain had abated. The

234

groom reverted to the dais with his friends, enjoying an occasional witty joke; it sometimes fell short of wit, but they elicited a hiccup of laughter anyway.

Lutfun and Prema stood on both sides of the bride. They held her arms and slowly walked her out of the door, down the passageway towards the podium. Her shaded eyes were downcast inside her transparent sequin veil. She had the most surrealistic feeling of being semi-suspended. Off the floor through the air, in her aunt's good hands, she felt she didn't know her own house. Where she was born and raised these last twenty-five years, running along this passageway. The yard had transformed too. The house looked unrecognisable through this prism of a heavy makeover. Just as the bride was all dolled up herself.

There she was. Prema lifted her saree a little bit at her feet. She climbed the two low steps and sat down gently next to the groom. Mila blinked. The groom too exuded unfamiliar newness. He smelled fresh, perfumed, and bathed. She could smell his understated cologne, as he could smell hers. But they hadn't looked at each other even once.

By now other people, Mila's friends, her cousins had all clambered the small podium. They kneeled behind the bridal couple to watch the ritual. A flimsy, transparent red scarf was laid over the couple's heads. An assortment of two traditional sweets, Firni, and Zarda, were placed in small silver-spooned bowls on a tray before the wedded couple. Lutfun performed the ritual. She took Mila's hand and planted a dollop of rice pudding, or the Firni, in the middle of her palm. She stretched Mila's hand across towards the groom's mouth. He swiped it with the tongue. The groom now returned the courtesy to Mila, whom Prema assisted.

Irfaan stole a sly look at Mila. He saw her downcast

235

eyes covered in shaded layers. A careless lip touch on Irfaan's soiled palm marked a red lipstick, as Mila licked her share of sweets, off his palm. This faded red bore testament of a secret kiss in full public view; in the moment, he wished the stain would never erase.

Mila's jovial friends and cousins noted this and found an excuse to be naughty. Prema unveiled Mila's face and lifted it by the chin for everyone to see the new bride. Another long mirror was placed before the newlyweds for their private eyes only. Irfaan gazed at her, grinning unabashedly through the mirror.

His sisters-in-law chirped behind him, "What did you see? Tell us, tell us."

He answered gleefully, "A full moon."

Then there was more joyous clamour. Mila lowered her head further, but Irfaan noticed a coy smile.

After a couple of hours, it was nearly over. The last ritual was the exchange of the garlands. The couple now stood upon the podium, as the guests did on the grounds. Irfaan couldn't resist anymore. He reached out for Mila's hand from under her silk veil and pressed it. Mila didn't press it back. Something went awry within her. This new life, in a new house, all this experience, leaving The House of Chowdhury, her mother, Lutfun and Prema, Grandma, and her uncles, the orchard, her bedroom, even the window, the roof garden beckoned her. Everything beckoned her, memories, one too many. Where she grew up, her entire life suddenly stopped breathing. She was having difficulty breathing. Oh! Where was her breath, now? She should respond to those signals by pressing Irfaan's hand back or deal with his wrath later. Well, that was another story.

Irfaan continued to signal. Her hands clasped in his, they walked towards the car. Her eyes were downcast; the grip of this strangeness numbed her. Then suddenly, two strong arms held her. They slammed her against a man's chest. No less, but her own father. He began to cry. She cried; her father cried; a drop from pure delight to pure grief. There they were, father and daughter united in separation. She clung to him, like a hanging bat on a wire. She was leaving them now to become someone's wife, a new becoming, a newness tore her in the gut, as though, as of this moment her past had died.

Prema came forward and extricated Mila from her father. She held her from behind and walked her towards the bridal car. Mila sniffled and didn't stop to see the expensive floral decoration over the car. A chauffeur opened the door of the passenger seat in the back of the car. Mrs Khan, her new mother-in-law, entered first, followed by Mila and then Irfaan. Irfaan's father took the front seat next to the drive. The car drove slowly through a milling crowd; a peacock danced in the rain.

Pizzazz

Blood oranges were endowed with a certain pigmentation. I called it the fruit's pizzazz, because of its lustre, which defined it and gave it the distinctive characteristics of dark flesh. I wanted it to grow in my mother's orchard, but the gardener said it couldn't, because of the climate. If the blood orange didn't flourish in this soil, then neither did many things in this culture. All these fossilised old customs and habits.

One afternoon, I sat on the balcony of my mother's house. A brilliant midday sun shone yet another monsoon day. I took a sip of lemonade my mother had made with freshly-squeezed lemons. Lemons, which grew in our orchard. I was recovering at her place, from an illness. Lemons and limes were not the only citrus fruits that grew in this orchard – oranges too. Except, the blood orange.

The monsoon winds whipped up my spirits. The orchard glowed, revitalised as the winds touched it. The wet fern unfurled along the mossy edges on the orchard's brick fence. Nature's drama ensued. These were months of recapitulations. They always were. Recapping past events that happened not only in my life but also in the lives of the others. A maid once worked in our house some years ago. I found myself thinking about her. Her loyalty had far surpassed any other who worked for us then. Her name was Lily. She was our loving Lily of the Valley. She possessed an exceptional quality of gritty honesty.

I was in high school then. One evening, my friend had come for a sleepover. We decided to order a meal with mother's permission. It was a native delicacy, namely Biryani. When the order arrived, Lily came up to my bedroom to hand it to us. I took it, and closed the door so hard that it banged. We sat down on my bed and didn't think of sharing it with anyone, not even with Lily. However, as we began to gorge on our first mouthful, there was a knock. The door burst open. Lily entered. Instinctively, we covered the food, guarding it with our palms. Really, we were such mean little creatures in those days. We were delinquents and she looked befuddled.

In all this confusion, she spoke out, "No, no. I didn't come here to snatch a share. I came to tell you that your Maa is calling you."

Saying so, she marched out. It was awful.

I looked at my friend. "We should've offered her a couple of spoons, huh?"

"I reckon. But although she's poor, she is not greedy. Mind you, we do tend to underestimate their human qualities because of who they are," my wise friend replied.

"Yes, I'm so ashamed. My God, you're right."

"Yes, we have. Walled them out. I wish we were more inclusive."

"We should have shared our food with her."

This incident had shaken me. It was both unforgivable and unforgettable. In a way, it compelled me to decipher these centurion customs that had prevailed upon us. Many years had passed since, but the 'invisible' still teetered on the edge of the elite-dom. Class segregation was acute. They were treated as outsiders, even plague-ridden, by some upper-class.

Our glasses, cups and saucers, plates, everything were separate. On no account did we eat from their plates or drink from their glasses, as they didn't from ours. Fancy eating off their plates! Seriously, if we were to visit them in their huts, they would lay out their best dinnerware to fan our egos.

No matter, whatever had happened to our maid, it had never crossed my mind even once to find out. Where was she all these years? Was she happy? Was she even living? Generally, wealth blinded many paymasters. Such sick employers had high expectations that peasants would work for them 24/7, from the day they were born until they died; employers treated them like some kind of a machine to run errands at a minimum wage without sick leave, or a respite, or even a decent meal of dry bread and half-rotten food. Some paymasters even withheld their meagre salaries or didn't pay them at all, in case they decided to leave or escape.

Again, if an employer turned out lecherous by any stroke of bad luck, then the fully fledged or unfledged would be used brutally, then held culpable for crimes they never committed. Night in and night out. Day in and day out. Their under-classed guardians, would be rendered powerless to handle such situations. On the first count, they would be bashful and want to suppress it. On a second, they would be incapable financially to move the matter through horrendously circuitous courts.

In order to punish them for the unwarranted crime of the innocuous souls, the only solution for an employer was to kick them out on the street and pin them up with the burden of shame, while the privileged victimiser got away. Once the victim was on the streets, they were exposed to the horrors of street life – begging, and prostitution, and more, totally unleashed upon them.

Such was the sad state of the 'Invisibles', without whom this sense of a fancy class hierarchy wouldn't even prevail. In a way, it was them, these innumerable minions, who justified the notion of the class, although unwittingly. It was always in the interest of the rich that the poor had to remain poor. This idea of classlessness, a figment of imagination, was never going to be stamped out, not today, not in a million years, not in this society or anywhere else. I made a

240

mental note of the great Hollywood movie *Sabrina*, which could be construed on so many levels.

Enough said. I ventured to learn more about our Lily. Not out of any moral obligation or to pioneer a cause, such as the eradication of a stultifying class system, but out of genuine interest. I took my glass of lemonade and stepped out into the orchard. The citrus-infused breeze titillated my nostrils. Had there been a blood orange tree, that extra pizzazz would have flavoured the air today. The orchard lacked the potency of such vibrant glamour of its pigmentation.

Down the hollyhock path and fuchsia-strewn deep velvet and crimson, I met the gardener. He sat pruning under a tree. When he saw me, he greeted me with a smile. I smiled back. Then I went up to him and stood watching him weed and unearth the unwanted.

"Do you know where Lily is now?" I asked him.

He looked at me briefly and said, "Yes, madam. I do in fact."

"Where is she? Can you ask her to see me one day?"

He nodded. "Sure, I will. I'll call her today. I have her mobile number."

"She has a mobile phone?"

"Yes, she does. You'll see the transformation when she comes."

"Transformation?" I asked.

"Yes, I'll ask her to see you tomorrow."

"Okay. That would be really great."

I walked away feeling good that Lily had a mobile phone now. I heard the gardener speak on his mobile. Maybe, it was Lily. However, as I came around the bend of the verandah, I saw a woman standing with three children. Her mouth was red with betel juices. The woman saw me and came forward.

241

She greeted me. "Hello, madam. Do you remember me?"

She chewed the paan.

"Hmm, not really sure. I have been away for a long time now."

"I'm the gardener's wife, Jasmine." She curved her mouth to cup the paan juices, like open tulips held rainwater.

"Oh! Yes, of course. How are you?"

I didn't remember her.

"I'm very well. My husband just shouted out to me to come to say hello to you."

"That's nice. Please sit."

"That's okay, I'm good standing. These are my three kids."

I smiled at them. They hid behind their mother. I sat down on a nearby chair and waited for them to sit as well. There were plenty of garden chairs around. But they sat on the cold floor instead. While her children leaned against her and kept looking at me in awe, it was as though I were not human at all. To them, I probably looked that way. My mother came by in a bit and sat down in the next chair. The gardener, too, had walked up to us.

"I'm finished for the day," he said.

"Okay, you can go now. Here, take this. Buy them lollies."

My mother gesticulated at the kids, as she handed over the generous tip.

The gardener took the tip from the mistress of the house. He extended both his arms towards her with a gracious smile and gently pulled the money.

In the meantime, the wife stood up and said to me, "Okay, madam, you will be around for some time now, won't you?"

"Yes, I think so," I said with a smile.

"I hope I'll see you again."

"Yes, I hope so too," I said.

The gardener then looked at me.

"I've given Lily a call. She said she would come over tomorrow to see you," he said.

"Very good, then," I said.

The family sauntered out of our compound. The gardener's wife had a gaudy sari on. Her children looked healthy.

I inclined my head towards Mother. "How come they still sit on the floor?"

Mother laughed and said, "Old habits die hard."

"Some customs never change, in spite of affluence, isn't that right?" I asked.

"Customs and affluence are two different issues. Money cannot always change customs and social practices, as it cannot change subtle human mannerisms. Some mannerisms are innate."

"Surely education could help. No? Yes?"

"It could in some cases, but not a whole lot, not in one generation anyway. Maybe in many generations to come, if at all."

I pondered and looked forward to seeing Lily the next day. I even thought of giving her an old sari of mine and some money for her children, just as Mother did to the gardener's family. Mother and I sat quietly, gazing in the full monsoon afternoon, and inhaled the fresh fruity smells.

"Let me ask you something," Mother said after a pause. "Would you be happy marrying your son or daughter off to a class of the "Nouveau Riche?"

"Hmm, I haven't given it much thought, but what if they were good individuals? What then?" I asked.

"Exactly, what then? Are you prepared to make such allowances and adjustments? The mental wavelength, sophistication, family traditions, and so many trade-offs to be made. New money individuals may amass plenty of wealth, but they also cling to cultural crudity and embarrassing cringe like pith to the rind. However, I am not saying that aristocrats are entirely flawless without their own share of sins. Still…"

"Not entirely flawless? They're the ones with all the flaws, really, Mother."

Mother pursed her lips. An uncomfortable stillness descended on the balcony. I wanted this demarcation to go away. I wanted society to be built on equality, rather than this deplorable hierarchy. I thought there was a conspiracy in keeping the poor, poor. And I often had been told off on account of it. I had been branded as cynical, even inimical, distrusting the upper class, who in my view went to great lengths to keep the poor, always in a one-down situation to feel powerful themselves.

By now the sun had wafted. The late afternoon had doused into a feverish heaviness. My mother left me to my ponders. A maid came out to ask me if I required anything. I smiled at her and said, no. She began to tell me that I shouldn't be sitting here anymore. A storm was about to break out. This girl's loyalty was admirable. Like our rare Lily, her cares and caresses were beyond the limits of the salary range of peasant servitude. While her own family could be perishing in punishing squalor, under a leaky roof in some remote and unadorned corner of the earth, she was keeping me well rugged-up against this nature's incoming disaster. I had tears.

The next morning, I showered early in anticipation of Lily. Lily had told the gardener that she was on her way. Eagerly, I pulled a relatively new sari out of my suitcase which I thought I would give her. I also took some money out of my purse. The doorbell finally rang. Our maid opened it. I stood in the middle of the room to greet her. She stepped over the threshold.

Was this Lily? The gardener did warn me of a transformation. But this? Lily was nearly three times over-weight. She wore a burqa, and underneath an expensive, glittery silk sari. She had her three sons with her, and she carried a pricey fruit hamper of oranges, grapefruit, and apples – a gift for Mother. She walked across the room with a huge beam and came right up to me and gave me a terse hug. I realised that hugging was imported, and common among the elites, not a tradition per se, especially in the villages. But Lily was now upwardly mobile, and trying to learn it to ingrate into her culture. The hugging was terse; she needed more practice to make it natural.

"Oh my God, the moment I heard about you, I just felt I had to rush to see you," she declared.

"I'm so glad too that you could come, Lily. Please, have a seat."

I invited her to sit in one of our aged sofas. I sat her down next to me. Mother didn't mind. But maids scurried with a kitchen stool. She sat down with her legs splayed, leaning against the headrest, as though she had earned all this. As though she had earned an age-old title and a family lineage.

"How are you?" I asked.

"I'm really good," she said. "Sorry, I got held up in the traffic. Our driver is a novice. He still can't handle rush hour traffic."

"That's okay," I said. "What else?"

"My husband has a fish hatchery. He is doing very well. We have a huge house. My children go to a paying school. The chairman of the village is my husband's first cousin. We have a huge refrigerator and an exotic, modern stove. Say, do you have an iPhone? I'll send you a video of my house and the new stove."

Of course, I had an iPhone. But it wasn't the latest, flashy like the one she clutched in-between her two rugged hands. Neither did our old stove have a sheen. She said it all in an unbroken breath, and I swallowed it all in an uninterrupted gulp. It was unbelievable. It was laudable too that out of trillions of under-classed people, she was one of very few to break through the veneer of class convention. Lily, who had trembled at the sight of my father's formidable personality. Lily, who would retreat to the kitchen's darkest corner for comfort, had now come to tell me this. A long way away, this rare breed, this new air of confidence, here's a success story, a far cry from the shy Lily. The incidence of the Biryani crossed my mind inadvertently, to brush blush on my high cheek-bones.

Once she had told me everything, our conversation began to stall, awkward that there was nothing else to say. I told her that I had a sari for her and a tip for the kids.

She blurted out, "I don't take handouts. I'm well off."

Her bluntness shocked me. I must have looked like a real idiot. She smiled at me and stood up. She took her three sons, who had leant against her the whole half-hour we had been chatting.

"I'll see you before I leave. I must go into the kitchen for now. I want to catch up with tea gossip."

Ah, tea! An insensitive oversight, I should have offered her tea, like we normally do to our guests. However, she can't have forgotten her comfort zone of the "otherness" of similar mindsets, the social mingle and the familiar tinkles of cups and saucers, the unwritten laws of forbiddance to use the master's fine bone china.

Society had set boundaries which were difficult to break down. Complex transformations often didn't happen in many generations. All the crudity and the loudness couldn't be replaced by the finesses, regardless of the wealth. Mother's moot point, that one had to be high bred to acquire nuanced social skills, seemed to have prevailed in this instance. However, if her rags to riches was possible, so was this in time.

Homecoming

Quasu was growing up, fast. He was now five years of age and was able to enjoy the wedding. Nazmun Banu sat with their tea, at teatime in the orchard. Autumn leaves had covered much of it.

"My Quasu is special in so many ways," Prema declared.

"Of course he is," Lutfun answered.

"His teacher at school said that he is doing wonders with his studies. He's far ahead of the rest of the boys in his class."

"That's lovely. We all want the best for him."

Nazmun Banu yawned and looked around the orchard.

"Your brother Ashik said, we may now have enough money to send Quasu to an expensive English medium school. Our business is doing really well," Prema said.

"That's awesome news. But I hope you won't move out. The house feels a bit empty already, without Mila."

"Yes, how time flies. Mila was born just the other day. And now? It will be the same for Quasu too. He will grow up like slithering sands through our fingers," Lutfun said.

Lutfun didn't have any children. But she didn't miss much either with Quasu being around. Little Quasu kept her busy.

"What else does Quasu's teacher tell you?" Nazmun Banu asked.

"Oh, are you kidding me, sister?" Prema asked.

These were good at heart, happy go lucky, slightly amoral people. But the reason for rivalry was unimaginably mundane. While Prema could marry Ashik by divorcing her ex-husband, Nazmun Banu couldn't divorce. She couldn't even if she wanted to, because in the eyes of her in-laws, she was the righteous wife, holy and pure. She remained shackled to the same place.

When Prema paused to rest from bragging about Quasu,

which she had been doing often to almost everyone's disapproval, Luftun chimed in, "Tea anyone?"

"No, no, Quasu would be home soon. I must get his juice ready," Prema said.

She rose from her chair to go indoors, while Lutfun and Nazmun waited around and looked at each other.

"Oh! She just wouldn't stop now, would she?" said Nazmun. "Every time we are together, must she brag about how great Quasu is? My Quasu, my Quasu is the best, he is this and that and what have we? As though we don't know what Quasu is. As though we don't love him enough."

"That's just her. Yes, I know it can be irritating. But you know what?" Lutfun asked.

"What?"

"I have seen her other children from her ex coming around here and asking the maids if they could see her."

"Really? Gosh! What would our amma say?"

"Mother-in-law knows. She looks the other way," Lutfun said.

"What a mess! Really! Say, how do you know?" Nazmun asked.

"One day, amma and I were sitting together under the neem tree. She saw them enter through the main gate and asked the gateman. She didn't ask them to come inside or anything but she overheard them asking about their mother."

"Hmm, how sad. I really feel sorry for those kids."

Nazmun looked away at the orchard aimlessly and sighed. Lutfun was quiet too. After some time, she rose from her chair and ambled through the autumn orchard. She looked at the plantain tree and the ripe mangoes. A bunch of mangoes hung over her. She reached out for one. She twisted it clockwise and anticlockwise before she pulled it off. She tossed the mango up and down in the air a few times, then as the sun downed leaving red streaks in the autumn sky, she returned to where Nazmun had been sitting downcast, amongst the circle of chairs.

"Should we go in, now?" Lutfun asked.

Nazmun looked up at Lutfun and said, "Mila didn't call today, did she?"

"Not that I know. Why?"

"I wonder how she is in that new place with her in-laws."

"She will be back tomorrow after the Walima," Lutfun said.

"Yes, of course. She didn't mention a honeymoon yet," Nazmun said.

"They only wedded yesterday."

"Yes."

"Have you decided what you are going to wear for the Walima?" Nazmun asked.

"Yes, my pink Kanjivaram with the pearl and ruby necklace. What about you?"

"I'll wear my white Kathan silk, with the diamonds."

Nazmun rose and stood abreast to Lutfun, as they walked towards the balcony to enter the house. The balustrade of the balcony was covered in green overhanging vines, trees, money plants, and rhododendron fell like a delicate curtain. Lutfun decided that they needed some trimming. As they had entered the room, they saw Mrs Chowdhury sitting quietly by the window. Her walking stick was with her.

They didn't know where Prema had disappeared with Quasu. But the telephone suddenly rang in the hallway, breaking this cosmic silence of dusk.

"Oh! Who could that be?" Nazmun hissed.

But before they could reach the phone, Prema had already come out of her bedroom and had picked it up.

"Hello," she answered, organising her sari over her shoulder.

"Hello, this is Mila. Is that you Choton?"

"Yes, beta it's me. How are you?"

"We're well. Sorry, I couldn't call you earlier today. We had to go to a feast given in our honour, the newlyweds."

"That's great. Enjoy every bit, Maa. How are your in-laws, Mr and Mrs Khan?"

"They're well. And so is Irfaan. Anything new there?" Mila asked.

"No, not particularly. The house feels empty, now that you have gone. The decorations are still there. Some have been taken down. The yard is a mess at the moment with wires everywhere."

"It's a lot of work. Yeah?"

"Yes, it is. Quasu misses you a lot, love. But he's really doing well in class. He's at the top of the world right now."

Lutfun and Nazmun overheard this conversation from the other room. Luftun suppressed a giggle, while Nazmun blurted out rolling her eyes, "Here we go again."

"Shh, keep your voice down, she'll hear us," Lutfun said.

Nazmun continued to look at Prema until she finished her conversation and the receiver was handed to her. Prema signalled them to come forward. First, Nazmun then Lutfun. The conversation went well over an hour. They talked about girly stuff, about the in-laws, and parties, and the honeymoon. They were planning to go on a honeymoon soon. They were still undecided whether it would be Cox's Bazaar or Rangamati. Then Mila let Lutfun in on a secret about the wedding night. Lutfun giggled and hid her face from the gazing Prema and Nazmun, so they wouldn't hear. They moved away.

251

"And then what happened?" Lutfun asked.

"He took me in his arms first. I lay there on his chest, listening to his heartbeat. He held me tight, then tighter, until we both had goosebumps all over us. He kissed me first on my forehead, nose, lips. And then..."

"And then? What? Tell me?" Lutfun asked.

"I'll tell you later after we come over."

"Yes, the Walima celebration is tomorrow. See you soon."

"See you tomorrow."

Mila hung up. It wasn't Lutfun's intention to smoke out what had happened on the wedding night, but Mila's spontaneity drew her into her own romance with her husband, Mila's uncle Sheri. Why would anyone be so inclined to find out about such intimacy? But they were. Lutfun was just as eager to listen as Mila was eager to tell. They would have to wait until the Walima.

The Walima celebrations, usually took place one or two days after the wedding ceremony. This ceremony was hosted by the groom's family, after which the bridal couple returned to the bride's father's house and stayed there for a couple of days, before they went back to the in-laws or to their own homes. However, Mila's case was different. They decided to go on a honeymoon straight from her father's house after the Walima.

The next day, Mila's mother and aunts at The House of Chowdhury were making preparations. There was much to be done. They had to decorate Mila's room. Loads of garlands were brought in. Lutfun and Prema took them into Mila's bedroom. Prema walked up first and towards the wooden shutters. She opened them and a flurry of dust flew everywhere. Autumnal sun filmed through the dust particles. Lutfun looked at the bed and decided to put a cover on. She walked up to the old Mahogany almirah and opened its ornate doors. Lutfun rummaged through the shelves. Accidentally, she opened the drawers and underneath tons of rubbish, she found some old pictures. They were mostly Mila's friends, but one friend Lutfun recognised. That was Rahim Ali, in his round spectacles.

She kept looking through and found some letters too. Rahim Ali had written Mila letters. Lutfun felt an urge to open them. She couldn't tell if they were in a relationship. Perhaps, it was unrequited and had remained like an undying ember of indeterminate direction. She opened one of many letters. Beautiful words which tried over and over to tie a bond and had cajoled her to come closer. Words which flowed like a river, rain and moon drops. Poetry, which expressed how they had sat in the rain. She, by his side. Her head lay on his chest. She held him tight and he held her until a raindrop fell on her lips. He held her chin and licked it off her luscious lips. Romance was born. He carried her indoors. A flash of lightning clapped; a storm brewed. The words were magical and sounded perfectly romantic in poetry.

"Hey, what're you doing there? Have you found some bedclothes?"

Prema's shrill, agitated voice brought Lutfun back to the present. She closed the drawer in a hurry and pulled out new bedclothes, neatly packed in a wrapper on one of the shelves. Nazmun Banu may have bought them some time ago and stuffed them in here. She gave the wrapper to Prema. But Prema saw her absent-mindedness.

"Everything okay?" she asked, as she pulled the bedclothes out all at the same time.

"Yeah, sure," Lutfun said. "Nice bedclothes."

Prema held one end of it and Lutfun the other, and they made the new bed together. Lutfun held a lump in her

253

throat, wondering how far this relationship between Rahim Ali and Mila had progressed. Lutfun felt betrayed that Mila had not confided to her about these many letters. The bed was made in silence. They stretched the sheets out without a single crease and tucked them under the mattress. In the meantime, a maid named Shimul entered the room with a hand full of rose garlands. The three decorated the bed. Some of the heavy garlands were laid across the mosquito net stand. The rest of the roses were spread evenly on the bed. Prema, Lutfun, and Shimul stood back to look at the decoration. The roses looked brilliant in the autumn sun which streamed through the open shutters. A light fragrance pervaded the air, as a prelude to the romance which was going to ensue.

They left the room with the windows open to air it for a while. Unless there was a strong wind, there was no reason to close the shutters. Let the room bask in the glow of the mellow autumn sun. As the trio walked out of the room, they found Nazmun Banu in the corridor. She had a bottle of mango pickle jars in her hands. Nazmun looked at them and peeked into the room through the narrow opening of the doors, as Prema was closing it. Nazmun smiled. She liked what she saw. Then she saw Shimul, the maid, who was also standing with them. She handed the pickle jars to Shimul. Shimul took them, and walked to the stairs to go up to the roof. Out on the roof, she put them down on the cemented floor on its far end, in full sunlight. The light shone like diamond glitterings on the aluminium jar covers, as she lined them up on the roof's edge, next to each other. She squinted against the autumnal dazzle. She stopped to glance at the night-flowering jasmine hanging over the mossy walls. There were a few flower petals scattered on the roof. The stem of the shiuli, or rather jasmine, was a potential orange dye, which could be used on clothes. She sauntered towards the flowers dropped off their stems, and picked up two handfuls. She pouched them in her sari and ran downstairs. A gusty wind blew a strand of hair across her face.

The Walima was just two just hours away. The members of the House of Chowdhury were getting dressed. Shimul rushed from one room to the next, running errands for them. Lutfun needed a hairpin to be put in place on her French Knot. Prema needed Shimul's help with the sari. Shimul sat down on the floor and held the fall of the sari's pleats, as Prema neatly pleated at the top and secured them by tucking the edge in the petticoat around the waist. Nazmun Banu couldn't find her matching blouse and called out for Shimul. Shimul flitted to her room and pulled it from under the piles of saris and jewellery boxes on the bed. When they were ready and inside the respective four cars, comfortably seated, the cavalcade took off towards the Walima venue, the Malibagh ladies centre. Shimul saw them out and returned to her tiny room in the servant wing, at the back of the house. She let out a sigh.

Shimul realised that the servants were either napping now, or cooking up bridal meals in the kitchen at the advent of the newlyweds' homecoming, Mila and Erfaan's. She walked calmly up to her room under the staircase, pulled a dented aluminium pan sitting on a slat-wall in the corner of the room. The pan had the gatherings of shiuli flowers, which she had been picking and saving here for a while now. She sat down on the floor next to it and began to separate the saffron-coloured stem off the flower white petals. Once it was all done, she went to the kitchen. The stoves were off-limits at the moment. Pots and pans occupied the stoves' craters. Shimul leaned against the door and waited for a stove to be free. She wanted to boil some water to douse the shiuli stems to unlock the colours. She had a white sari, a gift from Mrs Chowdhury a while back.

She decided to colour the sari in the shiuly saffron. This was the only time she was free before the bridal party returned.

Shimul walked over to her room. Hardly any sunlight entered it. There was an opening through the roof from which a slight ray broke through. In the dim light, she looked in the direction of her belongings. They were her bedding and a battered trunk. She went over to the trunk, sat down, and opened it. The white sari was on top. She only had a couple of clothes, which she wore every day. She took the sari out of the trunk and rubbed over it. The fabric felt smooth and new. It was a hundred percent cotton. She dropped the lid to the trunk and exited the room. Back in the kitchen, her infusion of saffron was in a pan. She unfolded the sari and pressed it in the infusion. She moved the fabric around in the colour. She put a lid to the pan and left it by the door, allowing the colour to seep through the fabric for a few hours.

She walked through the dark yard feeling forlorn. She thought of her own wedding day. She thought about how it ended suddenly one day when her husband married for the second time. He had jilted her and hurt her. She had stopped living, breathing. One day, she decided to leave and come to Dhaka. She found employment in the House of Chowdhury through a friend's recommendation. She decided this was a life of freedom. People must marry because of social custom. But there was no other freedom than earning one's own keep. Trapped in a loveless, broken marriage was like a wheel locked to its spokes. Tied up ruthlessly. The wedding party would be back soon. Shimul found this moment to reflect on her life as a maid. It was still freedom; she was free.

This was a silent house, at the moment. Except for Mrs Chowdhury, everyone had left. It gave her an opportunity to ruminate. She sat by the window in an easy chair. Her eyes were closed. She was old as was this house, a repository of her values and traditions. Mila growing up and getting married. The dramas played out over spanning generations. Tea gatherings in the orchard; the songs, the laughter, the romance, and also the grief, had all tied up to give the house character. This was not just a house anymore; it breathed the history of the Chowdhury family. It was meaningful to her. The House of Chowdhury was an extension of her.

The Journey

Wise people believed that the journey was more important than the destination.

The wheel of fortune revolved in two directions. That it slipped backwards and sometimes moved forwards. After about three decades, old Brown's fate was about to change today. And it happened mysteriously enough. There was no logic as to why or how things occurred; they just did, without any rhyme or reason. Circumstance lent itself favourably, leading to his success on this fateful foggy winter of 1875.

A sound of fury distracted them; wind-lashed across. The horses swerved a bit off course, but Brown's young apprentice, Peter, handled it skilfully. Brown took his wallet out of his shirt pocket and looked at a picture, of a little girl in a polka dot frock. He put his wallet away. Peter had been here before. They were on their way to the Carpenter abode. After about an hour's ride, they could see their house. It sat on a vast land which was now in full view. Their cart drew closer to the house; the horse trotted gently down the gravel path and stopped under the porch, at a pull of Peter's reins. With a sigh, they looked at one another. Peter and Brown disembarked. Someone flung the front door open. Lydia and Jim Carpenter came out and greeted them, but not Rose. There was some trepidation.

"Hello, how's it going?" Jim beamed cordially.

"Good, pretty good."

Peter managed a nervous smile.

"And how about you, Brown? Doing okay, old man?"

"Yes, yes, not too bad."

Peter could smell butter from here. Some drifted across in the winds to tickle his nostrils amiably.

"Is Rose not here?" Brown asked.

"Of course, she is. She's toiling away in the kitchen cooking for us and the two of you."

"Oh, I thought it was just a meeting, no food involved," Peter interjected.

"Look, I don't know. I just carried out the instructions that Jim gave me," Lydia smiled.

"Well, typically, it would be lunchtime by the time you got here. So, why not?" Jim said.

"Sure, sure, why not?" Brown mumbled.

As they all approached the main entrance together, and walked in through the door, Peter inclined his head. He saw Rose, in the adjacent kitchen area. She was leaning over a hot stove in the sunlight that had filtered through the kitchen windows. She looked at Peter and smiled. Peter smiled back and shrugged. Rose held a hot plate of burned drumsticks.

"Oh, dear. Don't worry, just leave them out here," Lydia said.

"I'll eat them!" Peter offered, graciously as he overheard.

Rose laughed at that and then turned to Brown. They walked towards the next room. Peter lingered in her presence slightly, before he joined them. They sat down in a bright floral sofa. Peter looked around and thought it was quite a charming room with many stuffed animals displayed on the mantel shelf. However, as he observed Brown, Peter found him absorbed in thoughts.

Brown was thinking about little Rosie. As a toddler, her first word for food was 'nun' for 'yum' which had emerged when Brown had given her a piece of cheese to taste. From then onwards, everything from water to pudding was 'nun', 'nun' and yet more 'nun' until she learnt 'yum' a few months later. A smile formed around the corners of his lips.

It was quite obvious that his mind wasn't on socialising this afternoon. Sitting on the far end, he felt edgy; he held the cushioned handle of the sofa in a tight grip. He wanted to get to business straight away. He asked Jim Carpenter if he could take a walk with him on the farm. Lydia guessed just as much and studied Peter. Peter avoided making eye-contact. He continued to gaze at the animal posters on the walls. Lydia sat quietly for a moment and then stood, mumbling that she needed to help Rose in the kitchen. Peter nodded, his lips compressed.

From this angle where Peter was sitting, he could see Rose tinkering with pots and pans and burnt drumsticks. She had her back towards him. Her wiry arms moved fast and her rounded hips swung inadvertently when she shifted her posture. Peter felt like being closer to her. He felt like touching those arms. He gazed at her until she'd turned around with a jolt and caught him dreaming. She suppressed a smile and waited for him to come over. Rose was accustomed to men drooling over her. But Peter did just the opposite. He rose from the sofa hurriedly and walked out. Rose put down the metal pot on a wooden table placed beside the stove and ran after him, feeling slighted. She always had the upper hand where her men were concerned. She was the one who turned them down, not the other way round.

Finding Peter was easy. He was sitting under a desolate apple tree. On this wintry morning, the apple tree looked like the sunless Hades of skeletal branches. The branches reached out like dendrites of the neural system. She stood calmly before him. Peter looked up.

"Why have you come?" she asked.

"What do you think?"

"I don't know. I'm asking you," she said.

"If I said I heard about you from Farmer Brown and wanted to meet you, would you believe me?"

"That would amuse me. It's flattering, but…"

"But what?"

"I don't know."

"As much as I want to Rose…"

"I don't understand. What is it then?"

"I don't know," he said.

Both Rose and Peter remained quiet after that. They knew not what to do next. Peter glanced at Rose and smiled. A lock of her curls had tumbled over her forehead in the wind.

Peter took a sharp breath and said, "Gosh, Rose. You're pretty."

He put a hand out and tried to play with her curls on her forehead. He twirled them around his fingers. She did nothing to stop it. Rose extended her hand towards Peter; her long fingers touched the tip of his. Peter enclosed her fingers into his masculine palm.

"Do you ever think of getting married, Peter?"

"Hmm, interesting question."

Peter smiled at her small inquisitive face and caressed her rosy cheek, touching it with his index finger. He put a protective arm around Rose and had a random thought of big ocean waves lapping on the shore.

"What're you thinking, Peter?"

"Nothing. How 'bout you, Rose? Do you think about marriage?"

"Yeah, I think about it but I'm afraid of long-term commitment."

"Afraid? Why?"

"That's just how I am."

Peter raised his eyebrows slightly. And looking away, he saw Brown and Jim walking towards them down the gravel path. Grim face, pursed lips, deep scowls. Brown and Jim were within view, Rose and Peter both stood up and waited for them. As they came closer, Brown looked at Rose; extending an arm, he suddenly broke down. Hundred years of ice seemed to have melted down in a rivulet.

"Wha? What is it?" she stammered.

Words froze. Brown couldn't talk. Rose shied away from his open embrace. He sat down on the bench, a tired old man who had lost so much and found it again, never to let it go. But he felt she had fallen and slipped in quicksand.

Jim asked Rose to come inside with him but had invited neither Brown nor Peter. Leaving them out, he took Rose by the shoulder and stalked inside. Rose's skirt swayed swiftly on the gravel path. It didn't occur to him that Rose was an adult now and she could choose her own life.

Indeed, the picture in old Brown's wallet came in handy; the picture of a small girl wearing a polka dot dress was the same dress Rose had among her possessions when the Carpenters had adopted her from the orphanage. In fact, that was her only belonging. This dress. Near match, photographs were there in Jim's album too that posed a striking similarity to the little girl's picture in Brown's wallet. There were no doubts in Brown's or Jim's mind that this was the same girl… Rose, Brown's little Rosie; no mistaken identity. Oh! Rosie was alive and well after all these years. Thirty years, those thirty long years, when Rose was abducted at five and sold to a stranger who had brought her to the orphanage for care. Her mother, Emma, Emma must be contacted at once! It was now up to Peter to collect the broken pieces. For Brown was completely devastated and beyond anyone's note-worthy reproach or approval. Grief and joy; sympathy and admonitions were tied up in one huge confusing emotion.

Brown put a hand on Peter's arm and Peter slowly led him to the cart. This house of welcome seemed cold. Those doors were now firmly locked. They returned to the buggy

262

and Peter drove them out of the Carpenter's premises. The long journey back, gave Brown sufficient time to settle down.

"Now that I've finally found her, I want Rosie to come home to live with us, Peter. I must write to Emma at once."

"Tell me, please, how did it all happen?"

"How did it happen?"

"Yes, Farmer Brown, how did it happen?"

"Well, I took Jim for a walk as you already know."

"Hmm."

"Then after a bit of chit-chat about the weather and our farms generally, I broached the subject. I took my wallet out and simply showed him Rosie's picture. He didn't say anything for a very long time and then he said, 'Who're you? How did you get hold of this picture in that dress?' I said because this is my Rosie and I believe your Rose and my Rosie are the same people. 'I need to sit down,' he said. 'Oh God, give me some breathing space.' So he sat down and I, beside him until he found his bearings back. 'Yes, yes, we brought her home in that dress. She had grown out of that dress by then but it still fitted her, a tight fit that is; even after three years. Rose was eight at the time. They don't feed them much in that orphanage, you know?' he said and I said, 'I know, I know all about Badgerys' Creek orphanage.' 'You do? Hey, you do, right?' he said. 'Then you must also know that Rose is ours now. No power in this world can take her from us. We adopted her legally from the orphanage.' 'Is that a threat?' I asked. By now, I started to panic, trying to get Rosie back from him. 'You do know that Rosie was stolen from us,' I said. 'Stolen? No, no I don't. They never told us anything about her past,' he said. 'Well, one day when we are both a little calmer, I shall tell you all about it. For now, let's just go back to Rosie,' I said. 'Lydia, Lydia would still have that dress in the closet

263

somewhere.' He was panicking too, you see. 'I don't need to see it. I only want to know if this is my Rosie.'

Farmer Brown paused and Peter looked at him through the corner of his eyes. He nodded and kept nodding, reinforcing his belief. "I had only one thing on my mind, Peter. To find out for sure, if indeed that was my little girl."

It was becoming dark and misty. Peter had a strange thought that had nothing do with these worldly affairs: what if every life on earth had stopped giving birth? He envisaged a dead world where 'Time' would still continue to rule but a subjectless state – an empty planet; a ghastly, empty, blue planet, just like the red or the frozen, the dwarf or any of the other planets in the universe, without a speck of life. What sort of a world would that be? Seeing Peter engrossed in thoughts, Brown said nothing.

"Now that you've found Rose, are you any wiser?" asked Peter, suddenly.

Brown was pensive for a while and then replied quietly, "Well, I should've thought of the orphanage. I guess it never occurred to me that she could be in the orphanage since she wasn't an orphan. But I know now that it was a mistake. It was a massive oversight and slip-up. I relied on the police to find her and was just happy in the thought that Rose's body wasn't found. To me, it meant she was alive. What more could I have asked for? What a fool I had been!"

"Yeah, I just hope it's not too late to bring Rose home."

"What do you mean?"

"Well, Rose has a home. A safe house that has protected her all those years. Why would she leave it?"

"Because I'm her biological father."

"And they raised her with all the love they could muster. A choice between infinite love and kinship? What's it going to be?"

"Blood's always thicker, no matter what happens."

264

"Orphanage is not a safe-haven. You should've done better and looked for her there. The Carpenters saved Rose from their atrocities."

Brown remained quiet.

"We need to get home. I am drained," Brown said.

"So am I."

Dusk had fallen over the gumtrees along the side-road. The horse rode through dirt and pebbles on the uneven track. The drive was lonely and dark. Brown struck a match in the dark and bent over to light a small lantern that hung by the carriage.

"Do you think Rose knows by now?" Brown asked, twiddling his thumb.

"I really don't know," Peter said, honestly.

Brown kept up his gaze as the horses darted down the dirt road. He speculated that Rosie must be thrilled to hear about the existence of her biological father.

"We must make another trip tomorrow to Emma's parent's house."

"Is that where she is?"

"I'm pretty sure."

"You don't know that. You haven't been in touch since she left you."

"We'll send a telegram before we go. I have their address somewhere."

"Are your parents-in-law still alive?"

"Don't know. Doesn't seem like it. It has been a long thirty years, now."

"When Emma left, you were still young. Why did you not take another wife?"

"Another wife? Emma's the only one for me: the love of my life."

Peter felt foolish. Love was something he hadn't factored in. "How does one feel when in love?"

265

"You'll know. Do you feel anything for Rose?

Peter smiled. "She's a beauty."

Brown nodded. "She looks like Emma when I had first met her, an angel in the garden of Eden. I was smitten and I still am."

They were home. Peter drove in through the gates of the farm and parked the cart up at the door. He jumped off as did Brown and they unharnessed the horse and walked it inside the stable by the barn. They entered through the kitchen door later, as the farm slept in silence, they plodded up the staircase.

The next morning Brown woke up with a smile. Much work was needed to be done today. First and foremost was to get in touch with Emma. He sat down to write a letter and found Emma's parent's address. He wrote several drafts and crunched them up in paper balls. At last, he wrote:

Dear Emma,

How are you? I know it has been a long thirty years since you left me. You were angry with me because I couldn't find little Rosie. Well! I got news. Good news. I hope this will find you in good health. Oh! Emma, Emma Brown. Guess what? I found Rose. I found her for you, my darling little bird. She is well. She has grown into a beautiful, confident lady.

Yours forever,

Brown

PS. Please write back to me as soon as you receive this.

Brown sat with the note in his hand for a while, thinking of mailing it in the afternoon post. In the unlikely event of Jim not passing on this vital information to Rose, it would have a harrowing effect in all families. To avoid this, something

266

else needed to be planned. This time around, Brown must do it right. Then he thought of Peter. What if Peter could be persuaded into a relationship with Rose? Cupid's bow must cast a stiff bull's eye. He went downstairs to search for Peter. Peter was in the sty mixing fodder for the pigs. Bent deep over the hog trough, his arms stirred the corn and the soybean meal. He realised much later that Brown had entered.

"What's up?" he asked, looking up.

"I'm sending Emma a letter."

"Good." Peter stood straight up.

"Something needs to be done. Rose must see her mum," Brown said.

"Of course, she must." Peter nodded.

"I got a plan," Brown said.

"Well?"

"Marry Rose," Brown said.

"Are you crazy? She'll never have me this way," Peter said.

"Why not? Can you think of another plan?"

"One day, I'll start a business and you'll be a part of it," Peter said.

"Sounds good. What about Rose?"

"Let me handle this. Now, you go inside and make yourself a nice cuppa. By the looks of it, you didn't get any sleep last night, did ye' now?" Peter asked.

Brown scratched his stubbles slovenly and looked at Peter's honest to goodness face.

"Trust me," Peter whispered.

"I trust you, Peter, you're the best thing that's happened to me after Rose and Emma."

Brown left after that and Peter sat down beside the wallowing pigs. The first thing that came to his mind was to make money. He had heard about the Gold-Rush and people's mad punting over it in New South Wales. He decided to join them in search for Gold before he proposed to marry Rose Brown. At the moment, she was Rose Carpenter but soon to be wedded to Peter Baxter, becoming Rose Baxter. What's in a name?

About the Author

Mehreen Ahmed is widely published and critically acclaimed by Midwest Book Review, DD Magazine, The Wild Atlantic Book Club to name a few. Her short stories are a winner in The Waterloo Short Story Competition, Shortlisted in Cogito Literary Journal Contest, a Finalist in the Fourth Adelaide Literary Award Contest, winner in The Cabinet of Heed stream-of-consciousness challenge. Her works are three-time nominated for The Best of the Net Awards, nominated for the Pushcart Prize award, two-time nominated for Aurealis Awards. Her book, *The Pacifist* is an announced Drunken Druid's Editor's Choice.

She has written a novel, novellas, short stories, flash, and micro-fiction. She was born and raised in Bangladesh. Currently, she lives in Australia.

Literary, Scholarly Publications

Cambridge University Press, Routledge, University of Hawaii University Press, Michigan State University Press, ISTE, Callej. org. Journal, Learner Autonomy Special Interest group (IATEFL, LASIG), Independence, University of Kent, Canterbury, The Sheaf, University of Sackachewan Press.

Perception Magazine (Syracuse University), ElliipsisZine, Oddball Magazine,The Talon Review (North Florida University), Door is A Jar Magazine, Litterateur RW Magazine, Scissors and Spackle, Flash Boulevard, Ponder Savant, Phenomenal Literature, Crêpe & Penn, Flash Frontier, Ginosko Literary Journal, BrownBag Online, The Cabinet of Heed, Straylight Magazine (Wisconsin-Parkland University), Melbourne Culture Corner, Cogito Literary Journal, Breathe Everyone Magazine, Literati Magazine, Active Muse, Dreaming in

Fiction, Anti-Heroin Chic, Love in the time of Covid Chronicle: Doors, Wellington Street Review, Setu Bilingual Journal, Impspired Magazine, The Writers and Readers Magazine, KREAXXXION Review, Thorn Literary Magazine, 3 Moon Magazine, Sage Cigarettes, FlashBack Fiction, Portand Metrozine, The Piker Press, Nthanda, CommuterLit, Angel City Review, Anthroposphere: The Oxford Climate Review, and more.

Like to Read More Work Like This?

Then sign up to our mailing list and download our free collection of short stories, *Magnetism*. Sign up now to receive this free e-book and also to find out about all of our new publications and offers.

Sign up here:
   http://eepurl.com/gbpdVz

Please Leave a Review

Reviews are so important to writers. Please take the time to review this book. A couple of lines is fine.

Reviews help the book to become more visible to buyers. Retailers will promote books with multiple reviews.

This in turn helps us to sell more books… And then we can afford to publish more books like this one.

Leaving a review is very easy.
Go to https://smarturl.it/v46hcv, scroll down the left-hand side of the Amazon page and click on the "Write a customer review" button.

Other Books by Mehreen Ahmed

The Pacifist

Published by Cosmic Teapot

In 1866, Peter Baxter's misfortune ends the day he leaves Badgerys Creek orphanage. Unsure of what to do next, Peter finds himself on a farm run by Mr Brown. An aging man, Brown needs help and is happy to give Peter a place to live in exchange for his labor. Unbeknownst to Peter, Brown's past is riddled with dark secrets tied to the same orphanage, which he has documented in a red folder.

During a chance encounter, Peter meets Rose. Peter cannot help but fall in love with her beauty, grace, and wit; however, he fears that his affection will go unrequited as a result of his crippling poverty. But fate changes when Peter joins the search for gold in Hill End, New South Wales. Striking it rich, he returns to Rose a wealthy man. Peter is changed by his new found affluence, heading towards the mire of greed. Will Rose regret her relationship with Peter?

Meanwhile, Rose has her own troubled history. One that is deeply entwined with Brown's past and Peter's future.

"An Australian masterpiece" (*Amazon*)

Order from Amazon:

Hardrback: ISBN 978-1-988762-03-6
Paperback: ISBN 978-1-988762-06-7
eBook: ASIN B06XYRRZVW

Moirae

Published by Cosmic Teapot

Nalia finds herself trapped in a strange and inescapable lucid dream. Danger looms ahead for her friends. Pressured out of their homes in the Lost Winds, every step threatens them with persecution and death.

Taking a daring route on a treacherous sea, they seek asylum in a new land. Will they make it to their destination? Will Nalia's dream of finding peace in Draviland become the utopia that she desperately desires, or are the dangers of this new land even worse than her home?

Set in a real time, stream-of-consciousness narrative, this story takes you on a sweeping literary journey.

"I can't imagine a more difficult style of writing to undertake, yet Ahmed has created a vibrant story full of intriguing and delightful images." (*Amazon*)

Order from Amazon:

Hardback: ISBN 978-0-995331-61-7
Paperback: ISBN 978-0-995331-60-0
eBook: ASIN B01LYMIGTW

The Blue, Red Lyrae
Published by Impspired

The Blue, Red Lyrae is a twin novella book, Offing and The
Cheshire Grins. They have both been written in a stream-of-
consciousness style. Either way both stories are tied like the
constellations of the lyre of the deep skies. Hence, the title The
Blue, Red Lyrae, meaning the colours of two of five main
constellations. Blue is indicative of hot and red, indicative of
cold, an existential allusion to life, dancing at the cosmic tune
of a symbolic harp that Lyra stands for.

Order from Amazon:

Paperback: ISBN 979-8-562270-81-8
eBook: ASIN B08NKB861J

Other Publications by Bridge House

Resilience

by Jim Bates

Remembrance Day is special for one grandfather. Which story of he and his brother at the lake will John remember today? Blake loves his garden but he's not so sure about the rabbit. Tyler stands up to his dad while hunting crows. What really did happen in the room at the Inn on the Lake? Why doesn't Quinn run away anymore?

"*Resilience* is an absolute gem. A collection of twenty-seven beautifully written short stories that deal with the central theme of its title." (Amazon)

Order from Amazon:

ISBN: 978-1-914199-00-4 (paperback)
978-1-914199-01-1 (ebook)

Whisky for Breakfast

by Christopher P. Mooney

The thirty-five stories in Mooney's debut are dominated by a
cast of characters who colour outside of society's lines. They
are hustlers, prostitutes, addicts, gangsters, killers, thieves,
beasts. They are the dangerous, the lost, the lonely, the sick,
the suicidal, the broken-hearted. Men and women, defeated by
life. Their depravity is real, yet the writing in this
uncompromising collection of transgressive fiction, always
carefully crafted, evokes the sense that their humanity is not
yet lost. In *Whisky for Breakfast*, nothing is off limits.

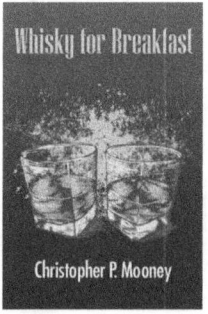

"A terrific read, often shocking and full of memorable
characters. This is an excellent collection of short stories and
would highly recommend." (*Amazon*)

Order from Amazon:

Paperback: ISBN 978-1-907335-89-1
eBook: ISBN 978-1-907335-90-7

In Fields of Butterfly Flames

by Steve Wade

Ostracised by betrayal, isolated through indifference, gutted
with guilt, or suffering from loss, the characters in these
twenty-two stories are fractured and broken, some irreparably.
In their struggle for acceptance, and their desperate search for
meaning, they deny the past. Some abandon responsibility,
others are running from something or someone. Some flee their
homes and their homelands, while others return home, only to
find themselves even more marginalized and estranged.

"It's not too often when a book can make you physically react
to the words. Haven't read anything as visceral, gripping and
real as this in a long time... Highly recommend!" (*Amazon*)

Order from Amazon:

Paperback: ISBN 978-1-907335-87-7
eBook: ISBN 978-1-907335-88-4

www.ingramcontent.com/pod-product-compliance
Lightning Source LLC
Chambersburg PA
CBHW070857180626
46817CB00003B/804